KnuckleHeadz" Genre: Urban Suspense / Action Drama

by

Jayson Swann

2.

Front Matter

Chapter 1: Graduation Day Dreams and Desert Realities

The Las Vegas sun, a relentless, unforgiving orb, beat down on the city, turning the asphalt into a shimmering mirage. Graduation day. The air vibrated with a peculiar mix of elation and a gnawing, unspoken anxiety. For Marcus, Jamal, Chloe, David, and Aisha, this was it. The culmination of years spent navigating textbooks, navigating friendships, and navigating the labyrinthine streets of a city that promised everything and delivered it with a double-edged sword. The campus, once a sanctuary of learning, now felt like a launching pad, its familiar brick and mortar fading into the background as their gazes turned towards the distant, glittering horizon of the Strip. It was a beacon, a siren song of opportunity, a promise of a future painted in neon and fueled by possibility. Yet, beneath the veneer of celebratory smiles and the rustle of dispensed diplomas, a current of uncertainty ran deep. The desert, vast and indifferent, stretched out before them, a stark, literal representation of the unknown that lay beyond the structured confines of their academic lives. The heat wasn't just physical; it was a tangible manifestation of the pressure bearing down on them, the weight of expectations, the ghost of past struggles, and the daunting prospect of forging a path in a world that often rewarded ruthlessness over righteousness.

Marcus, his jaw tight, adjusted the collar of his slightly too-tight graduation gown. He was the leader, the one with the plan, or at least the one who projected that he did. His ambition burned bright, a fire stoked by the ever-present specter of his family's mounting debts. He saw the diploma not as an end, but as a key, a means to an end. The conventional paths, the cubicle farms and the entry-level salaries, felt like a slow, agonizing descent into the very quicksand he was desperate to escape. His gaze flickered to a knot of older guys by the parking lot, their hushed conversation punctuated by knowing nods and furtive glances. He strained to catch snippets, the words "easy money," "quick turnaround," and "no questions asked" slicing through the festive din. It was a whisper, a dark counterpoint to the triumphant cheers echoing from the auditorium, a temptation that promised a faster, albeit dirtier, route to the life he craved. The worn tires of his beat-up sedan, parked amongst a sea of gleaming luxury vehicles that seemed to mock his present reality, served as a constant, painful reminder of his current limitations. The contrast was a punch to the gut, a visual representation of the chasm between the life he dreamed of and the one he was living.

Jamal, ever the strategist, leaned against a palm tree, a casual observer yet keenly aware of every nuance in the crowd. His street smarts, honed in the unforgiving alleys and backstreets of Vegas, made him a natural at reading people and situations. He saw the flicker of desperation in Marcus's eyes, the subtle tightening of Aisha's grip on her purse. He felt the collective yearning for something more, something *bigger*, than the predictable rhythm of a nine-to-five existence. He caught the hushed exchanges too, the coded language that spoke of a different kind of hustle, one that operated in the shadows, away from the prying eyes of authority. It was a dangerous allure, a shortcut that promised to bypass the years of struggle and sacrifice that his friends, and he himself, had braced for. The city itself seemed to pulse with this undercurrent of illicit opportunity, a hidden engine humming beneath the dazzling facade of the Strip.

Chloe, her artistic sensibilities finely tuned, felt the palpable tension beneath the surface of forced celebration. Her fingers, usually stained with paint or charcoal, were clenched at her sides. The glint of opportunity in Marcus's eyes was mixed with a familiar desperation she'd seen before, a look that always preceded trouble. She watched as Jamal subtly steered Marcus away from the older men, a silent acknowledgment of the dangerous currents swirling around them. Chloe harbored her own quiet vulnerabilities, a fear that her dreams of capturing the city's vibrant, chaotic soul on canvas would remain just that—dreams—if she couldn't find a way to break free from the economic constraints that tethered her. The art world was as competitive and cutthroat as any back alley deal, and the thought of compromising her vision, of painting for survival rather than expression, was a chilling one.

David, the quiet observer, the one who processed the world through a lens of numbers and logic, remained on the periphery. He saw the calculations in Marcus's ambition, the risk assessments in Jamal's calculated nonchalance, the yearning in Chloe's artistic gaze, and the protective fire in Aisha's loyalty. He understood the allure of the Strip, its seductive promise of instant gratification, but his mind was already dissecting the probabilities, the potential pitfalls, the inevitable consequences of chasing those ephemeral promises. He noticed the subtle shifts in their group dynamic, the way Marcus's inherent leadership was being tested by the very pressures that sought to define their futures. He saw the unspoken anxieties that hung in the sweltering air, as thick and suffocating as the desert heat.

Aisha, her fiery spirit simmering beneath a veneer of forced composure, felt the unease settle like a shroud. Her loyalty to her friends, particularly to Jamal, was fierce, a protective instinct honed by shared experiences and the unspoken understanding that they were all they had. But even her unwavering devotion couldn't entirely mask the growing apprehension that something was shifting, that the familiar camaraderie was being subtly eroded by forces they were only beginning to comprehend. She saw the glances exchanged, the hushed conversations that seemed to exclude her, the glint of temptation in Marcus's eyes that spoke of desperation, not just ambition. The vastness of the desert, stretching out in every direction, seemed to mirror the overwhelming uncertainty of their collective future, a future that was suddenly feeling less like a canvas waiting for their dreams and more like a trap sprung with no easy escape. The cheers and laughter around them felt hollow, a thin veneer over the true anxieties that pulsed beneath the surface of this momentous day.

As the day bled into the electric embrace of the night, the graduation party pulsed with an infectious energy, fueled by cheap champagne and the heady sense of freedom. Laughter spilled out into the warm air, punctuated by the distant thrum of bass from a nearby club. But beneath the revelry, the whispers of a different kind of future, one that promised swift escape from the grind, began to take root. Marcus, his earlier anxieties amplified by the celebratory mood, found himself gravitating towards a group of older men, their faces etched with a kind of hardened experience. Their conversation was low, punctuated by knowing nods and the occasional sharp, clipped laugh. Marcus caught phrases like "guaranteed payout," "connections," and "off the books." It was a dangerous siren song, a melody of instant gratification that played directly to his deepest anxieties. He saw the worn-out fabric of his father's old suit, the one he'd borrowed for the occasion, and the gnawing pressure of impending bills. The allure of a quick fix, a shortcut around the years of struggle, was becoming increasingly potent. He felt a familiar sense of impatience, a burning desire to transcend the limitations that had defined his life thus far.

Jamal, ever perceptive, noticed Marcus's drift. He, too, had overheard the whispers, the subtle insinuations of lucrative opportunities that skirted the edges of legality. He understood the magnetic pull of easy money, the intoxicating promise of a life unburdened by financial worries. His own street instincts told him that these weren't just idle boasts; there was a seriousness to the hushed tones, a veiled invitation to a world where the rules were different, and the rewards were far greater. He saw the gleam in Marcus's eyes, a dangerous mix of hope and desperation, and knew that the seeds of temptation had found fertile ground. The contrast between their own sputtering vehicles and the sleek, powerful machines cruising the Strip's dazzling boulevard was a stark visual reminder of what they lacked, and what these whispers seemed to offer.

Chloe, sketching idly in a notebook, felt a prickle of unease as she observed Marcus engaging with the older men. She recognized the predatory glint in their eyes, the way they seemed to be sizing him up. Her own artistic soul recoiled at the thought of any pursuit that compromised integrity, but she also understood the desperate need to escape the limitations of their current circumstances. She saw the way Jamal subtly shifted his position, a silent guardian, intercepting Marcus's gaze and offering a subtle shake of his head. It was a silent communication, a shared understanding of the precipice they were teetering on.

Aisha, her hand resting protectively on Jamal's arm, felt the shift in the atmosphere. She saw the way Marcus's focus had narrowed, his attention drawn to the darker currents flowing beneath the celebratory surface. Her loyalty to Jamal, her fierce desire to protect him and their friends, made her hyper-aware of any potential threat. She didn't fully understand the implications of the hushed conversations, but she sensed a dangerous undertone, a deviation from the path they had all, in their own ways, believed they were on. The night air, usually vibrant and full of promise, now seemed charged with a subtle menace, the glittering lights of the Strip casting longer, more ominous shadows than usual.

David, ever the observer, processed the scene with his characteristic detachment, filing away the interactions, the subtle cues, the unspoken anxieties. He saw the allure of the fast life, the promise of wealth and escape, but his mind was already calculating the odds, the inherent risks involved in such propositions. He recognized the desperation that fueled Marcus's gaze, the street wisdom that guided Jamal's subtle interventions, the artistic sensitivity that made Chloe recoil from the darker undertones, and the fierce loyalty that made Aisha a vigilant protector. The intoxicating mix of celebration and underlying tension was a complex equation he was still trying to solve, a prelude to decisions that would irrevocably alter their lives. The city, in its dazzling, indifferent glory, was about to play a much larger role than any of them could yet comprehend.

Later that night, the pulsating glow of the Las Vegas Strip served as a dramatic backdrop for a pact sealed under the dazzling glare of neon. The iconic Fountains of Bellagio, their water dancing in choreographed bursts, seemed to mirror the chaotic energy simmering within the group. The air vibrated with a potent mix of exhilaration and a burgeoning sense of dread. Fueled by bravado, a shared frustration with their current circumstances, and a desperate yearning for something more, they made a promise to each other, a silent vow to explore the fringes of legality, to test the boundaries of their world. The dazzling marquees, advertising fortunes to be won and dreams to be had, now seemed to cast long, ominous shadows, a stark contrast to the youthful recklessness that propelled their decision.

Marcus, emboldened by the shared commitment, felt a surge of defiant energy. He saw this as their collective escape route, their chance to break free from the constraints that had held them captive for so long. The thought of finally outmaneuvering the system, of claiming the life he believed he deserved, was intoxicating. He looked at his friends, their faces illuminated by the shifting kaleidoscope of light, and saw a reflection of his own desperate hope.

Jamal, ever the pragmatist, offered a more measured, yet equally determined, perspective. He saw the inherent dangers, the potential pitfalls, but he also recognized the power of their collective ambition. His street smarts whispered warnings, but his ambition shouted louder, promising control and influence. He viewed this pact as a strategic move, a calculated risk that, if managed correctly, could yield significant rewards. He met Marcus's gaze, a silent acknowledgment of their shared purpose, but his mind was already dissecting the potential angles, the ways to navigate this treacherous new terrain.

Chloe, though hesitant, felt an undeniable pull towards the shared adventure. Her artistic eye was captivated by the raw, unfiltered energy of the moment, the sheer audacity of their pact. The thrill of stepping into the unknown, of defying expectations, resonated with her yearning for something beyond the ordinary. Yet, a knot of apprehension tightened in her stomach, a quiet fear that the lines they were about to cross were more defined, and more dangerous, than they imagined. She saw the potential for creative inspiration in the city's underbelly, but also the risk of losing herself in its shadows.

Aisha, her loyalty unwavering, stood by Jamal, her expression a mixture of determination and concern. She believed in their collective strength, their ability to face any challenge together. But even as she offered her support, a small voice of caution whispered in the back of her mind, a premonition of the perilous path they were embarking upon. She saw the unbridled ambition in Marcus's eyes and the calculating gleam in Jamal's, and worried about the direction their shared dreams might take.

David, as always, remained a quiet observer, his mind meticulously cataloging the risks and potential rewards. He saw the pact not as a romanticized rebellion, but as a complex equation with a high probability of failure. Yet, he also recognized the inherent logic in their desire for change, the undeniable pressure of their circumstances. He understood that their shared secret, this pact forged under the neon glow, was a powerful binding agent, but also a fragile one, susceptible to the harsh realities they were about to confront. The neon lights, usually symbols of joy and celebration, now seemed to paint long, ominous shadows across their faces, a harbinger of the darkness that lay ahead. It was a moment charged with the reckless optimism of youth, a dangerous cocktail of ambition, desperation, and the intoxicating allure of the forbidden.

Their initial foray into this clandestine world was marked by a palpable sense of adrenaline, a stark departure from the monotonous routines of their former lives. It began with seemingly minor hustles, the kind of tasks that felt more like dares than criminal enterprises: keeping watch for a few hours, facilitating small, discreet exchanges, acting as diversions. The thrill of operating outside the established norms, of navigating the city's hidden currents, was intoxicating. David's knack for numbers, his ability to spot patterns and assess risks with uncanny accuracy, proved surprisingly invaluable. He could predict the flow of traffic, identify potential surveillance blind spots, and calculate the optimal timing for their movements, his analytical prowess a quiet anchor in their burgeoning recklessness.

Jamal's street smarts, honed through years of navigating complex social dynamics and territorial boundaries, were equally crucial. He knew the players, the unspoken rules of engagement, the subtle cues that signaled danger. He could sense when a situation was about to turn south, when to push and when to retreat, his instincts a finely tuned radar in the unpredictable urban landscape. He became their guide, their navigator through the shadowy alleys and backrooms where these transactions took place.

Chloe, initially hesitant, found herself unexpectedly drawn into the thrill of it all. Her artistic eye, trained to notice the minutiae of composition and detail, allowed her to pick up on subtle discrepancies that others missed. She could spot a counterfeit bill from a distance, recognize the tell-tale signs of surveillance equipment, and recall the exact placement of security cameras from a single glance. Her perception, sharpened by years of artistic observation, became an unexpected asset, adding a layer of sophistication to their simple operations. The ease with which they navigated these initial ventures, the seemingly effortless flow of their actions, began to breed a dangerous sense of confidence, a false illusion that their actions were consequence-free, a mere game played out in the periphery of a larger, more legitimate world.

Marcus, driven by the urgent need to alleviate his family's financial burdens, saw these early successes as validation. He pushed for more, for bigger opportunities, his ambition overriding any nascent caution. He felt the intoxicating rush of control, the satisfaction of orchestrating these small victories. The money, though initially modest, represented a tangible shift, a crack in the edifice of their former limitations.

Aisha, while supportive of her friends, couldn't entirely shake the gnawing unease that had settled within her. She saw the growing confidence, the subtle shift in their demeanor, and worried that they were becoming too comfortable, too accustomed to operating in this gray area. Her innate sense of morality, her deeply ingrained loyalty, made her question the long-term implications of their actions. She found herself constantly glancing over her shoulder, a nascent paranoia beginning to take root, a feeling that they were dancing on the edge of a precipice.

Even in these nascent stages, as the initial thrill of their clandestine activities began to wane and the reality of their chosen path started to solidify, subtle cracks began to appear within their once-unshakeable bond. Marcus's ambition, a powerful engine driving him forward, began to manifest as a growing impatience with any perceived hesitation or caution from the others. Minor disagreements, once easily smoothed over by shared laughter and camaraderie, now carried a sharper edge, fueled by the underlying pressure of their escalating ventures and Marcus's increasingly autocratic tendencies. He started to see dissent not as healthy debate, but as an impediment to progress, a threat to the momentum they had so carefully built.

Jamal, reveling in his newfound influence and the tangible financial gains, began to subtly challenge Marcus's leadership. He saw Marcus's growing impulsiveness as a potential liability, a weakness that could jeopardize their operations. Jamal's own strategic mind, sharpened by his street-level education, craved a more calculated approach, one that prioritized long-term gain over short-term risk. His suggestions, initially offered as collaborative input, began to carry a tone of subtle correction, a quiet assertion of his own burgeoning authority within the group. He was becoming increasingly comfortable with the faster pace of their illicit lifestyle, the financial freedom it afforded him, and found Aisha's growing unease a frustrating obstacle to his own burgeoning aspirations.

Aisha's discomfort deepened with each passing week. The moral implications of their actions, once a nagging whisper, had grown into a persistent chorus of doubt. She found herself increasingly at odds with Jamal, whose embrace of their new reality seemed to blind him to the ethical compromises they were making. Their conversations, once filled with shared dreams and affectionate banter, were now strained, punctuated by her pleas for caution and his dismissive reassurances. She saw the way he reveled in the newfound respect, the almost fearful deference they commanded, and feared he was losing himself in the intoxicating illusion of power. The dynamic between them, once a pillar of their group, was starting to fracture, creating a palpable tension that spread like a ripple effect through their interactions.

David, ever the quiet observer, meticulously cataloged these subtle shifts, these nascent fissures in their foundation. He saw the escalating risks, the increasing boldness of their ventures, and recognized the dangerous trajectory they were on. His analytical mind was working overtime, processing the data, projecting the potential outcomes, and a growing sense of unease settled upon him. He understood that the intoxicating pull of easy money was amplifying not just their ambitions, but also their insecurities, subtly altering their perceptions of themselves and each other. The shared innocence that had once bound them was slowly eroding, replaced by a complex web of conflicting desires, growing paranoia, and the subtle but undeniable allure of a life lived on the edge. The camaraderie that had defined their graduation day was being tested, strained by the very promises of freedom and prosperity they had so eagerly embraced.

The air, thick with the scent of cheap perfume and the cloying sweetness of spilled liquor, vibrated with the discordant symphony of graduation night. Laughter, sharp and brittle, punctuated the rhythmic pulse of music thumping from portable speakers. Marcus, feeling the scratchy wool of his borrowed suit against his skin, watched the spectacle unfold from the periphery, his mind a thousand miles away, wrestling with the stark realities that awaited them beyond the neon-drenched illusion of the Strip. The diploma, clutched loosely in his hand, felt less like a key and more like a hollow promise, a testament to a system that demanded more than it gave. The weight of his father's worn-out wallet, the faded bills inside barely enough to cover the mounting utility bills, pressed down on him like a physical burden. The whispers he'd overheard earlier, fragments of conversations about "off-book deals" and "guaranteed payouts," snagged at his thoughts, offering a tantalizing counter-narrative to the narrative of struggle and scarcity that had defined his young life. He saw the gleaming chrome of a passing sports car, its occupants silhouetted against the vibrant glow of a casino marquee, and the contrast was a physical ache in his chest. It was a stark visual metaphor for the chasm between the life he yearned for and the one that seemed to stretch out before him, an endless expanse of effort for meager rewards. The very air seemed to hum with the silent promise of an easier way, a quicker path to the glittering prizes that Vegas so readily displayed.

Jamal, leaning against a dented Ford Taurus that had seen better days, his eyes scanning the crowd with practiced ease, felt the same undercurrent of discontent rippling through their small circle. He caught Marcus's restless gaze, the subtle clenching of his jaw, and understood the unspoken desperation that fueled it. The conventional path, the one lauded by teachers and counselors, felt like a slow, arduous climb up a mountain with no guarantee of a summit. He'd seen it play out too many times: the promises of education turning into student loan debt, of hard work leading to dead-end jobs. The whispers of alternative routes, of opportunities that existed in the city's shadowed corners, resonated with a primal instinct for survival, a learned cunning that whispered of shortcuts. The sheer opulence on display – the shimmering dresses, the expensive jewelry, the effortless swagger of those who seemed to possess everything – served as a constant, gnawing reminder of their own material limitations. He watched as Marcus's eyes lingered on a group of men in sharp suits, their hushed conversation punctuated by gestures that spoke of confidence and illicit dealings. Jamal felt a prickle of unease, a gut feeling that Marcus was being drawn into something that could unravel their carefully constructed facade of normalcy.

Chloe, her sketchbook tucked protectively under her arm, her eyes absorbing the vibrant chaos of the night, felt a different kind of pressure. The artistic dreams that had once seemed so vibrant and attainable now felt fragile, susceptible to the harsh realities of economic survival. She understood the yearning for a life beyond the confines of their struggling neighborhood, the desire to break free from the limitations imposed by circumstance. She had seen the flicker of ambition in Marcus's eyes, the same spark that ignited her own creative spirit, but it was now tinged with a desperation that worried her. She noticed Jamal's subtle efforts to steer Marcus away from the more questionable conversations, a silent acknowledgment of the danger lurking beneath the surface of their celebration. Her own art, her passion, felt like a luxury she might soon have to sacrifice for practicality. The thought of compromising her vision, of trading her brushes for a soul-crushing job just to make ends meet, was a prospect that chilled her to the bone. The glittering promises of the Strip, she knew, often came with a hidden cost, a price that could be steeper than any of them were prepared to pay.

Aisha, her arm linked with Jamal's, felt the familiar warmth of his presence, a grounding force in the whirlwind of the night. But even his reassuring presence couldn't entirely quell the growing sense of unease that had begun to settle over her like a fine layer of desert dust. She saw the restless energy radiating from Marcus, the way his gaze kept drifting towards the edges of the party, towards the older men who seemed to exude an aura of dangerous confidence. She caught the hushed exchanges, the coded language that hinted at opportunities far removed from the legitimate world they had just graduated from. Her loyalty to Jamal, her fierce protectiveness of their small group, made her hyper-aware of any potential threat. She felt the subtle shift in Marcus's demeanor, the way his focus narrowed when those hushed conversations began, and a knot of apprehension tightened in her stomach. The vast, indifferent desert that surrounded their city seemed to mirror the overwhelming uncertainty of their future, a landscape that offered both possibility and peril in equal measure. The cheers and laughter around them felt increasingly hollow, a thin veneer over the anxieties that pulsed beneath the surface of this momentous day.

"Yo, Marcus, you good, man?" Jamal's voice, a low rumble against the backdrop of the party, cut through Marcus's reverie. He gestured towards the group of men who had captured Marcus's attention. "Those cats look like they ain't here to wish you congrats."

Marcus forced a smile, trying to shake off the unsettling feeling. "Nah, man, just... thinking. This whole graduation thing, it's like a door, right? But the key ain't in the books, you know?" He gestured vaguely towards the gleaming towers of the Strip, their lights a beacon in the encroaching darkness. "Look at that. They ain't getting there by showing up to class. There's another way."

Jamal followed his gaze, his expression unreadable. "Another way usually means a steeper price, my dude. And more often than not, that price ain't paid in dollars." He clapped Marcus on the shoulder, a gesture meant to be reassuring but carrying an undertone of caution. "We just got out. Let's not jump back into something worse."

Chloe, overhearing their conversation, chimed in, her voice tinged with a familiar concern. "Marcus is right about one thing, though, Jamal. We can't just go back to the same old grind. My mom works double shifts just to keep the lights on. College tuition? That's a fantasy. This diploma feels like a golden ticket, but the gatekeeper's asking for a king's ransom." She fiddled with the edge of her sketchbook. "I'm trying to figure out how to get my art seen, how to make a living from it, but every gallery owner I talk to wants connections, wants experience I don't have. It's like you need to be already successful to even have a chance."

Aisha, her brow furrowed, squeezed Jamal's arm. "But what kind of 'other way,' Marcus? The whispers I'm hearing... they don't sound like good people. They sound like trouble." She looked at Marcus, her eyes pleading for him to be sensible. "We promised we'd stick together, remember? That we'd look out for each other."

Marcus met her gaze, his own eyes burning with a fierce, desperate intensity. "And I am looking out for us, Aisha! This isn't about playing games; this is about survival. My dad's talking about selling the house. Selling the house! And for what? So he can keep paying for my little sister's braces? I can't just stand by and watch them drown. This... this is a chance. A real chance." He lowered his voice, leaning in conspiratorially. "Those guys... they're talking about moving product. High-end stuff. Quick turnaround. Minimal risk, big reward. They need people who can be discreet, people who aren't already on the radar."

Jamal's expression darkened. "Moving product? Marcus, that's not a 'quick turnaround,' that's a fast track to prison. Or worse. You're talking about getting mixed up with real criminals."

"Criminals who are living the life, Jamal!" Marcus retorted, his voice rising slightly, drawing the attention of a few nearby partygoers. "While we're out here scraping by, living check to check, they're living large. They've got the cars, the clothes, the respect. And they got it because they weren't afraid to take a chance." He gestured towards the expensive vehicles parked haphazardly around the lot, their sleek lines and polished surfaces a stark contrast to the sputtering engines and dented fenders of their own rides. "Look at them. That's the kind of life that's out there for the taking. We're graduating from high school in the middle of the biggest playground in the world, and we're supposed to go get some entry-level job that pays minimum wage? That's not freedom, that's a cage."

Chloe shifted uncomfortably, the intensity of Marcus's words unnerving her. "But Marcus, at what cost? Is it worth it if it means looking over your shoulder every second? If it means losing yourself?" She thought of the vibrant colors she loved to use, the way she blended hues to create something beautiful and new. She feared that this path would only drain her of color, leaving her with a monochrome existence of fear and regret. "I want to create something, not destroy myself."

"You create what you can with the means you have, Chloe," Marcus said, his tone dismissive. "Right now, the means are limited. But this... this changes that. This gives us the capital, the freedom, to pursue whatever we want later. Think about it. We get this done, we make enough to set ourselves up, then we can go back to being artists, go back to school, whatever. It's a temporary solution to a permanent problem."

Jamal scoffed. "Temporary? Nothing about this screams 'temporary,' Marcus. Those guys you're talking to, they don't just let people walk away when they're done. You get in, you're in. And they don't care about your artistic aspirations or your family's bills. They care about their bottom line." He looked at Aisha, seeking her silent agreement, and saw it reflected in her wide, worried eyes. "We need to be smart about this. We need to be realistic."

"Realistic is my dad losing his job next month because the company's downsizing," Marcus shot back, his voice raw with emotion. "Realistic is me not being able to afford textbooks next semester. Realistic is seeing my mom break her back for pennies. I'm tired of being realistic. I want to be successful. And if the path to success isn't paved with the rules they taught us in school, then so be it." He turned his back on them, walking towards the group of men, his shoulders squared with a defiant resolve that chilled Jamal and Aisha to the bone. The music seemed to fade, the laughter receding, as Marcus stepped into the orbit of the older men, drawn by a gravitational pull of desperation and ambition.

The contrast between the vibrant energy of the graduation party and the hushed, intense conversations happening just yards away was a stark illustration of the crossroads they now faced. The sleek, powerful machines cruising the Las Vegas Strip, their headlights slicing through the humid night air, represented more than just wealth; they were symbols of a different kind of power, a different way of navigating the world. For Marcus, burdened by the weight of his family's financial struggles, these machines, and the lifestyles they embodied, represented an escape. The diploma in his hand, a hard-won symbol of academic achievement, felt increasingly irrelevant against the backdrop of such tangible, ostentatious success. He'd overheard snippets of conversation earlier, whispers of lucrative opportunities that skirted the edges of legality, promising swift financial rewards for those bold enough to seize them. The idea of a shortcut, a way to bypass the years of struggle and uncertainty that conventional paths entailed, was a siren song, a melody of instant gratification that resonated deeply with his burgeoning impatience. He looked at the worn tires of his family's aging sedan, a constant reminder of their limitations, and then his gaze swept across the street to a gleaming black SUV, its tinted windows concealing whatever luxuries lay within. The disparity was a palpable ache, a constant thrumming reminder of what he felt he and his family deserved, and what they were currently denied.

Jamal, ever the keen observer of the urban landscape, noticed Marcus's drifting attention, the way his focus narrowed as he caught the eye of one of the older men.

Jamal's own street smarts, honed in the labyrinthine alleys and backstreets of Las Vegas, had taught him to recognize the subtle cues of opportunity, but also the glint of danger in a predator's eyes. He understood the allure of easy money, the intoxicating promise of a life unburdened by financial anxieties. The casual confidence of the men Marcus was drawn to wasn't just a product of wealth; it was an aura of control, a sense that they operated by their own rules. He saw the desperation in Marcus's eyes, a potent mix of ambition and a genuine need to alleviate his family's burdens, and knew that the seeds of temptation had found fertile ground. The whispers he too had overheard spoke of a different kind of hustle, one that operated in the shadows, away from the prying eyes of authority, and the rewards, he knew, were far greater than anything a minimum-wage job could offer.

Chloe, her artistic sensibilities always keenly attuned to the nuances of human interaction, felt a prickle of unease as she watched Marcus gravitate towards the group. There was a predatory glint in their eyes, a way they seemed to be sizing him up, assessing his potential. Her own artistic soul recoiled at the thought of any pursuit that compromised integrity, but she also understood the desperate need to escape the limitations of their current circumstances. She saw the way Jamal subtly shifted his position, a silent guardian, intercepting Marcus's gaze and offering a subtle shake of his head, a wordless communication of shared concern. The thought of her dreams, of capturing the city's vibrant, chaotic soul on canvas, remaining just that—dreams—if she couldn't find a way to break free from the economic constraints that tethered her, was a chilling prospect. The art world was as competitive and cutthroat as any back-alley deal, and the idea of compromising her vision for survival was a bitter pill to swallow.

Aisha, her hand resting protectively on Jamal's arm, felt the shift in the atmosphere, the subtle tension that began to permeate the festive air. She saw the way Marcus's focus had narrowed, his attention drawn to the darker currents flowing beneath the celebratory surface. Her loyalty to Jamal, her fierce desire to protect him and their friends, made her hyper-aware of any potential threat. She didn't fully understand the implications of the hushed conversations, but she sensed a dangerous undertone, a deviation from the path they had all, in their own ways, believed they were on. The vastness of the desert, stretching out in every direction, seemed to mirror the overwhelming uncertainty of their collective future, a future that was suddenly feeling less like a canvas waiting for their dreams and more like a trap sprung with no easy escape. The neon lights, usually symbols of joy and celebration, now seemed to paint long, ominous shadows across their faces, a harbinger of the darkness that lay ahead. The intoxicating mix of celebration and underlying tension was a complex equation, a prelude to decisions that would irrevocably alter their lives.

"You know," Marcus began, his voice low and measured as he rejoined his friends, his eyes still alight with a dangerous glint, "I was thinking. All this talk about college, about getting a degree... it's a long game. A really long game. And honestly, for most of us, it's a gamble with pretty stacked odds against us." He gestured towards the passing cars, his gaze lingering on a sleek, black sports car that purred past them. "That's not a gamble. That's a statement. That's someone who decided they weren't gonna play by the rules. Someone who understood that sometimes, you gotta create your own opportunities."

Jamal met Marcus's gaze, his own eyes holding a mixture of apprehension and a grudging understanding. "And what kind of opportunities are you talking about, Marcus? Because those guys you were just talking to... they don't exactly scream 'legitimate business.'"

"Legitimacy is a concept for people who have the luxury of time and resources," Marcus countered, his tone hardening. "We don't have that luxury. My dad's talking about selling the house. Selling the house! So we can keep paying for my sister's braces and my mom's medical bills. This isn't just about me anymore, man. This is about all of us. We're all in the same boat, same struggling neighborhood, same dead-end prospects. Unless... unless we decide to be something different." He paused, letting his words hang in the air. "I heard them talking about moving product. High-end stuff. And they're looking for reliable people who can be discreet. People who aren't already on the radar."

Aisha's breath hitched. "Moving product? Marcus, are you serious? That's... that's dangerous."

"Dangerous is my dad losing his job," Marcus shot back, his voice laced with frustration. "Dangerous is my mom working triple shifts and still barely making ends meet. Dangerous is watching our futures slip away because we're too afraid to take a risk. Those guys? They're making bank. They're living the life we're all dreaming about. And they got there because they weren't afraid to get their hands a little dirty." He looked at his friends, his eyes pleading for them to understand. "This is our chance. Our one shot to break free from all this. We do this, we make enough to set ourselves up, and then... then we can go back to whatever we want. Go to college, start a business, whatever. But we need capital. And this is the fastest way to get it."

Jamal shook his head slowly, his gaze steady. "Fastest doesn't always mean best, Marcus. And 'getting our hands dirty' usually means getting them caught. These guys you're talking to, they're not playing for participation trophies. They're playing for keeps. And if you get caught, you don't just go to jail; you lose everything. Your freedom, your future, everything." He thought of the countless stories he'd heard on the streets, the cautionary tales of those who chased the fast life and ended up behind bars, their dreams shattered.

Chloe, her artistic sensibilities often at odds with the harsh realities of their world, felt a tremor of fear run through her. "But what if we get caught? What if this 'opportunity' lands us in jail? Then what? No college, no art, just… nothing." She clutched her sketchbook tighter, a fragile shield against the encroaching darkness. "I want a life, Marcus, not just a quick payday that ends in a cell."

"We'll be smart about it," Marcus insisted, his voice firm. "We'll be careful. David's good with numbers, he can help us figure out the angles, the timing. You, Jamal, you know the streets, you know how to read people. Chloe, your eye for detail, you can spot things others miss. And Aisha… you're the heart, you keep us grounded." He looked at them, his gaze intense, searching for a flicker of agreement. "This is our chance to rewrite the script. To stop being the background characters in other people's stories and start writing our own. We can do this. Together." The weight of his words settled heavily upon them, the allure of escape and prosperity warring with the gnawing fear of consequence. The distant, dazzling lights of the Strip seemed to beckon, promising a different destiny, a life far removed from the struggles they had always known.

The hum of the city was a low thrum against their ears, a counterpoint to the frantic beat of their own hearts. Las Vegas, bathed in the lurid glow of a million neon signs, was a mirage of possibility, a glittering expanse that seemed to promise everything and nothing all at once. For Marcus, the diploma clutched in his hand felt increasingly like a meaningless prop, a paper testament to a system that had ultimately failed to provide the escape he craved. The words of the men he'd spoken to earlier echoed in his mind, a seductive whisper of a life lived on a different track, one paved with quick returns and calculated risks. He felt Jamal's steady gaze on him, a silent question hanging in the air. Chloe's subtle apprehension, Aisha's worried frown – he saw them all, but the lure of an easier way, a faster ascent, was a powerful current pulling him forward.

"So, what's the play, Marcus?" Jamal's voice was low, cutting through the distant din of traffic and the nearer sounds of the revelers scattered across the park. The air, still heavy with the desert heat, was beginning to cool, but a different kind of heat was building within their small circle. The celebratory mood of graduation had begun to curdle, replaced by a shared, unspoken anxiety about the looming future.

Marcus met Jamal's gaze, his own eyes reflecting the kaleidoscope of lights from the Strip that painted the sky in hues of electric blue, searing pink, and pulsating green. "The play, man, is that we're not gonna play their game anymore. We ain't gonna be the ones stuck working double shifts for minimum wage while these cats out here... they're living like kings." He gestured broadly towards the glittering skyline, a testament to a world that operated by different rules, rules that seemed infinitely more appealing. "I talked to them. They're looking for people. People who can move product. High-end stuff. Said it's about discretion. About being smart. About being reliable."

Aisha leaned closer to Jamal, her voice a soft murmur. "Product, Marcus? What kind of product? This sounds... heavy." The unease that had settled over her earlier had deepened, the casual mention of illegal activity sending a shiver down her spine. She thought of her younger siblings, of the innocent trust they placed in her. This was not the future she envisioned for them, or for herself.

"It's not about what the product is, Aisha, it's about what it does," Marcus argued, his voice gaining an edge of defensiveness. "It's about the money. The capital. Enough to get us out of this hole. Enough to actually *live*. Think about it. Chloe, your art... you could have a studio, the best supplies. Jamal, you could finally get that car you've been dreaming of, one that doesn't sound like it's gonna fall apart every time you turn the key. We could all have... more." The word hung in the air, charged with the weight of their collective desire.

Chloe fiddled with the strap of her sketchbook, her gaze fixed on the vibrant light show that was currently dancing across the facade of a nearby casino. "More of what, Marcus? More risk? More looking over our shoulders? I want to create beautiful things, not become part of something ugly." The allure of financial freedom was undeniable, but the cost, she suspected, was far greater than mere monetary exchange. She pictured her canvases, the vibrant colors she painstakingly blended, and wondered if this path would strip all the color from her life.

"It's a calculated risk, Chloe," Marcus insisted, his tone firm. "We'll be smart. We'll be careful. We're not going to be stupid about this. We'll stick together. That's the most important thing. We've got each other. We can watch each other's backs. This is our pact. Our way out." He looked at each of them in turn, his eyes burning with a conviction that was both compelling and alarming. "We've graduated. We're adults now. And we have a choice. We can choose to follow the path they laid out for us, the one that leads to more of the same, or we can forge our own. We can take what's ours."

Jamal remained silent for a moment, his gaze sweeping over the scene. The Strip, in all its gaudy glory, was a siren song of temptation, a testament to a world that rewarded audacity and often punished caution. He saw the desperation in Marcus's eyes, the genuine yearning for a better life, and he understood it. He felt it himself, a dull ache of dissatisfaction with the limited horizons that had been presented to them. But he also saw the precipice, the dangerous edge of legality that Marcus was so eager to step over. "A pact, huh?" he said, his voice carefully neutral. "And what exactly are we pact-ing for, Marcus? A quick payday that lands us in federal prison?"

"We're pact-ing for a future," Marcus shot back, his voice rising slightly. "A future where we're not defined by where we came from, but by what we're willing to do to get where we're going. This isn't about being reckless; it's about being resourceful. It's about seizing an opportunity when it presents itself, even if it's not the one they taught us about in school." He paused, his gaze sweeping over the dazzling display of lights, the relentless energy of the city. "Look at all this. This is out there for the taking. And we're supposed to settle for less because it's the 'safe' option? That's not safe; that's surrender."

Aisha's hand tightened on Jamal's arm. "But Marcus, what if 'taking what's ours' means taking it from someone else? What if it means hurting people?" Her mind conjured images of the families she'd seen struggling in her own neighborhood, the fear in their eyes when the bills piled up. She didn't want to be the cause of that fear.

"We're not hurting anyone," Marcus said, though a flicker of uncertainty crossed his face before he masked it. "We're just... facilitating a transaction. Moving goods. It's business. And we'll be smart about it. We'll take what we need, set ourselves up, and then we can do whatever we want. We can even go back to school then, with money in our pockets, not debt. This is just a stepping stone."

Jamal sighed, running a hand over his face. "A stepping stone that could crumble beneath our feet and send us falling into a pit we can't climb out of. Marcus, I hear you. I do. I want a better life just as much as you do. But there are lines, man. Lines you don't cross if you want to sleep at night." He looked at Chloe and Aisha, seeing the fear and uncertainty reflected in their eyes. He couldn't let Marcus lead them all down a path that could end in ruin. "We're a team, yeah. But a team doesn't throw its players to the wolves. We need to find another way."

"Another way that's going to take us twenty years to get anywhere?" Marcus scoffed. "No thanks. I'm not waiting that long. This is happening tonight. The deal's set. They need people for a run tomorrow. And they're paying good money. Money we can use to actually *start* our lives, not just... exist." He turned, his gaze fixed on the vibrant heart of the Strip, the pulsing, electric core of the city that held both promise and peril. "Who's with me?"

The silence that followed was thick with unspoken anxieties and nascent rebellion. The distant sounds of the city seemed to amplify the quiet desperation that had settled over them. The neon lights, usually a symbol of Vegas's vibrant energy, now seemed to cast long, distorted shadows, painting their faces in hues of uncertainty and apprehension. The very air crackled with the weight of the decision Marcus was pushing them towards. He had laid it all out, a tempting offer disguised as a lifeline, a shortcut through the minefield of their futures.

Jamal met Marcus's intense gaze, his own expression a mixture of concern and a grudging respect for his friend's audacity, even if he thought it was misguided. "Look, man, I get wanting to break free. I really do. But this... this feels like jumping off a cliff because you're tired of walking uphill. We need to be smart about this. We need a plan that doesn't involve... this." He gestured vaguely towards the shadows where Marcus had spoken with the older men earlier, a space that seemed to hum with a dangerous energy.

Chloe, her fingers tracing the worn edges of her sketchbook, finally spoke, her voice barely a whisper. "But if we say no, Marcus, what then? Will you still be our friend? Will we still be a team?" The fear of fracturing their bond was as potent as the fear of the unknown path Marcus proposed. She valued their friendship above all else, but she also valued her own integrity.

Aisha's eyes darted between Marcus and Jamal, her heart caught in the middle. She trusted Jamal's cautious instincts, but she also saw the genuine desperation in Marcus's plea. His desire to help his family was a powerful motivator, one she understood deeply. Her own family had faced similar struggles, and the weight of responsibility was a heavy burden for all of them. "Marcus," she began, her voice gentle but firm, "we can find another way. We always do. We're smart. We're capable. We don't have to do this."

Marcus's jaw tightened, a familiar stubbornness settling over him. "Another way that takes years, Aisha? Years that my family doesn't have? Years where my dad could lose everything? This is it. This is the chance. And if you're not with me, then maybe... maybe we're not as close as I thought we were." The words hung in the air, a subtle threat, a test of their loyalty. He needed them, but more than that, he needed their agreement, their validation of his choice. He saw it as a test of their collective will, a declaration of independence from the limitations that had defined their lives.

Jamal stepped forward, placing a steadying hand on Marcus's shoulder. "That's not fair, man. This is about all of us. And we can't make a decision like this if you're trying to guilt us into it. We're your friends, Marcus. That means we tell you when we think you're about to walk into a burning building." He met Marcus's gaze, his own eyes reflecting a deep concern. "But if you're set on this... if this is the path you're choosing... then we're not letting you walk it alone. We're in this together. Whatever happens."

A slow smile spread across Marcus's face, a mixture of relief and triumph. He clapped Jamal on the back, the gesture firm, a silent acknowledgment of their shared commitment. "That's what I'm talking about," he said, his voice regaining its earlier confidence. "That's the pact. We do this, and we do it together. We're gonna make it. All of us." He looked out at the sprawling, glittering cityscape, the neon lights reflecting in his eyes, a silent promise of a future radically different from the one they had just left behind. This was more than just a graduation night; it was the beginning of something new, something dangerous, something that would bind them together in ways they couldn't yet comprehend. The pact, sealed not with a handshake but with a shared, defiant gaze towards the intoxicating glow of the Las Vegas Strip, was their declaration of war against the ordinary, a reckless gamble on a future they would build on the shaky foundations of illegality and untested courage. The night was young, and the city, with its endless temptations and hidden dangers, awaited.

The city's heartbeat, a relentless rhythm of engines and distant sirens, was the only soundtrack to their first clandestine steps. Graduation hats and diplomas were hastily stowed away, replaced by a nervous energy that thrummed beneath their skin. Marcus, ever the architect of their descent, had orchestrated this initiation with a precision that belied the chaotic nature of their chosen path. The initial meeting point was a dimly lit alcove behind a seedy pawn shop, the air thick with the metallic tang of desperation and stale cigarettes. It was a far cry from the manicured lawns of their alma mater, a stark reminder of the chasm between their dreams and the reality they were now embracing.

Their first 'assignment' was deceptively simple: act as inconspicuous observers for a meet-up happening across the street in a dimly lit bar, a place that reeked of cheap whiskey and broken promises. The instructions were clear: blend in, note who came and went, and report any unusual activity. It was meant to be a test of their ability to remain unseen, to become shadows in the periphery of the city's underbelly. Marcus had stressed the importance of anonymity, of melting into the background, a skill he'd honed through years of observing the silent negotiations that happened in the margins of society.

David, surprisingly, took to the role with an almost detached professionalism. His mind, accustomed to dissecting complex algorithms and predicting market trends, now turned its analytical prowess towards human behavior. He noticed the subtle tells – the way a man nervously adjusted his collar, the almost imperceptible glance towards the door, the coded greetings exchanged between individuals. He saw the patterns emerge, the subtle choreography of illicit dealings, and found a strange satisfaction in decoding it. His initial apprehension had morphed into a focused intensity, his eyes scanning the street with the sharp focus of a predator assessing its prey. He was good at this, a realization that sent a shiver of both excitement and unease down his spine. He mentally cataloged the vehicles parked nearby, noting license plates, the makes and models, mentally cross-referencing them with the few faces he recognized from Marcus's earlier introductions. He noticed the subtle shift in the way people walked when they were carrying something significant, the almost imperceptible tension in their shoulders. It was like a secret language, and he was beginning to understand the grammar.

Jamal, on the other hand, relied on his ingrained street smarts. He possessed an innate understanding of the city's pulse, a sixth sense for danger that had been forged in the crucible of his upbringing. He could read the mood of a street, the unspoken warnings in the atmosphere, the subtle shifts that signaled trouble brewing. His presence was a constant anchor for the group, his steady demeanor a calming force against the rising tide of adrenaline. He kept a watchful eye on Marcus, his brow furrowed with a mixture of concern and a grudging respect for his friend's unwavering conviction. He noticed the way the other patrons of the bar subtly avoided eye contact with certain individuals, the hushed conversations that abruptly ceased when they entered the room. He'd seen this kind of environment before, and he knew the unspoken rules. He kept his posture relaxed, his gaze casual, but his senses were on high alert, absorbing every detail, every nuance. He discreetly signaled to Marcus when a car that had been idling for an unusual amount of time finally pulled away, its headlights momentarily illuminating the faces inside.

Chloe, despite her initial trepidation, found herself surprisingly captivated by the visual narrative unfolding before her. Her artistic eye, trained to perceive nuance and detail, noticed the subtle interplay of light and shadow, the unspoken communication in body language, the way the city itself seemed to breathe with a life of its own. She found a strange beauty in the grit and grime, the raw authenticity of the scene. Her sketchbook, usually filled with vibrant colors and delicate lines, remained closed in her bag, but her mind was sketching with an intensity she'd never experienced before. She noticed the way the neon lights painted the faces of the passersby, casting them in dramatic, almost theatrical hues. She saw the weariness etched onto the faces of those who hurried by, the determined stride of those who seemed to know their destination, and the hesitant steps of those who seemed lost. It was a living canvas, and she was a silent observer, absorbing the textures and tones of their illicit world. She observed the clandestine exchange of a small package, a quick, almost invisible transaction that took place under the cloak of darkness, and felt a surge of understanding that surprised her.

The ease with which they operated was both exhilarating and terrifying. There was no immediate consequence, no flashing lights or angry shouts. Just the quiet hum of the city, indifferent to their small transgression. This lack of immediate repercussion fostered a dangerous sense of invincibility, a fragile illusion that they were somehow immune to the repercussions that had ensnared so many others. They had slipped through the cracks, emerging on the other side with their anonymity intact. The experience was like a baptism by fire, a first taste of a forbidden fruit that left them craving more. The adrenaline coursed through their veins, a potent elixir that masked the underlying fear and uncertainty. They had successfully navigated their first foray into the unknown, and the intoxicating rush of accomplishment was a powerful motivator, a whisper of promise in the deafening silence of their uncertain futures. Marcus, observing his friends, felt a surge of pride, a confirmation that his vision was taking root. He saw the subtle shift in their demeanor, the newfound confidence that settled upon them like a second skin.

Their subsequent tasks escalated subtly, moving from passive observation to more active participation. The next step involved delivering a small, unmarked package to a specific location, a drop that required precision and discretion. Marcus had emphasized the importance of not knowing the contents, of being merely a conduit, a ghost in the machine. The package was no bigger than a deck of cards, its weight surprisingly substantial. The instructions were to leave it in a designated public restroom, tucked away in a specific stall, and to be gone before anyone else entered. It was a test of nerve, a challenge to their ability to perform under the subtle pressure of potential discovery.

David meticulously mapped out the route, identifying multiple entry and exit points, calculating the optimal time to execute the drop to minimize the chances of encountering anyone. He saw it as a logistical puzzle, a series of variables to be managed. He researched the building's layout online, noting security camera blind spots and potential surveillance areas. His mind raced with contingencies, with backup plans for every conceivable scenario. He visualized the act itself, breaking it down into discrete, manageable steps. He knew the importance of leaving no trace, of making their presence as ephemeral as possible. He considered the best way to conceal the package within his clothing, ensuring it wouldn't be noticeable.

Jamal, ever the pragmatist, scouted the location beforehand, his casual demeanor masking his keen observation. He noted the usual foot traffic, the types of people who frequented the area, and the general atmosphere. He paid attention to the subtle cues that indicated potential trouble – the individuals who seemed overly aware of their surroundings, the lingering cars with tinted windows. He saw the drop as a tightrope walk, a delicate balance between efficiency and caution. He knew the importance of projecting an air of nonchalance, of appearing to be just another person going about their day. He practiced his walk, his gaze, ensuring he wouldn't draw any unwanted attention. He saw the potential for a swift and clean execution, but he also felt the ever-present hum of risk.

Chloe, tasked with being their distant lookout, positioned herself in a nearby café, the aroma of coffee a stark contrast to the tense anticipation she felt. Her artistic sensibilities were heightened; she saw the scene as a tableau, each individual a character in a unfolding drama. She noted the way the light fell on the entrance of the restroom, the ebb and flow of people entering and exiting. She felt a knot of anxiety tighten in her stomach as Marcus disappeared inside, his movements swift and purposeful. Her heart pounded in her chest with every passing second, each tick of the clock amplifying her apprehension. She saw a man exit the restroom shortly after Marcus entered, his expression unreadable, and her breath hitched. Had he seen Marcus? Had the drop gone awry?

The moment Marcus emerged, his face impassive, Chloe let out a silent breath of relief. The simplicity of the act, the lack of any immediate visible consequence, was disarming. It was almost too easy. This ease, however, was precisely what made it so dangerous. It was a seductive invitation, a subtle erosion of their caution. The thrill of successfully completing the task was a potent drug, dulling the sharp edges of their fear and amplifying the allure of this new life. They had proven themselves capable, adaptable, and, most importantly, discreet. The pact they had made under the neon glow of the Strip was beginning to solidify, not through grand gestures, but through these small, incremental steps into the moral gray. Each successful mission chipped away at their inhibitions, leaving them more susceptible to the siren call of illicit gains.

The sense of accomplishment was palpable, a heady concoction of adrenaline and burgeoning confidence. Marcus, with a subtle nod of approval, led them to another secluded spot, a deserted stretch of alleyway behind a closed-down cinema, the faded posters a ghostly testament to forgotten dreams. Here, amidst the graffiti-scarred brickwork and the faint smell of decay, they received their next instructions. This time, it involved a more direct exchange, a meeting with a contact who would be recognizable by a specific item of clothing – a faded blue baseball cap worn backward. The transaction was described as a simple handover, a transfer of information for a sum of money.

David, ever the strategist, had already begun to analyze the potential risks associated with a direct face-to-face interaction. He had considered the variables of identification, the potential for a setup, and the need for a swift and clean exit. He had identified the optimal vantage points from which to observe the meeting, noting escape routes and potential hiding places. He had even researched the local police patrol patterns, trying to gauge the likelihood of encountering law enforcement in the vicinity. He approached it like a chess game, anticipating his opponent's moves and planning his own counter-moves. He was developing a system, a framework for navigating these increasingly complex situations.

Jamal, his senses honed by years of navigating the city's less reputable corners, surveyed the designated meeting area with a practiced eye. He noticed the subtle signs of recent activity – a discarded cigarette butt, a scuff mark on the pavement that seemed out of place. He was acutely aware of the predatory nature of their new environment, the constant need to be vigilant. He kept his gaze steady, his posture relaxed, projecting an aura of casual disinterest. He knew the importance of blending in, of becoming invisible within the urban landscape. He could sense the subtle shifts in the atmosphere, the almost imperceptible changes that signaled potential danger. He saw a figure lingering in the shadows of a doorway across the street, seemingly innocuous, but his instincts told him otherwise.

Chloe, her artistic eye always drawn to the details, noticed the way the late afternoon sun cast long, distorted shadows, creating an atmosphere of mystery and unease. She observed the subtle body language of the few people who passed by, noting their hurried pace and averted gazes. She felt a growing sense of trepidation, a prickle of awareness that this was more than just a simple exchange of information. She saw the nervous way Marcus fidgeted with his collar, the slight tightening of Jamal's jaw, and recognized the shared tension that now bound them. The thrill of the previous 'hustles' was beginning to be tempered by a more profound understanding of the stakes involved.

The man with the blue cap arrived precisely on time, his movements fluid and unhurried. He exchanged a brief, almost imperceptible nod with Marcus, a silent acknowledgment that sealed their unspoken transaction. The exchange itself was over in a matter of seconds – a small, folded piece of paper passed from the stranger's hand to Marcus's. There was no conversation, no unnecessary interaction, just the silent completion of a clandestine task. The lack of fanfare, the sheer mundane nature of the act, was almost more unsettling than any overt display of danger. It normalized the illicit, making it seem like just another transaction in the vast marketplace of the city.

As Marcus slipped the paper into his pocket, a faint smile touched his lips, a flicker of triumph in his eyes. He met Jamal's gaze, a silent communication passing between them – they had done it. They had navigated another precarious step, their nascent skills proving more than adequate. The money that was exchanged for the information was handed to Marcus, a wad of bills that felt both liberating and corrupting in his hand. It was more than he'd made in weeks of menial labor, a tangible reward for their newfound enterprise. Chloe, from her vantage point, observed the entire exchange, her heart still thrumming with a mixture of fear and fascination. She saw the subtle nod of approval Marcus gave to Jamal, a silent acknowledgment of their shared success. The ease with which it had happened was unnerving, a seductive promise of future rewards. This was not merely about survival anymore; it was about aspiration, about the rapid accumulation of resources that could fundamentally alter their trajectory. The city, in its relentless embrace, was slowly, surely, pulling them deeper into its intricate web.

The air, still thick with the residual adrenaline of their recent endeavors, carried a new scent – that of opportunity, sharp and intoxicating. The wad of cash in Marcus's pocket was more than just paper; it was a tangible symbol of their departure from the mundane, a promise of a future unburdened by the grinding realities of their previous existence. Yet, even as this newfound wealth began to settle, a subtle shift in their dynamic became apparent, a barely perceptible tremor beneath the surface of their shared ambition. Marcus, emboldened by their consistent success, found his strategic mind already racing ahead, pushing the boundaries of their current operations. He spoke of expanding, of seeking out more lucrative opportunities, his eyes alight with a feverish ambition that bordered on recklessness.

"We're good at this," Marcus declared, his voice low but resonant as they regrouped in a grittier, more anonymous corner of the city, a pawnshop's back alley that offered a stark contrast to the earlier cinema's faded glamour. "We've proven we can move unseen, unheard. But staying small, staying hidden, that's how you get caught eventually. We need to think bigger." His gaze swept over the others, a silent challenge in his eyes. He was no longer content with simply observing and executing small tasks; he craved a more significant role, a leadership position in the clandestine economy they were tentatively exploring. He envisioned them as key players, not just foot soldiers, and his words painted a picture of a future that was both thrilling and daunting. He began to outline a new proposal, a more complex operation that involved a greater degree of risk, a deeper dive into the city's more dangerous currents.

Aisha, however, felt a growing unease gnawing at her conscience. The initial thrill had long since subsided, replaced by a prickling awareness of the moral implications of their actions. The money was indeed a powerful lure, a quick fix to the financial anxieties that had plagued her for years, but it came at a cost she was beginning to question. "Bigger, Marcus?" she asked, her voice softer, laced with a note of apprehension that stood in stark contrast to his fervent excitement. "We're barely a month into this, and you're already talking about… taking bigger risks. Don't you think we should be more careful? What if this is too much?" Her gaze flickered towards Jamal, hoping for a shared sentiment, but he met her concern with a steady, almost impassive expression.

Jamal, on the other hand, found the influx of cash to be a welcome balm to years of struggle. His pragmatism, usually a source of stability, was now being nudged by the allure of financial freedom. He'd always been the one to keep them grounded, the voice of reason born from necessity, but the ease with which they were acquiring resources began to chip away at his usual caution. "Careful is one thing, Aisha," he countered, his tone firm but not unkind. "But being afraid to move is another. We're not hurting anyone. We're just… facilitating things. And this money," he gestured, a subtle shift in his posture indicating his growing comfort with their new reality, "this money changes things. It means we don't have to live like we used to." He saw it as a deserved opportunity, a chance to finally escape the cycle of poverty that had defined his life, and he was unwilling to let apprehension derail it. He felt a surge of protectiveness towards the group, but it was now tinged with a desire to secure their collective future, a future that seemed suddenly within reach.

David, ever the detached observer, meticulously cataloged the escalating risks inherent in Marcus's ambitious plans. He saw the logical progression, the inevitable increase in scrutiny that came with larger operations. He mentally dissected the potential pitfalls, the increased likelihood of detection, the more sophisticated countermeasures they might encounter. His analytical mind was working overtime, creating elaborate risk assessments and contingency plans, but he kept these calculations largely to himself, a silent observer of their diverging perspectives. He noted the subtle shifts in their communication, the way Marcus's pronouncements were met with a mixture of eagerness and apprehension, and he began to understand that their shared journey was becoming increasingly individualized. He saw the pattern: ambition leading to increased risk, which in turn amplified both opportunity and danger. He felt a growing detachment, a sense of observing a complex equation unfold, the variables constantly shifting.

Chloe, caught between Aisha's moral reservations and Marcus's unbridled ambition, found herself attempting to bridge the growing divide. She understood both sides of the argument, the need for caution and the undeniable allure of their newfound success. "Maybe we can find a middle ground," she suggested, her voice a gentle attempt to soothe the rising tension. "Marcus, we can be smart about this, take calculated steps. Aisha, we're not going to do anything reckless. We're all in this together, remember?" She tried to inject a sense of unity into their conversations, to remind them of the pact they had made, the shared dream that had propelled them into this dangerous world. But even as she spoke, she felt the subtle pull of the easy money, the intoxicating whisper of a life free from the constraints of their former struggles. It was a seductive force, a powerful current that was subtly altering their relationships and amplifying their individual desires and insecurities.

Marcus, however, was already moving beyond the realm of suggestion. He had a new contact, a potential supplier for... items that could significantly enhance their capabilities. The specifics were vague, shrouded in the usual coded language, but the implication was clear: this was a step up, a move into a more serious league. He presented it not as a choice, but as a natural progression, a necessity for their continued success. "This guy," Marcus explained, his voice dropping to a conspiratorial whisper, "he can get us the gear. Better comms, maybe even something for... protection. We can't operate in the shadows forever without making sure we can defend ourselves." He was projecting an image of a seasoned operator, someone who understood the harsh realities of their chosen path.

Aisha's eyes widened in alarm. "Protection? Marcus, what are you talking about? This is exactly what I'm worried about. We're not street thugs. We're supposed to be smarter than this." Her voice trembled slightly, the fear becoming more palpable. The idea of acquiring weapons, of engaging in anything that could lead to violence, pushed her further into her moral quandary. She looked at Jamal, her plea for understanding clear in her gaze.

Jamal, however, saw it differently. He understood the underlying logic, the pragmatic necessity of such a move in their world. "Aisha, it's not about being thugs," he explained, his tone measured. "It's about survival. If things go south, and they can, we need to be prepared. Marcus is thinking ahead. It's a business decision." He tried to reframe it, to present it as a practical consideration rather than a descent into criminality. The money he'd accumulated allowed him a new perspective, a sense of agency he hadn't possessed before. He was no longer just reacting; he was planning.

David, meanwhile, had already begun researching the types of equipment Marcus might be referring to, the potential legal ramifications, and the increased risks associated with possession and use. He saw the trajectory as a clear escalation, a move that would undeniably place them higher on the law enforcement radar. He noted the subtle but significant change in Marcus's demeanor, a growing confidence that bordered on arrogance, and the way Jamal's initial pragmatism was morphing into a more hardened acceptance of their new reality. He also observed Chloe's increasing efforts to mediate, her role as the group's conscience becoming more pronounced, yet her own hesitations were also becoming more apparent to him. He saw the subtle way her eyes would linger on him, a mixture of curiosity and concern, as if seeking his opinion, his validation.

Chloe, feeling the pressure of their diverging paths, found herself increasingly exhausted by the constant effort to maintain equilibrium. "Marcus, we need to talk about this. All of us," she insisted, her voice firm. "This is getting out of hand. We started this to get out of a bad situation, not to create new, even bigger problems." She believed in their collective potential, but she was starting to fear that their individual desires were eclipsing their shared purpose. She saw how the intoxicating allure of easy money had begun to magnify their existing insecurities. Marcus's ambition, Aisha's moral quandaries, Jamal's newfound comfort with risk, and even her own quiet apprehension were all being amplified, creating subtle but significant fissures in their unity. She realized that their initial innocence was rapidly fading, replaced by a more complex, more dangerous understanding of the world and their place within it.

The ease with which they had acquired their first significant sums of money had indeed been a powerful catalyst. Marcus, in particular, seemed to revel in his newfound influence, his decisions carrying an unspoken weight that the others were increasingly reluctant to challenge. He started making decisions unilaterally, relaying information and instructions as faits accomplis rather than proposals for discussion. This shift was subtle at first, a mere preference for efficiency over consensus, but it began to breed a quiet resentment, particularly in Aisha, who felt her concerns were being systematically ignored.

"He's changing, isn't he?" Aisha confided to Jamal one evening, their conversation taking place on a dimly lit street corner, far from Marcus's current preoccupations. The cash she had received was tucked away, its presence a constant reminder of their shared enterprise, but also a source of internal conflict. "He's not the Marcus we knew from graduation anymore. It's like... the city is eating him alive."

Jamal, however, was experiencing his own transformation. The financial stability was a revelation. He was able to send more money home to his family, to start paying off debts that had once seemed insurmountable. This sense of empowerment was addictive. "He's adapting, Aisha," Jamal replied, his voice steady. "This world... it demands you adapt. You're still thinking too much about 'before.' We're in a new game now. And Marcus, he's playing to win." He saw Marcus's ambition as a necessary driver, a force that was propelling them forward. He didn't necessarily agree with every decision, but he understood the underlying logic. The ease of their early successes had made him more confident, more willing to accept the inherent risks. He found a strange satisfaction in the efficiency of their operations, the smooth execution of tasks that once would have seemed impossible.

David, observing this nascent friction, felt a growing sense of trepidation. He saw the seeds of division being sown, not from external threats, but from within. Marcus's unchecked ambition and Aisha's mounting unease were creating a dynamic tension that felt unsustainable. He meticulously documented the instances of unilateral decision-making, the increasingly dismissive responses to Aisha's questions, the subtle ways Jamal seemed to be aligning himself with Marcus's more aggressive strategies. He recognized the intoxicating pull of the easy money, how it amplified individual desires and masked underlying insecurities. Chloe's attempts to mediate were admirable but increasingly futile against the tide of ambition and the allure of wealth. He felt a growing sense of detachment, like a scientist observing a potentially volatile reaction.

Chloe, feeling increasingly isolated in her attempts to maintain a sense of collective morality, found herself gravitating towards David, seeking a shared understanding of the unsettling shifts. "It's like we're all on different paths now," she confessed to him during a brief, hushed conversation while Marcus was preoccupied with a phone call and Aisha had stepped away to compose herself. "Marcus wants to push forward, no matter the cost. Aisha's terrified of where it's leading. And Jamal... he's changed too. He sees the money, and it's blinding him to the danger." She spoke softly, her voice laced with a weariness that extended beyond the physical demands of their operations. The intoxicating nature of their illicit gains was subtly altering not just their actions, but their very perceptions of right and wrong, of loyalty and self-preservation. The shared dream was beginning to fragment, replaced by a complex web of individual motivations and escalating anxieties.

The incident that truly highlighted the growing cracks involved a more substantial delivery, one that required a higher level of coordination and carried a greater risk of exposure. Marcus, eager to impress a new, more influential contact, bypassed some of the usual precautionary steps, prioritizing speed and discretion over thorough reconnaissance. He had decided that a direct, late-night drop at a less populated industrial area would be more efficient.

"We don't need to overthink this," Marcus had stated dismissively when Aisha raised concerns about the location and the timing. "It's a simple handover. I'll handle it."

Jamal, though initially hesitant about the deviation from their established protocols, was swayed by the potential payout and Marcus's confident assertion. "Marcus is right, Aisha," he'd said, his voice betraying a subtle shift towards rationalizing Marcus's impulsiveness. "We've done riskier things. Plus, this is a big payday. We need this." He saw it as a calculated risk, one that would ultimately benefit them all. The money was too tempting to ignore, and Marcus's conviction, however misguided, was persuasive.

David, however, had already conducted a preliminary assessment of the area, identifying potential blind spots in surveillance and noting the increased likelihood of encountering law enforcement patrols due to the proximity of a major thoroughfare.

He had mapped out multiple escape routes and calculated the optimal window for the exchange, but his meticulous plan was largely ignored. He saw the potential for disaster in Marcus's haste, the way the ambition was overriding common sense. He made a mental note of the time Marcus departed, the precise minutes ticking by as Marcus navigated the city's darkened arteries, a solitary figure driven by an increasingly insatiable hunger.

Chloe, tasked with providing remote observation from a vantage point overlooking the industrial district, felt a knot of anxiety tighten in her stomach. The area was eerily quiet, the only illumination coming from the distant glow of the city skyline and the occasional passing headlights. She saw Marcus's car pull up to the designated meeting point, a desolate stretch of road beside a disused warehouse. The silhouette of another vehicle appeared shortly after, its headlights cutting through the darkness. The exchange was brief, a fleeting moment in the vast emptiness of the night. But as Marcus turned to leave, Chloe's heart leaped into her throat. A patrol car, its siren eerily silent, was cruising slowly down the adjacent street, its headlights sweeping across the scene just as Marcus's car accelerated away.

Marcus, however, managed to evade immediate detection, his quick reflexes and knowledge of the back routes serving him well. He returned to their meeting point, a secluded park on the city's outskirts, his face a mask of relief and exhilaration. He had narrowly avoided a potentially disastrous encounter, a brush with the law that had been a direct consequence of his own impatience.

"See? I told you it would be fine," Marcus declared, a triumphant grin spreading across his face as he handed over the substantial payment to the others. "Just a little bit of pressure, that's all."

Aisha, however, was visibly shaken. "A little bit? Marcus, we were almost caught! That was too close. This is not 'fine.' This is reckless." Her voice was tight with fear and anger. The near-miss had solidified her deepest anxieties, confirming her fears that Marcus's ambition was leading them down a path of no return. The easy money no longer felt so liberating; it felt tainted, dangerous.

Jamal, while acknowledging the close call, remained pragmatic. "We weren't caught, Aisha. That's what matters. We got the money, and we learned from it. Marcus drove well." He was still focused on the outcome, on the tangible reward, and downplayed the severity of the risk. The financial boost was too significant for him to easily dismiss the operation as a failure.

David, observing the exchange, noted the subtle flinch in Aisha's shoulders, the forced nonchalance in Jamal's tone, and the defiant gleam in Marcus's eyes. He saw how the intoxicating pull of easy money was amplifying their individual traits, pushing them further apart. Marcus's ambition was becoming arrogance, Aisha's caution was morphing into outright fear, Jamal's pragmatism was hardening into a selective blindness, and Chloe's attempts at mediation were becoming increasingly strained. The seeds of division, once barely visible, were beginning to sprout, threatening to unravel the fragile bond that had brought them together on graduation day, a stark reminder that the desert realities they had embraced were far more complex and perilous than their initial dreams had ever allowed. The very success they had sought was, ironically, becoming the source of their potential downfall, each triumph a step further away from innocence and closer to a dangerous precipice. The city, in its infinite capacity for both reward and ruin, was shaping them, molding them into something new, something the innocent graduates who had once dreamed on manicured lawns could never have imagined.

Chapter 2: Escalation and Entrapment

The city, once a canvas of dreams and anxieties, had become their playground, its underbelly a sprawling network of opportunities, each more enticing, and more treacherous, than the last. The initial exhilaration of their small successes had morphed into a calculated confidence, a dangerous evolution that saw them shedding their old lives with an almost disconcerting ease. Marcus, his jaw set with a new kind of determination, no longer spoke of mere survival; he spoke of dominance, of claiming their rightful place in the shadows. The whispers of his family's mounting debt, a gnawing fear that had long been a constant companion, now fueled a relentless drive. He saw each operation, each illicit transaction, not as a risk, but as a necessary step towards a future where financial security wasn't a distant mirage.

"We're leaving crumbs on the table," Marcus declared, his voice carrying an edge of impatience as they gathered in the dim light of a converted warehouse loft, the scent of stale coffee and ambition thick in the air. "These small-time jobs? They're for beginners. We're past that. My father's breathing down my neck, Aisha. Bills are piling up like a bad habit. We need a big score, something that sets us up for good, something that makes them forget we ever scraped by." He tossed a neatly folded wad of cash onto a battered metal table, the crisp bills a stark contrast to the grimy surroundings. It was more than they had made in their first three operations combined, a testament to their growing audacity, but Marcus saw it as merely an appetizer. His gaze, sharp and calculating, fell on Jamal, sensing a kindred spirit in his pragmatic ambition.

Jamal, his usual quiet demeanor now imbued with a subtle swagger, had indeed been orchestrating more complex schemes. The thrill of orchestrating intricate plans, of outmaneuvering the unsuspecting, had become his own brand of intoxication. He found a perverse satisfaction in the meticulous planning, the careful calibration of risk and reward. His reputation, once confined to the fringes of their social circle, was beginning to solidify in these clandestine circles, whispered about with a mixture of respect and apprehension. The casino floors, once just a backdrop for their early ventures, now felt like his personal chessboard.

"Marcus has a point," Jamal interjected, his voice smooth and measured, as he carefully stacked the money Marcus had brought. "We've proven we can handle the pressure. We're clean, we're efficient. Why not leverage that? I've been scouting a few... possibilities. High-stakes games, private clubs. The buy-ins are steep, but the payouts are astronomical. And there's a steady flow of... 'discreet' merchandise moving through those circles too. We could be the distributors. We're already connected to people who need what they're selling." He unrolled a city map, pointing to a cluster of upscale establishments in the city's most affluent district. The map, once a guide to their urban landscape, was now a blueprint for their ascent.

Aisha, however, felt a growing unease that was beginning to outweigh the initial thrill. The casual way they now discussed large sums of money, the nonchalant acceptance of increasingly dangerous propositions, sent a tremor of fear through her. The weight of Marcus's family debts, while understandable, felt like a justification for a descent she was finding harder and harder to accept. "High-stakes gambling, Jamal? Illicit merchandise? This isn't 'leveraging,' this is diving headfirst into a cesspool," she argued, her voice trembling slightly. "We're not equipped for this. We're not... those people. We started this to get out of debt, to have a little breathing room, not to become kingpins of the underworld." She looked around at their faces, searching for a flicker of her own apprehension, but found only a shared focus on the potential gains.

David, ever the observer, noted the subtle but significant shift in their collective demeanor. The easy camaraderie of their early days was being replaced by a more intense, almost predatory focus. He saw how the seductive allure of wealth was warping their perceptions, dulling their moral compasses. He had spent days meticulously analyzing the financial projections for Jamal's proposed ventures, calculating not just the potential profits, but the exponentially increased risks. The probability of detection, the potential for violent repercussions, the sheer scale of the legal ramifications – all of it pointed towards a trajectory that was becoming increasingly perilous. He found himself meticulously documenting every deviation from their initial, more cautious plan, creating a silent, internal record of their descent. He saw how easily they had accustomed themselves to a lifestyle far beyond their original means, shedding their old lives like a worn-out skin for the shine of ill-gotten gains. The quiet student who once fretted over student loans was being replaced by someone who calculated risks with the cold detachment of a seasoned professional.

"Aisha's right, Marcus," David said, his voice deliberately calm, a stark contrast to the simmering excitement around the table. "Jamal's proposals, while potentially lucrative, carry a significantly higher risk profile. The surveillance in those circles is far more sophisticated, and the clientele... they're not the type to forgive mistakes. Furthermore, the distribution of controlled substances, even on a small scale, escalates our legal exposure exponentially. We're talking about sentences that would make our current problems seem like minor inconveniences." He paused, letting his words hang in the air. "My projections suggest a nearly threefold increase in the likelihood of apprehension for these types of operations compared to our previous endeavors."

Marcus, however, waved away David's concerns with a dismissive flick of his wrist. "Sentences? David, we're not going to get caught. That's why we have you. You're our insurance policy, our 'analytical advantage.' Besides, my father's creditors aren't exactly the forgiving type. They're not going to wait for us to conduct a risk assessment. We need the money, and we need it now." His eyes, once filled with a hopeful ambition, now held a glint of desperation, a reflection of the mounting pressure from his own life. The easy money had become an addiction, a means to an end that was rapidly eclipsing any sense of caution.

Jamal, sensing Marcus's conviction, added his own calculated persuasion. "Think of it this way, Aisha," he said, his voice soft, almost conspiratorial. "We're not just moving product; we're providing a service. People want these things, and they're willing to pay top dollar for discreet delivery. We can control the flow, vet the clients. It's about managing the risk, not avoiding it entirely. And the games... I've developed a system. I know how to play the odds, how to spot the tells. We can't just stick to petty jobs forever if we want to truly escape." He gestured to the money, a tangible symbol of their new reality. "This is freedom, Aisha. Isn't that what we wanted?"

Chloe, caught between Aisha's increasingly vocal anxieties and the unyielding determination of Marcus and Jamal, found herself struggling to maintain her equilibrium. She saw the undeniable appeal of the lifestyle, the luxury that was slowly beginning to permeate their lives – better clothes, nicer meals, a temporary reprieve from the constant worry. But she also saw the subtle changes in their personalities, the hardening of their edges, the growing disconnect from the people they used to be. The city, with its intoxicating blend of desperation and opportunity, was a powerful solvent, dissolving their former selves.

"It's not just about the risk, is it?" Chloe finally said, her voice barely above a whisper, directed more at herself than at the others. "It's about... who we're becoming. We used to talk about what we wanted to *do* with our lives. Now it feels like we're just focused on what we want to *have*." She looked at Marcus, whose gaze was fixed on the money, and then at Jamal, whose eyes held a calculating gleam. She felt a pang of loss for the naive idealism that had once bound them together. The shared dream had curdled, replaced by a more immediate, more tangible pursuit of wealth.

Their first foray into Jamal's proposed ventures proved to be a baptism by fire. The target was a private poker game held in the opulent penthouse suite of a downtown hotel, a clandestine gathering frequented by the city's elite and its less savory denizens. Jamal, armed with his meticulously crafted system and an uncanny ability to read people, was confident. Marcus, his face set in a mask of forced nonchalance, was eager for the larger payout. Aisha, though her hands were clammy with anxiety, had agreed to act as a lookout and point of contact, a role she performed with a nervous efficiency. David, as always, was analyzing the digital landscape, looking for potential security vulnerabilities and monitoring police frequencies, his fingers flying across his laptop keyboard in a quiet corner of their rented safe house.

The atmosphere inside the suite was thick with cigar smoke and the hushed clinking of chips. The air crackled with tension, a palpable energy that fueled the high stakes. Jamal, at the center of the table, moved with a practiced ease, his calm demeanor a stark contrast to the growing desperation of his opponents. He played his cards with a precision that was almost surgical, each raise, each fold, a calculated maneuver. Marcus, stationed at the bar, nursed a drink, his eyes scanning the room, his mind already calculating the potential profit from the merchandise he was scheduled to discreetly deliver later that night. He was a coiled spring, ready to strike when the opportunity arose.

Aisha, positioned discreetly in the hotel's lobby, kept a constant vigil, her eyes darting towards the elevators, her heart pounding with every approaching footstep. She had been instructed to signal Marcus with a prearranged text if any unusual activity was detected, anything that deviated from the expected flow of guests. The casual disregard for security that the high rollers exhibited was both a testament to their perceived invincibility and a significant risk factor for the group. They moved with an entitlement that suggested they believed themselves above the law, a dangerous assumption that Aisha prayed Marcus and Jamal would not fall prey to.

Jamal's initial success was astounding. He managed to win a significant sum, enough to make their previous earnings seem like pocket change. The tension in the room shifted, his opponents growing more aggressive, more desperate. It was at this critical juncture that Marcus made his move. He approached Jamal, a subtle nod indicating the time was right for the merchandise exchange. The discreet handover of a small, nondescript package was executed with practiced efficiency, a silent transaction amidst the clamor of the game.

However, the evening's fortunes took a sharp turn. One of the losing players, a man with eyes that held a dangerous glint, began to grow suspicious of Jamal's seemingly effortless wins. His inquiries became more pointed, his accusations more veiled but no less menacing. The celebratory mood began to sour, replaced by an undercurrent of suspicion and hostility.

"You're too lucky, my friend," the man sneered, his voice low and gravelly. "Almost as if you know what cards are coming." He flicked a subtle glance towards Marcus, whose presence in the room had also drawn his attention.

Jamal, ever the poker face, offered a disarming smile. "Just a good night, my friend. And perhaps a little intuition."

But the seed of suspicion had been planted. As Jamal prepared for another hand, the man made a sudden, aggressive move, knocking over the table, scattering chips and cards across the opulent carpet. The ensuing chaos was a signal. Two burly men, who had been positioned discreetly near the entrance, moved swiftly to intercept Jamal.

This was Marcus's cue. He reacted instantly, not with aggression, but with calculated evasion. He shoved past the melee, heading for the exit, the package he had just acquired clutched tightly in his hand. His escape plan, meticulously laid out by David, involved a specific service elevator and a pre-arranged rendezvous with Chloe, who was waiting in a nondescript van a few blocks away.

Jamal, however, was not so fortunate. The losing player, anticipating this exact scenario, had his men corner him. A brief, brutal struggle ensued, and Jamal found himself roughly subdued. The merchandise, intended for distribution, was now in the hands of their adversaries. Aisha, witnessing the escalating violence from the lobby, felt a cold dread seize her. She immediately sent the prearranged signal to Marcus, her fingers fumbling with her phone, the words of her earlier warnings echoing in her mind.

David, monitoring the police scanner, heard the faint crackle of a dispatch call concerning a disturbance at the hotel. His brow furrowed as he cross-referenced the information with the intel he had on the players involved. He knew instantly that their carefully constructed operation had gone spectacularly wrong. He sent an urgent, encrypted message to Marcus: "Abort. Rendezvous at secondary safe house. Jamal compromised."

Marcus, already in motion, received the message and adjusted his escape route. He bypassed the intended rendezvous with Chloe, opting instead for a more circuitous and dangerous path through the city's labyrinthine alleyways. The near-miss with the patrol car during their previous operation had made him acutely aware of the potential for surveillance. He felt a surge of adrenaline, a primal instinct for self-preservation overriding any sense of loyalty to Jamal. The weight of the merchandise in his pocket felt like a leaden burden.

Chloe, receiving David's updated intel, understood the gravity of the situation. Her role shifted from passive observer to active participant in Marcus's escape. She intercepted him at a predetermined point, the van's engine a low rumble in the pre-dawn quiet. As Marcus scrambled into the passenger seat, his face grim and streaked with sweat, she saw the unmistakable signs of a close call.

"Jamal's been taken," Marcus stated flatly, his voice devoid of emotion. "The merchandise... they got it." He tossed the package onto the dashboard, its contents now irrelevant. The adrenaline was beginning to recede, replaced by a chilling realization of their vulnerability.

Chloe, her hands steady on the steering wheel, her eyes fixed on the road ahead, absorbed the news with a grim stoicism. "David said. We need to lay low. That hotel... it's probably crawling with security and, worse, police by now." She knew this was more than just a failed operation; it was a direct consequence of their escalating ambition, a brutal reminder of the razor's edge they were treading. The easy money had come with a steep price, and they were now facing the first installment.

Back at the safe house, David was meticulously erasing any digital footprints, dismantling their communication network, and preparing for an immediate relocation. The smooth operation had devolved into a chaotic scramble for survival. He felt a detached sort of grim satisfaction in the efficiency of his damage control, even as the implications of Jamal's capture weighed heavily on him. He knew that Jamal's silence, or lack thereof, could have devastating consequences for them all. The stakes had been raised, not incrementally, but catastrophically. The glamour of their illicit pursuits had evaporated, replaced by the cold, hard reality of their precarious existence.

Aisha, still in the lobby, managed to slip away unnoticed in the ensuing confusion, her heart still hammering against her ribs. She made her way back to her own small apartment, the wad of cash she had earned from the operation feeling cold and heavy in her pocket. The exhilaration of their earlier successes seemed like a distant memory, replaced by a gnawing fear and a profound sense of regret. She had wanted freedom, but this felt like a gilded cage, each step further trapping them in a cycle of escalating danger. The ease with which they had shed their old lives now felt like a betrayal, a surrender to a darker impulse. The city, which had promised so much, was now showing its teeth, and she feared they had stepped too far into its predatory embrace. The notion of a future unburdened by financial anxieties was now overshadowed by the very real threat of imprisonment, or worse. The game had indeed changed, and the rules were proving to be far more unforgiving than they had ever imagined. The allure of instant wealth had blinded them to the long-term consequences, and now, the shadows were beginning to close in. The ease with which they had become accustomed to a lifestyle far beyond their original means was now being eclipsed by the stark reality of their vulnerability. They had shed their old skins, but the new ones were already showing the first signs of tearing under the immense pressure.

Las Vegas. The name itself was a siren song, a shimmering mirage on the horizon of their ambition. It was a city built on dreams and broken promises, a glittering facade that masked a churning, avaricious heart. For Marcus, Jamal, Aisha, David, and Chloe, it represented the ultimate stage, a place where their carefully honed skills could be amplified, their ambitions unleashed without the suffocating constraints of their previous lives. The initial sting of their botched Las Vegas operation, the chilling capture of Jamal, had done little to dampen Marcus's resolve. Instead, it had ignited a burning, almost desperate need to recoup their losses and, more importantly, to prove that they were not to be underestimated. The city, with its neon glow and intoxicating promises, was not just a destination; it was a crucible.

The aftermath of Jamal's capture had been a whirlwind of frantic activity, a desperate dance in the shadows. David, ever the pragmatist, had immediately initiated their emergency protocols. The safe house was abandoned, their digital footprints meticulously scrubbed. Marcus, fueled by a potent cocktail of guilt and adrenaline, had managed to evade any immediate pursuit, thanks to Chloe's sharp driving and David's pre-planned escape routes. Aisha, her initial terror slowly giving way to a cold, steely resolve, had reached out to a contact within the city's less savory circles, a person she'd cultivated during their initial scouting phase. This contact, a man named Silas, operated on the fringes, a facilitator of sorts, someone who knew people who could make problems disappear, or, more relevantly, someone who could provide the resources and introductions needed to navigate the treacherous landscape they now found themselves in.

"We can't go back to what we were," Marcus declared, his voice hoarse, as they huddled in a dingy motel room on the outskirts of Vegas, the silence punctuated only by the distant hum of traffic. The camaraderie that had once defined them was strained, replaced by a palpable tension, a shared awareness of their precarious situation. "Jamal's gone, and if we don't make a move, if we don't recover what we lost, we're finished. They'll find him, they'll squeeze him, and he'll sing like a canary." His eyes, usually sharp and focused, were shadowed with fatigue and a gnawing anxiety. The weight of Jamal's absence, the potential consequences of his capture, pressed down on him with suffocating force.

Aisha, surprisingly, was the one who seemed to regain her composure first. The fear that had gripped her at the hotel lobby was still present, a cold knot in her stomach, but it was now tempered by a pragmatic understanding of their predicament. "Silas is our best bet," she said, her voice steady. "He owes me a favor, a big one. He can get us access to places we couldn't even dream of before. But it comes with a price, and that price isn't just money." She looked at each of them, her gaze lingering on Marcus. "He's going to want something in return, something that will pull us even deeper."

Silas, when they finally met him in a dimly lit backroom of a nondescript bar frequented by those who preferred the shadows, was a man who exuded an aura of quiet power. He was older than them, his face etched with the lines of a life lived on the edge, his eyes sharp and unnervingly perceptive. He listened intently to Aisha's recounting of their misfortunes, his expression unreadable. When she finished, he leaned back, a faint smile playing on his lips.

"Jamal, eh?" Silas mused, his voice a low rumble. "A talented young man. A shame he got caught playing in the big leagues without the proper credentials." He turned his attention to Marcus. "You want to get him back? Or at least, you want to recoup your losses? That's a dangerous game you're playing, Marcus. The people who took your friend don't play by the same rules."

Marcus met his gaze, a flicker of defiance in his eyes. "We're willing to pay. We're willing to do what it takes."

Silas chuckled, a dry, rasping sound. "Willingness is cheap. I need something more. I need you to understand that this city... it's not just about gambling and cards. It's about influence. It's about access. You want to play in this arena, you need to be connected. And connections, my friends, are not easily bought." He steepled his fingers. "There's a casino, a new one, 'The Mirage.' Very exclusive. Very... discreet. The owner, a man named Viktor, he's always looking for new talent, new ways to increase his 'assets.' He's also got a... problem. A rival is trying to muscle in on his territory, and Viktor needs a certain problem solved, permanently."

David, his analytical mind already whirring, spoke up. "And what exactly would this 'problem' entail?"

Silas's smile widened. "A rival businessman. A man who likes to operate in the open, which is, of course, unacceptable to Viktor. He wants him removed from the equation. Discreetly. No fuss. No mess. And in return, Viktor will overlook your previous... indiscretions. He'll even provide you with the means to get Jamal back, assuming he's still in one piece."

The proposition hung in the air, heavy and foreboding. Aisha felt a chill snake down her spine. This was a step beyond anything they had ever contemplated. This wasn't just about acquiring wealth; it was about taking a life. The line they had been so careful to tiptoe around had just been obliterated. Marcus, however, saw it as the only path forward. The desperation in his eyes had hardened into a grim determination. The pursuit of easy money had morphed into a desperate fight for survival, and the city of Las Vegas, with its intoxicating blend of opportunity and danger, was rapidly becoming their prison.

"We'll do it," Marcus said, his voice firm, betraying none of the turmoil raging within him. Chloe, who had remained silent, her gaze fixed on the intricate patterns of the bar's worn carpet, gave a barely perceptible nod. She understood the stakes. Their shared future, their very freedom, depended on their ability to navigate this treacherous new landscape. The siren call of vice had not only lured them to Vegas but had also ensnared them in its depths, a gilded trap from which escape seemed increasingly impossible.

The following days were a blur of covert preparations. David, utilizing his considerable technical skills, managed to glean as much information as possible about Viktor's rival, a man named Carmine Rossi. Rossi was known for his brash public persona and his ostentatious displays of wealth, a stark contrast to the shadowy dealings that fueled Viktor's empire. He was also, according to David's intel, a creature of habit, his routine as predictable as the ticking of a clock. This predictability, David theorized, would be their greatest weapon.

Chloe, with her innate ability to blend into any environment, was tasked with the initial reconnaissance. She spent hours observing Rossi, mapping his movements, identifying his security protocols, and pinpointing potential vulnerabilities. The opulent casinos and exclusive nightclubs of the Strip, once symbols of aspirational luxury, now felt like the hunting grounds for a desperate pack. The glittering facade of Vegas concealed a brutal, unforgiving ecosystem, and they were the new predators, driven by necessity.

Marcus and Aisha, meanwhile, worked with Silas to gather the necessary tools and information. Silas provided them with untraceable communication devices, sophisticated surveillance equipment, and, most importantly, access to Viktor's inner circle. This access came with its own set of demands. Viktor, a man who measured loyalty in blood, expected absolute discretion and unwavering commitment. He was not a man to be crossed, and the consequences of failure were not merely financial; they were existential.

The plan, as it began to coalesce, was audacious, bordering on suicidal. Rossi was scheduled to attend a private charity gala at one of the city's most exclusive hotels. The event was a high-profile affair, attended by the city's elite, the very people who ostensibly upheld the law. This made it the perfect cover for their operation. The chaos and anonymity of such a large gathering would provide the ideal backdrop for their discreet, albeit brutal, task.

David had identified a critical window of opportunity: the brief period between Rossi's arrival at the hotel and his entrance into the main ballroom. A service tunnel, rarely used and poorly monitored, ran beneath the hotel, offering a potential ingress and egress point. Marcus, armed with specific instructions and a weapon provided by Silas, would intercept Rossi in the tunnel. Aisha, stationed nearby, would act as a secondary lookout and provide a swift exit strategy, coordinating with Chloe who would be waiting with a nondescript vehicle on a side street.

The night of the gala arrived with a palpable sense of dread. The air in Las Vegas crackled with an electric energy, a symphony of distant music and the rumble of luxury vehicles. As Marcus and Aisha approached the hotel, disguised as catering staff, the sheer opulence of the scene was almost overwhelming. The glitz and glamour, however, served only to underscore the grim reality of their task. The allure of power and status, the very things that had drawn them to this city, were now pushing them towards a precipice. They were no longer just running from debt; they were actively participating in the city's dark underbelly, mistaking recklessness for control, ambition for a legitimate path.

David monitored their progress from a nearby van, his fingers flying across his laptop keyboard, a digital phantom orchestrating their every move. He had secured access to the hotel's security feed, a risky endeavor that could easily expose them, but one he deemed necessary. Chloe, parked a few blocks away, her engine idling, was a silent, watchful presence, a lifeline in the unfolding drama.

"He's here," David's voice crackled through Marcus's earpiece, a tense whisper. "Rossi's arriving now. Security detail is light, as expected. He's moving towards the service entrance."

Marcus's heart hammered against his ribs. He caught Aisha's eye; a shared glance of grim understanding passed between them. They moved with practiced efficiency, melting into the shadows of the service corridors, the scent of disinfectant and stale air a stark contrast to the perfume and champagne wafting from the ballroom above. The weight of the small, deadly package in Marcus's pocket felt like an anchor, pulling him down into the abyss.

They reached the mouth of the service tunnel, a dark, gaping maw. "Aisha, you take position by the emergency exit," Marcus instructed, his voice strained. "Keep your eyes peeled. I'll go in."

Aisha nodded, her face pale but determined. She moved silently, disappearing into the maze of corridors, her earlier anxieties now channeled into a focused vigilance. Marcus took a deep breath and stepped into the tunnel. The darkness was absolute, broken only by the faint glow of his hidden comm device. He could hear the distant thrum of the city, a muffled reminder of the world above. He was a hunter, stalking his prey, but he was also a hunted man, acutely aware of his own vulnerability. The temptation of Vegas had led them down a path paved with good intentions, but it had quickly devolved into a descent into true darkness. The intoxicating blend of wealth and power had proven to be a potent drug, and they were now addicts, willing to pay any price for their fix, even if that price was their souls. The line between desperation and depravity had become alarmingly blurred, and in the suffocating darkness of the service tunnel, Marcus felt the full weight of that realization crushing down on him. He was no longer just a student trying to escape debt; he was a criminal, his hands already stained with the potential for bloodshed. The siren call of vice had drawn them into the heart of the storm, and the true cost of their ambition was about to be revealed.

The sterile, sterile white of the motel room felt like a shroud. Chloe traced the condensation ring left by her lukewarm coffee, each circular imperfection mirroring the growing unease in her gut. Marcus's pronouncement – "We'll do it" – echoed in the oppressive silence, a death knell for the naive aspirations that had lured them to this gilded cage. She'd nodded, a traitorous gesture born of a desperate hope that this would be the last, the ultimate sacrifice to reclaim Jamal and their fractured lives. But even then, a cold tendril of dread had coiled around her heart, whispering of the irreversible step they were taking. Silas's proposition wasn't just a transaction; it was a descent into a moral abyss, a place where the sharp edges of their ambition would be ground down into something ugly and unrecognizable.

The subsequent days had been a disorienting kaleidoscope of clandestine meetings and hushed discussions. David, hunched over his glowing screens, dissected Viktor's rival, Carmine Rossi, with the clinical detachment of a surgeon. Chloe found herself drawn into his meticulous process, not as a participant, but as an observer, her artist's eye picking up nuances David's data streams couldn't convey. She studied the grainy surveillance footage of Rossi, a man who radiated an almost aggressive confidence, his tailored suits screaming wealth, his every gesture a performance. It was during these sessions, poring over Rossi's public appearances, that Silas's chillingly pragmatic request emerged. "Viktor needs a certain... alteration to Rossi's public image," Silas had explained, his voice smooth as aged whiskey. "Something that will discredit him, make him vulnerable. Something that looks... authentic." He'd then turned his unnervingly sharp gaze on Chloe. "You're an artist, aren't you? You have a way with details."

The words, innocuous on their surface, had landed with the weight of a death sentence. Chloe's art had always been her sanctuary, a space where she could translate emotion into form, where beauty and truth converged. To wield that talent for deception, for manipulation, felt like a violation of her very soul. Yet, here she was, tasked with crafting a lie that would be indistinguishable from truth. David, oblivious to her internal turmoil, had readily agreed to her involvement. "Chloe can handle the visual aspects," he'd declared, his focus entirely on the technical execution. "We need something that can be subtly integrated into Rossi's digital footprint, something that looks like a genuine leak, a private indiscretion."

Chloe's initial task was to create a series of forged social media posts and leaked private messages that would paint Rossi as a corrupt, untrustworthy figure. She spent hours in the suffocating anonymity of a rented studio, the hum of the city a distant, mocking lullaby. Her fingers, usually guided by inspiration, now felt like blunt instruments, forced to contort her innate skill into something insidious. She crafted witty, damning captions for fabricated photographs, invented conversations laden with double entendres and veiled threats, all designed to erode Rossi's carefully constructed public persona. Each keystroke, each pixel manipulated, felt like a betrayal of her own artistic integrity. She found herself sketching in the margins of her notebooks, not the vibrant landscapes she once loved, but jagged, anxious lines, a visual manifestation of her inner conflict. The colors she chose became muted, somber, mirroring the darkening of her spirit.

The first set of fabricated documents was submitted to David, who reviewed them with a critical, appraising eye. "This is good, Chloe. Almost too good," he'd said, a hint of admiration in his tone. "The facial expressions, the subtle inconsistencies in the lighting... it's masterful. Rossi won't suspect a thing." His praise felt like a barbed compliment, highlighting the very perversion of her talent that was tearing her apart. She saw her ability not as a gift, but as a weapon, a tool that was corrupting her from the inside out.

Marcus, caught in the whirlwind of planning the physical assassination, seemed oblivious to the subtle erosion of Chloe's spirit. His focus was solely on the immediate danger, on ensuring the operation's success and Jamal's retrieval. Aisha, however, noticed. She saw the subtle tension in Chloe's shoulders, the way her eyes flitted away from any direct gaze, the almost imperceptible tremor in her hands when she held a pen. One evening, as they huddled in a nondescript diner, the clatter of plates and the murmur of conversations a thin veneer over their clandestine world, Aisha placed a hand over Chloe's.

"Are you okay?" Aisha's voice was soft, laced with genuine concern.

Chloe flinched, then forced a smile. "Just tired. This is all... a lot."

"It's more than a lot, Chloe," Aisha said, her grip tightening. "I see how this is affecting you. This isn't what you do. This isn't who you are."

Tears welled in Chloe's eyes, hot and sudden. "But what choice do we have, Aisha? They took Jamal. Marcus feels responsible. We're in this deep. If this is what it takes..." Her voice cracked. "If this is how we get out, how do we say no?"

Aisha squeezed her hand. "We don't say no to surviving, Chloe. But we have to be careful not to lose ourselves in the process. There's a difference between doing what's necessary and becoming what we're fighting against."

The words resonated deeply within Chloe. She was doing what was necessary, but at what cost? Her art was her voice, her way of making sense of the world. Now, her voice was being twisted, used to sow discord and distrust. She found herself unable to sketch, the blank canvas mocking her inability to create something genuine. Instead, she started painting over old pieces, smearing vibrant colors with dark, muddy hues, creating abstract expressions of her guilt and despair. The lines became frantic, the forms distorted, a visceral representation of her fractured psyche.

As the date of the gala approached, Chloe's role evolved. Silas, impressed by her earlier forgeries, requested something more tangible, something that would directly implicate Rossi in a scandal during the event itself. "Viktor wants proof," Silas had explained, his tone devoid of emotion. "Something that can be 'discovered' during the gala. A private ledger, perhaps? Or encrypted communications detailing illicit dealings."

This was a far more complex undertaking, requiring not just visual deception but also a convincing imitation of data and technical sophistication. David, for all his brilliance, lacked Chloe's intuitive grasp of visual storytelling. He could build the digital framework, but Chloe needed to imbue it with a sense of verisimilitude, to make it feel real, lived-in.

Working with David, Chloe found herself immersed in the intricacies of data presentation, learning how to mimic the visual language of confidential documents. She designed spreadsheets that looked damning, created email trails that suggested conspiracy, and even sketched out the façade of encrypted messages, all the while feeling a growing sense of alienation from her own creativity. Her artistic process, once a joyous exploration, had become a grim, meticulous act of fabrication. She would spend hours analyzing the visual aesthetics of authentic documents, noting the fonts, the spacing, the subtle watermarks, all to ensure her forgeries were flawless. The irony was not lost on her: she was using her artistic talent to dismantle another person's life, all in the name of survival.

One afternoon, while David was busy coordinating logistics, Chloe found herself alone in their makeshift command center, a tangle of wires and screens. She had been tasked with creating a series of "leaked" documents that would appear to show Rossi engaging in illegal arms dealing, a far more serious accusation than mere corruption. She opened a blank document, her fingers hovering over the keyboard. Instead of typing, she found herself sketching again, this time a self-portrait. It was a distorted reflection, her eyes wide with a fear she couldn't articulate, her mouth a gaping void. As she worked, a wave of nausea washed over her. This was no longer just about compromised integrity; it was about actively participating in a potentially lethal deception. If these forged documents led to Rossi's demise, she would be complicit, her art a catalyst for murder.

She confided in Aisha again, her voice barely a whisper. "I can't do this, Aisha. This is... this is different. This could get someone killed."

Aisha's expression was grim. "I know. We're all aware of the risks, Chloe. But we're also aware of what happens if we don't do it. Marcus is convinced this is the only way to get Jamal back, and Silas... Silas is a dangerous man to disappoint." She looked at Chloe, her eyes filled with a mixture of empathy and resolve. "You're a brilliant artist, Chloe. You're creating something that looks real. That's your gift. But the consequences... those are on us, on Marcus and David and me. You're doing what you're asked, what's necessary to keep us all safe."

But Chloe couldn't shake the feeling that she was actively participating in the corruption. Her art, once a source of pride and self-expression, had become a source of shame. She started to avoid looking at her own work, her creations filling her with a deep sense of unease. The vibrant palette that had once characterized her art felt like a distant memory, replaced by a bleak, monochromatic world. She tried to channel her feelings into her art, painting abstract pieces that were dark and chaotic, filled with jagged lines and unsettling imagery. These paintings, however, offered no catharsis, only a stark reflection of her compromised soul.

The day of the gala arrived with a suffocating sense of inevitability. Chloe, tasked with a final visual flourish – a carefully crafted 'smoking gun' document that David would subtly plant in Rossi's briefcase – felt a profound sense of detachment. She completed the forgery with a mechanical precision that belied the turmoil within her. It was a masterpiece of deception, a testament to her skill, and a damning indictment of her current reality. As she handed the document over to David, their eyes met. In his, she saw a flicker of... something. Recognition? Sympathy? It was impossible to tell. David was a man of logic, not emotion, and his participation in this plan was purely transactional.

Later, waiting with Aisha in the shadows of a side street, Chloe watched as Marcus and Aisha, disguised as part of the catering staff, slipped into the hotel. She felt a strange, almost surreal sense of disconnect, as if she were watching a movie unfold. Her hands, usually so sure and steady, trembled as she gripped the steering wheel of their getaway car. She had played her part, a crucial one, in the elaborate charade. Her artistic talent had been twisted, its purpose perverted, and the compromise gnawed at her with an agonizing persistence. The vibrant dreams she'd harbored upon arriving in Las Vegas had been systematically dismantled, replaced by the grim reality of her complicity. She was no longer just an artist; she was a cog in a machine, a tool wielded by darker forces, her creativity sacrificed on the altar of survival. The neon glow of the city, once a beacon of hope, now felt like the cold, hard glare of a spotlight, exposing her deepest fears and the devastating compromises she had made. The art she had created, meant to be a testament to beauty and truth, had become a harbinger of destruction, a silent scream of her own lost innocence. She closed her eyes, the image of the forged document seared into her mind, a symbol of her artistic compromise and the irreversible path they had all embarked upon.

David's focus had always been on the meticulous architecture of systems, the elegant dance of logic and data that underpinned the city's humming infrastructure. He saw the world in algorithms, in predictable sequences that could be analyzed, manipulated, and ultimately, controlled. Chloe's artistic endeavors, while fascinating in their own right, remained a secondary consideration, a necessary component of Silas's overarching plan, but not the core of his own engagement. His true battlefield was within the glowing matrix of his monitors, a landscape of code and encrypted pathways where every decimal point, every fluctuating variable, represented a potential lever of power.

Silas's directive to destabilize Carmine Rossi's financial empire had initially presented David with an intellectual puzzle, a complex problem demanding a precise and multifaceted solution. He'd begun by meticulously mapping Rossi's known assets, tracing the flow of capital through shell corporations and offshore accounts with an almost obsessive zeal. He wasn't merely looking for vulnerabilities; he was constructing a digital blueprint, identifying the arteries and veins of Rossi's wealth, and then devising ways to constrict them. The initial stages were purely analytical, a cold, hard assessment of financial leverage. He identified key points of entry, discovered overlooked compliance oversights, and noted the intricate web of dependencies that kept Rossi's illicit operations afloat.

The true escalation, however, began when Silas hinted at more direct intervention. "Rossi's liquidity is his lifeblood," Silas had mused, swirling a glass of amber liquid that caught the faint light of David's screens. "We need to disrupt that. Not just inconvenience him, David. We need to choke him." The implication was clear, and it sent a shiver of both apprehension and exhilaration down David's spine. He wasn't just to analyze; he was to *act*.

This shift pushed David beyond the realm of passive observation into active manipulation. His first forays were subtle, almost imperceptible nudges to the financial currents. He exploited a minor currency fluctuation, subtly rerouting a fraction of a percentage point from one of Rossi's overseas accounts to a dormant holding company he'd previously established. It was a test, a probe to gauge the system's responsiveness and identify any immediate detection mechanisms. The transaction, small in isolation, was a calculated risk, a digital whisper that could easily go unnoticed. When no alarms blared, no suspicious activity reports were generated, David felt a surge of confidence. The system was more permeable than he'd anticipated.

This initial success emboldened him. He began to explore more aggressive strategies, always with the caveat of deniability, of creating a narrative that could be attributed to market volatility, regulatory oversight, or even Rossi's own internal mismanagement. He leveraged his understanding of algorithmic trading, crafting a series of phantom buy orders that created artificial spikes in the value of certain Rossi-controlled assets, only to pull them back at the last moment, leaving his target to chase phantom profits. It was a sophisticated form of psychological warfare, waged in the sterile landscape of financial markets. The thrill of outsmarting the system, of orchestrating these intricate maneuvers from the shadows, was becoming increasingly addictive. He would spend hours hunched over his keyboard, his fingers flying across the keys, his mind completely absorbed in the intricate dance of numbers. The world outside his illuminated workspace ceased to exist; there was only the glow of the screens and the promise of another successful manipulation.

His risk tolerance, always present but previously contained within the acceptable parameters of professional hacking, began to stretch. He started to explore deeper, more proprietary systems, those that governed the transfer of significant capital. Silas had provided him with access codes, obtained through means David didn't care to inquire about, granting him passage into territories previously uncharted. He found himself probing the security protocols of major financial institutions that had dealings with Rossi, looking for the digital backdoors that could facilitate the siphoning of larger sums.

Chloe's initial task, creating the visual fabrications to damage Rossi's public image, had been a necessary precursor. David understood Silas's strategy: the digital disruption needed to be supported by reputational damage. While Chloe meticulously crafted the illusion of Rossi's corruption, David was laying the groundwork for the financial catastrophe. He was building the digital trap, and Chloe was providing the bait.

One evening, while dissecting the financial records of a subsidiary that handled Rossi's shipping manifests, David discovered a pattern of overpayments to a specific logistics provider. The amounts were small, almost insignificant in the grand scheme of Rossi's vast enterprise, but the regularity was a glaring anomaly. It smacked of a kickback scheme, a common method for moving illicit funds. David recognized the potential. If he could subtly amplify this anomaly, make it appear far more significant than it was, he could create a powerful narrative of financial malfeasance that Chloe could then weaponize.

This required a delicate touch. He couldn't simply invent numbers; that would be too easily detected. Instead, he began to manipulate the data in a way that mimicked genuine accounting errors, introducing discrepancies in exchange rates, altering timestamps on recorded transactions, and subtly shifting decimal points in decimal amounts. It was like performing microsurgery on Rossi's financial records. Each alteration was meticulously logged in his own secure system, a shadow ledger of his interventions, creating a trail that, if discovered, would only point to a series of "unfortunate technical glitches" or "human errors."

The deeper he went, the more the ethical implications gnawed at him. He wasn't just a passive observer of criminal activity anymore; he was an active participant, an architect of deception. The thrill of the challenge, however, was a potent counterweight to his nascent guilt. He saw himself as a master chess player, strategically sacrificing pawns to achieve a larger objective. And his objective, as Silas had made clear, was the complete dismantling of Carmine Rossi.

He recalled Silas's earlier instructions: "Viktor requires Rossi to be rendered completely inert. His influence must be extinguished, David. Permanently." The word "permanently" had resonated with a chilling finality, suggesting that this wasn't just about temporary disruption; it was about annihilation. And David, with his unique skillset, was the instrument of that annihilation.

The financial systems he was now operating within were incredibly complex, a labyrinth of interconnected networks designed to be impenetrable. But David had always thrived in complexity. He saw the vulnerabilities not as barriers, but as invitations. He spent days tracing the intricate pathways of Rossi's investments, meticulously mapping out the flow of money from its origins to its final destinations. He discovered that a significant portion of Rossi's illicit gains were being funneled into a series of high-yield, short-term investment funds, managed by a discreet private equity firm. This was a critical vulnerability, a point where Rossi was concentrating his capital in a way that made it susceptible to rapid divestment or, conversely, a sudden freeze.

David began to craft a plan to exploit this concentration. He envisioned a scenario where he could initiate a massive, coordinated sell-off of Rossi's holdings within these funds, triggering a cascade effect that would plummet their value. To do this effectively, he needed to gain access to the trading platforms of the private equity firm. This was a far more significant undertaking than anything he had attempted before, requiring him to breach multiple layers of security, bypass sophisticated firewalls, and potentially even impersonate authorized traders.

The preparation for this operation consumed him. He spent weeks analyzing the firm's digital infrastructure, identifying the weakest points of entry. He studied their software updates, looking for zero-day exploits, and even researched the personal digital footprints of key personnel to identify potential social engineering vectors. He was building an arsenal of digital tools, each one designed for a specific purpose, a precise strike against Rossi's financial fortress.

His internal monologue became a constant battle between exhilaration and apprehension. He knew that such a direct and aggressive manipulation of financial markets carried immense risk. Discovery would not just mean his own downfall, but potentially the exposure of Silas and Viktor, a consequence he couldn't afford to contemplate. Yet, the sheer intellectual challenge, the opportunity to test the absolute limits of his abilities, was an irresistible siren song. He found himself increasingly detached from the real-world implications, viewing the entire operation as an elaborate, high-stakes game.

The ethical quandaries were no longer whispers; they were a persistent chorus. He was actively engaging in acts that, if discovered, would lead to severe legal repercussions, not only for him but for everyone involved. He was, in essence, orchestrating a sophisticated form of financial sabotage. The thought of the potential fallout – the ripple effect of market instability, the potential ruin of innocent investors caught in the crossfire – did cross his mind, but he quickly rationalized it away. Rossi was a criminal, a predator. David saw his actions as a form of justice, albeit one delivered through unconventional means. He was leveling the playing field, taking from the corrupt and, in theory, contributing to a larger, albeit clandestine, cause.

He remembered Chloe's struggle, her artistic integrity being compromised for their shared goal. He understood her pain, her internal conflict, but he saw his own engagement as fundamentally different. He wasn't corrupting a creative process; he was applying a skill set, a talent for logic and systems, to achieve a desired outcome. The lines between right and wrong had blurred so significantly that he no longer saw a clear distinction, only the immediate objective and the intricate path to achieving it.

The opportunity to execute the primary phase of his plan presented itself during a period of high market volatility, a perfect cover for a significant shift in trading activity. Silas provided the final go-ahead, a terse confirmation that set David's adrenaline coursing. He initiated the sequence, his fingers moving with practiced efficiency. He began by subtly altering the data feeds to the private equity firm, introducing minor errors that would slightly misrepresent the true value of Rossi's holdings. This was the precursor to the main event, designed to sow a seed of doubt, to make the subsequent, more significant manipulations appear as a natural consequence of existing market conditions.

Then, he unleashed the synchronized sell orders, crafted to overwhelm the automated trading systems. The sheer volume of the orders, timed to hit simultaneously across multiple platforms, was designed to trigger an automatic price collapse. He watched with a detached fascination as the numbers on his screen began to plummet. It was a digital avalanche, a controlled demolition of Carmine Rossi's financial empire. He felt a grim satisfaction as he saw the value of Rossi's portfolio erode with alarming speed. He had successfully weaponized the very systems that were meant to protect wealth, turning them into instruments of destruction.

As the market reacted, David continued to refine his actions, subtly adjusting the parameters of his sell orders to ensure the maximum possible damage while minimizing the risk of immediate detection. He was aware that this level of aggressive market manipulation would inevitably draw scrutiny, but he had built in layers of obfuscation, routing his commands through a series of anonymizing proxies, ensuring that any investigation would hit a dead end.

He knew this was a dangerous game, a tightrope walk over an abyss. Each keystroke, each executed command, was a calculated risk, a gamble with potentially devastating consequences. But the exhilaration of being at the center of such a complex and impactful operation, of wielding such immense digital power, was intoxicating. He was no longer just a hacker; he was a force of nature, shaping the financial landscape with his intellect and his code. The prick of his conscience, though still present, was increasingly muffled by the roar of his ambition and the thrill of the chase. He had crossed a threshold, and there was no turning back. He was all in, committed to seeing this elaborate financial demolition through to its destructive conclusion.

The air in the cramped apartment, once thick with the shared ambition of their early days, now felt heavy with unspoken dissent. Aisha watched Jamal across the worn table, the flickering screen of his laptop casting a ghostly light on his face. He was different. The hunger in his eyes hadn't lessened, but it had transformed, hardening into something almost predatory. He'd always been driven, fiercely so, but this... this was a new level. This was a dive into the deep end of the moral murk, and she was left treading water, growing colder with each passing moment.

Her initial unease had been a low hum, a subtle discord in the symphony of their shared purpose. She'd seen the way his eyes lit up when Silas spoke of "leveraging assets" and "strategic positioning," words that felt like thinly veiled euphemisms for something far more sinister. Then came the "opportunities," the whispered suggestions of bending rules, of finding loopholes that felt less like clever workarounds and more like deliberate sidesteps around basic decency. She remembered the first time Jamal had brought home a significant sum of money, not from a legitimate job, but from a "consulting fee" for a company that seemed to exist only on paper. He'd been so proud, so exhilarated, chalking it up to his burgeoning business acumen. Aisha, however, had felt a cold dread seep into her bones. It was too easy, too clean, and the source felt... tainted.

She'd tried to talk to him, her voice a hesitant tremor against his booming confidence. "Jamal," she'd begun, her hands twisting in her lap, "where did this really come from? Silas has been talking a lot, and some of it... it doesn't sit right with me."

He'd waved her concerns away with a dismissive flick of his wrist, his gaze still glued to the glowing screen. "Aisha, darling, you worry too much. This is how the game is played. We're playing smart. We're ahead of the curve."

"But is it... legal?" she'd pressed, the word tasting like ash in her mouth.

He'd finally looked up, his expression a mixture of impatience and something akin to pity. "Legal is for those who can't make their own way, Aisha. We're not playing by their rules. We're making our own."

That was the moment the first true crack appeared in the foundation of their shared world. His ambition, once a flame that warmed them both, had become a wildfire, consuming everything in its path, including, she feared, his conscience. Silas, with his smooth pronouncements and his aura of untouchable power, was clearly a corrupting influence. And Jamal, so eager to impress, so desperate for validation, was falling under his spell, hook, line, and sinker.

The escalation wasn't just financial; it was psychological. Silas, ever the puppeteer, had begun to weave a narrative of victimhood and entitlement. He'd paint Carmine Rossi as a villain, a leech on society who deserved to be bled dry, and then subtly, insidiously, imply that anyone who stood in his way, anyone who dared to challenge him, was a hero. Jamal absorbed this narrative like a sponge, his own moral compass spinning wildly off course. He started to see their actions not as illicit activities, but as righteous crusades, a necessary purging of corrupt elements from the city.

Aisha found herself increasingly isolated within their small circle. The others – the quiet tech guys David was working with, the edgy young women who ran errands for Silas – seemed to drink the Kool-Aid without question. They spoke in hushed tones of "disruption" and "recalibration," their eyes wide with a manufactured enthusiasm that Aisha couldn't replicate. She tried to connect with them, to find a sympathetic ear, but their conversations always circled back to the same themes: financial gains, avoiding detection, and the ever-present need to impress Silas and, by extension, Viktor.

Her attempts to pull Jamal back became more desperate, more direct. "Jamal, please," she pleaded one evening, after he'd returned from a clandestine meeting with Silas, his face alight with a dangerous excitement. "This isn't you. This isn't what we wanted. We wanted to build something, not... not become these people."

He slammed his fist on the table, making the coffee cups jump. "And what do you know about it, Aisha? You sit here, safe and sound, while I'm out here doing the dirty work! You think this is easy? You think Silas and Viktor would even give us the time of day if we weren't willing to get our hands dirty?"

The accusation stung. She wasn't being lazy; she was being principled. "It's not about getting our hands dirty, Jamal. It's about not letting them rot. There's a difference."

His jaw tightened, the muscles in his neck corded. "You don't understand the bigger picture. You're too caught up in the small stuff. Rossi is a cancer, Aisha. We're the cure. And sometimes, the cure is painful."

The gulf between them widened with every word. He saw her as naive, timid, an obstacle to his progress. She saw him as lost, blinded by greed and the intoxicating allure of power. Their conversations, once filled with laughter and shared dreams, became tense, punctuated by silences that screamed with accusation and disappointment. He would retreat into his work, into the glow of his screens, leaving her in the shadows, grappling with her growing disillusionment.

She started to notice the subtle changes in his behavior. The way he flinched at loud noises, a nervous habit he'd never had before. The way he constantly checked his phone, his eyes darting to every notification. The way he spoke in riddles, referring to operations and assets with a coded language that excluded her. He was becoming a stranger, a man she barely recognized, consumed by a world she couldn't, and wouldn't, enter.

The casualness with which he spoke of deceit was particularly unnerving. He'd relay stories of elaborate deceptions, of manipulated documents and fabricated identities, not with any sense of guilt, but with a kind of pride, as if these were badges of honor. He once recounted, with a chilling lack of remorse, how he'd had to "reframe" a significant financial transaction to avoid scrutiny, a euphemism for outright fraud. Aisha had felt physically ill. She remembered their early days, how they'd dreamt of building a legitimate business, something they could be proud of, something that would benefit their community. Now, their "business" was a phantom, a front for Silas's shadowy operations, and Jamal was its enthusiastic, amoral frontman.

Her attempts to involve him in their old life, in the things they used to love, met with blank stares or impatient dismissal. She'd suggest a walk in the park, a quiet dinner, a visit to a gallery. He'd invariably respond with, "Can't. Got to work." Or, "Silas needs me." The city, once a vibrant playground for their aspirations, had become a chessboard, and he was too engrossed in the game to notice the beauty of the world around him.

The emotional toll was immense. She felt a profound sense of betrayal, not just by Silas, but by Jamal himself. He had promised her a partnership, a shared journey. Instead, he had embarked on a solo expedition into a moral wilderness, leaving her behind to fend for herself. Their relationship, once their strongest asset, was crumbling, the foundation eroded by his recklessness and her unwavering ethical stance. She tried to hold on, to find a sliver of the man she had loved, but the man he was becoming was a terrifying stranger.

One rainy afternoon, she found herself staring at old photographs, their faces young and hopeful, full of uncomplicated dreams. They were planning a future, a future that felt solid and real. Now, their future was a nebulous, dangerous construct, built on shifting sands of deceit and danger. The disquiet that had been a low hum was now a deafening roar, a constant thrumming in her chest, a suffocating blanket of dread. She was trapped, not by any physical bars, but by the sheer momentum of their descent. She had tried to steer them back, to anchor them to their shared values, but the currents were too strong, the pull of power and illicit gain too alluring for Jamal. And as she watched him, increasingly distant and detached, she knew, with a sinking certainty, that she was losing him, and with him, a part of herself. The escalating recklessness was not just a problem for their operation; it was a tear in the fabric of her own life, a wound that bled into every aspect of her existence, leaving her adrift in a sea of fear and disillusionment. She was no longer just an observer; she was a casualty, caught in the collateral damage of a war fought in the shadows, a war that had consumed the man she loved and threatened to swallow her whole. The city, once a symbol of opportunity, now felt like a gilded cage, its glittering promise a cruel deception.

Chapter 3: The Weight of Betrayal

The city, a sprawling, indifferent beast, continued its ceaseless hum. For Aisha, that hum had become a symphony of anxiety, a soundtrack to Jamal's increasingly erratic behavior. He moved through their shared apartment like a phantom, his eyes either glued to a screen or lost in some distant, troubling thought. The earlier unease she'd felt had metastasized into a gnawing fear, a constant knot in her stomach that tightened with every clandestine phone call, every hushed conversation Jamal would abruptly end when she entered the room. The lines between their shared dreams and Silas's insidious influence had blurred so thoroughly that she could no longer discern where Jamal's desires ended and Silas's manipulations began.

She remembered the early days with a bittersweet ache. Their apartment, then a cramped but hopeful sanctuary, had been a space for late-night brainstorming sessions, fueled by cheap coffee and boundless optimism. They'd sketched out business plans on napkins, their voices ringing with conviction as they spoke of building something legitimate, something that would lift them, and their community, out of the shadows. Now, those same sketches felt like relics from a forgotten era, artifacts from a life that had been ruthlessly stripped away. Jamal's ambition, once a shared ember, had been fanned into a conflagration by Silas, and Aisha found herself standing on the periphery, watching her world burn.

Silas's insidious charm, a venomous sweetness that promised power and protection, had ensnared Jamal completely. He spoke of "necessary evils" and "calculated risks" with a chilling pragmatism that Aisha couldn't stomach. He'd painted Carmine Rossi not as a rival, but as a predator, and their actions not as criminal, but as preemptive strikes, a necessary cleansing of the city's underbelly. Jamal, eager to prove his worth, his mettle, had readily swallowed this narrative, his once-clear moral compass spinning wildly, calibrated to Silas's corrupt frequency. The justifications he offered for their increasingly dubious activities – the fabricated invoices, the offshore accounts, the carefully laundered funds – were delivered with the conviction of a zealot, leaving no room for dissent, no space for doubt.

"It's just business, Aisha," he'd say, his voice laced with a weariness that barely masked his growing arrogance. "You wouldn't understand the pressure, the complexities."

But Aisha *did* understand. She understood the gnawing fear of discovery, the moral compromises that chipped away at one's soul. She understood the insidious creep of guilt, the way a single transgression could pave the way for countless others. She understood the desperate need to maintain a façade of normalcy while the foundations of her life crumbled. She understood it all, perhaps too well, because she was living it, suffocating in its toxic atmosphere.

The isolation was the most crippling aspect. The others within their nascent organization, those who answered to Silas and, by extension, Viktor, seemed to exist in a different reality. Their conversations were coded, laced with jargon that veiled their illicit activities in a cloak of professional detachment. They spoke of "asset reallocation" and "strategic partnerships" as if discussing stock portfolios, their eyes devoid of the flicker of conscience that haunted Aisha. She'd tried to engage them, to find a common ground, a shared spark of humanity, but their focus remained rigidly on the next score, the next risk, the next step in Silas's elaborate game. They were cogs in a machine, and Aisha, with her inconvenient conscience, was a loose screw.

Jamal's descent wasn't merely a matter of financial impropriety; it was a profound shift in his very being. The man who had once debated philosophy with her for hours, who had championed fairness and integrity, was vanishing, replaced by a slick, calculating operator who saw the world as a series of opportunities to be exploited. His laughter, once a genuine expression of joy, was now often hollow, tinged with a cynicism that chilled her to the bone. He'd developed a nervous tic, a rapid blinking of his eyes when questioned too closely, and a habit of constantly checking his phone, his gaze darting to the screen with an almost primal vigilance. He was a man living on the edge, constantly looking over his shoulder, and the paranoia had begun to seep into their lives, poisoning the air they breathed.

One evening, as rain lashed against the windows, mirroring the tempest raging within her, Aisha confronted him again. "Jamal, we need to talk about this. Properly. Not about... 'reallocations' or 'consulting fees.' About what we're *doing*."

He was hunched over his laptop, the blue light illuminating his drawn features. He didn't look up. "We're surviving, Aisha. Thriving, even. This is the only way in this city. You want to be a victim, or you want to be a player?"

The question landed like a blow. "A player doesn't destroy everything they touch, Jamal! A player doesn't leave a trail of broken trust and compromised principles behind them." Her voice trembled, raw with a grief that felt ancient. "You promised me... you promised me we were building something good. Something real."

He finally pushed the laptop away, his chair scraping loudly against the floor. His eyes, when they met hers, were hard, devoid of the warmth she remembered. "And what's not real about this, Aisha? This apartment? The food on the table? The fact that Silas and Viktor are lining our pockets? That's real enough for me. Maybe you're just not cut out for this world. Maybe you're still dreaming of a life that doesn't exist."

The accusation, the dismissiveness, was a betrayal far deeper than any financial maneuver. He was no longer just disagreeing with her; he was actively discrediting her, devaluing her very perspective. She felt a chasm opening between them, a yawning void that threatened to swallow their shared history whole. She tried to recall the Jamal who had held her hand during her grandmother's funeral, who had comforted her when her career aspirations had hit a dead end, but that man seemed like a character from a novel, a memory from a different lifetime. This man, with his hardened gaze and his callous pronouncements, was a stranger.

The increasing secrecy was another wedge driven deep into their relationship. He would slip out at odd hours, his movements furtive, his explanations vague. He'd return with a restless energy, a glint of something dangerous in his eyes, but would offer no details, no context, only a curt dismissal if she pressed for information. The trust that had once been the bedrock of their partnership was eroding, replaced by a corrosive suspicion. She found herself scrutinizing his every word, dissecting his every action, searching for signs of the man she had loved, but finding only the architect of their shared downfall.

She started to notice the subtle ways Silas exerted his influence, not just on Jamal, but on their entire operation. Silas was a master manipulator, a puppet master who pulled strings with an invisible hand. He'd plant seeds of doubt, foster rivalries, and then subtly mediate, positioning himself as the indispensable problem-solver. Jamal, desperate for Silas's approval, his perceived wisdom, was a willing pawn in this intricate game. Aisha watched, helpless, as Jamal began to mirror Silas's calculating demeanor, his interactions becoming less about collaboration and more about calculated moves on a complex chessboard.

The weight of it all was crushing. The constant vigilance, the moral compromises, the gnawing fear – it was an unsustainable existence. She found herself longing for the simplicity of their early days, for the days when their biggest worry was making rent or landing a client. Those days now seemed impossibly distant, a dream from which she had been brutally awakened. The city, once a symbol of opportunity and a canvas for their ambitions, had become a labyrinth of deception and danger, and she was lost within its suffocating walls.

Jamal's transformation was more than just a deviation from their original path; it was a complete inversion of their shared values. He had become what they had sworn to fight against. He spoke with the same casual disregard for the law, the same ruthless pragmatism, that they had once condemned in the figures of power they'd hoped to usurp. He was embracing the very darkness they had intended to illuminate. The ambition that had once drawn them together now threatened to tear them apart, a stark testament to how easily the pursuit of power could corrupt even the noblest intentions.

The pressure was mounting, not just on Jamal, but on the entire fragile ecosystem they had built. Silas, always a step ahead, seemed to thrive in this escalating tension, his pronouncements growing bolder, his demands more insistent. He spoke of expansion, of larger operations, of a more significant footprint in the city's clandestine economy. And Jamal, caught in Silas's orbit, was swept along, his own apprehension masked by a veneer of determined confidence. Aisha could see the fear in his eyes, though, a fleeting shadow that betrayed the bravado. He was playing a dangerous game, and the stakes were rising exponentially, threatening to consume them all. The camaraderie they had once shared, the implicit understanding and support, was being steadily eroded by suspicion and the ever-present threat of exposure.

It was during this period that Marcus, the supposed steady hand at the helm, began to show cracks in his own composure. The constant threat of discovery, the sleepless nights, the pressure from Viktor – it was all taking its toll. His leadership, once characterized by a measured approach, was becoming increasingly autocratic. Decisions were made unilaterally, consultations became perfunctory, and dissent was met with thinly veiled warnings. He was trying to exert control in a situation that was rapidly spiraling out of control, his methods becoming more reactive than strategic.

Jamal, ever the opportunist, began to sense this shift, this vulnerability in Marcus. He saw the strain on Marcus's face, the impatience in his voice, and a new ambition began to bloom within him. It wasn't just about impressing Silas or Viktor anymore; it was about seizing power, about carving out his own domain. He started subtly undermining Marcus, questioning his decisions in hushed tones, planting seeds of doubt among the inner circle, subtly highlighting his own perceived competence and loyalty. He presented himself as the pragmatic alternative, the one who truly understood the nuances of their operations, the one who could navigate the treacherous waters ahead with more clarity than the increasingly beleaguered Marcus.

Aisha witnessed this subtle power play with a growing dread. The once-unshakeable bond between Jamal and Marcus, forged in shared ambition and mutual respect, was fraying, the threads of their friendship stretched taut, threatening to snap. Paranoia began to permeate their interactions. Every whispered conversation, every averted gaze, was interpreted through a lens of suspicion. Jamal would eye Marcus with a calculating intensity, while Marcus, sensing the shift, grew more guarded, his interactions with Jamal laced with a subtle distrust. The air in their clandestine meetings, once charged with focused energy, was now thick with unspoken animosity, the corrosive acid of distrust eating away at the foundation of their alliance. Loyalty, once the cornerstone of their operation, was being tested, and the results were devastating. The trust they had once held sacred, the unspoken pact that had bound them together, was eroding, leaving them exposed and vulnerable to the machims that lurked in the shadows, waiting to exploit their divisions. The weight of betrayal, it seemed, was a burden that was only just beginning to be tallied, and the ledger was already stained with the ink of broken promises and fractured friendships.

The air in the warehouse hung thick and heavy, saturated with the scent of dust, stale oil, and something metallic, something that Aisha had come to associate with the sharp edge of danger. The dim, flickering bulbs cast long, distorted shadows that danced like specters across the corrugated iron walls. This was it. The culmination of weeks of clandestine planning, of hushed meetings and coded messages, of the gnawing anxiety that had become Aisha's constant companion. The payoff was meant to be substantial, a king's ransom that promised to stabilize their precarious operation and, perhaps more importantly, offer a brief respite from the suffocating pressure of Viktor's watchful eye. Jamal had presented it as their golden ticket, a way to finally gain a foothold, to solidify their position and perhaps even begin to dictate terms rather than merely survive them.

But even as the adrenaline surged, a knot of unease tightened in Aisha's stomach. There was a palpable tension in the air, a static charge that had nothing to do with the impending transaction. Silas, ever the maestro of manipulation, had orchestrated this deal with meticulous precision. He'd parceled out information on a need-to-know basis, a tactic that had always fostered a subtle undercurrent of distrust, but this time it felt different. It felt deliberate, a calculated withholding of key details that left Aisha feeling exposed, a pawn on a board where the rules seemed to shift with every move. Jamal, too, seemed unusually taut, his usual swagger replaced by a nervous energy that he couldn't quite disguise. He'd been unusually secretive in the days leading up to this, his phone calls becoming even more furtive, his explanations for his absences clipped and evasive.

Marcus, usually the picture of calm control, paced the perimeter of the makeshift meeting space, his jaw set, his eyes scanning the periphery with an unnerving intensity. The strain of leadership, the constant tightrope walk between ambition and survival, was etching deeper lines onto his face. He'd been the one to broker the initial deal, the one to vouch for the buyer, a shadowy figure known only as 'The Ghost,' whose reputation for ruthlessness preceded him like a dark omen. The buyer was said to be connected to a rival faction, a group with whom they had a history of animosity, making this transaction inherently volatile. It was a high-stakes gamble, a dance on the precipice of their survival.

"Everyone in position?" Marcus's voice, usually a steady anchor, was strained. He addressed the small group gathered in the cavernous space: Jamal, Aisha, two of their most trusted operatives, and Marcus himself. Silas was conspicuously absent, a familiar tactic to maintain a degree of plausible deniability, leaving Jamal and Marcus to manage the volatile details on the ground.

Jamal nodded, his gaze fixed on a point somewhere beyond the warehouse doors. "All secure. The buyer is en route, ETA five minutes." His voice was steady, but Aisha detected the subtle tremor in his hands as he adjusted the collar of his jacket.

Aisha's mind raced, piecing together the fragmented information she possessed. They were here to receive a substantial quantity of untraceable arms, weaponry that would significantly bolster their defensive capabilities and open new avenues for their burgeoning operations. The payment was to be in untraceable bearer bonds, a hefty sum that would allow them to operate with a greater degree of autonomy, to finally break free from the suffocating grip of their benefactors, Viktor and his network. The risk was immense, the potential reward astronomical. Yet, the missing pieces of the puzzle gnawed at her. What were the specific terms of the exchange? What were the fallback plans if things went south? Silas had been maddeningly vague, citing security concerns, but Aisha suspected something more.

The crunch of tires on gravel outside sent a jolt of anticipation through the tense silence. Heavy-duty vehicles, dark and menacing, pulled up to the warehouse entrance, their headlights cutting through the gloom. The air crackled with an almost unbearable suspense. The doors to the warehouse groaned open, revealing the figures silhouetted against the harsh glare of the vehicle's headlights. They were heavily armed, their faces obscured by balaclavas, their movements sharp and precise. The Ghost's crew.

Jamal stepped forward, his hand resting on the concealed weapon beneath his jacket. "We're here for the exchange," he announced, his voice echoing in the vast space.

A gruff voice, amplified by a throat microphone, responded. "We have the goods. Where is our payment?"

Marcus gestured towards a nondescript crate, its contents wrapped in heavy canvas. "It's all there. Let's make this quick and clean."

As the two groups moved towards each other, a subtle shift occurred. It was almost imperceptible at first, a ripple in the charged atmosphere. Aisha noticed it in the way Jamal's eyes flickered towards Marcus, a brief, almost imperceptible exchange that spoke volumes. Then, as the exchange began, the first indication of the betrayal unfurled. Marcus's men, who were supposed to be securing the perimeter and monitoring their flanks, suddenly converged on Jamal's side, their weapons subtly but undeniably aimed not at the buyer's crew, but at Jamal and Aisha.

Confusion rippled through Aisha's small team. "What is this, Marcus?" Jamal demanded, his voice dangerously low.

Marcus didn't flinch. His expression was unreadable, a mask of grim resolve. "Orders from upstairs, Jamal. Viktor's decided you're a liability." The words hung in the air, cold and sharp as shards of ice.

Aisha's blood ran cold. Viktor. The unseen hand that had guided their every move, the architect of their precarious existence, had apparently decided to cut them loose. But this wasn't a clean severing; this was an execution. The realization struck her with the force of a physical blow. They had been set up. Silas, the ever-present puppet master, had played them all.

Chaos erupted. The buyer's crew, sensing the internal discord, remained frozen, their weapons still trained on the potential recipients of their goods. Marcus's men, their loyalties clearly divided, advanced with a chilling deliberation. It was a carefully orchestrated ambush, designed to eliminate Jamal and Aisha while simultaneously seizing the arms and potentially pinning the blame on them.

Jamal reacted with lightning speed, shoving Aisha behind a stack of crates. "Get down!" he yelled, drawing his weapon. Gunfire erupted, a deafening symphony of destruction that shattered the tense silence. The warehouse, moments before a stage for a clandestine transaction, had become a battlefield.

Aisha peered through a gap in the crates, her heart pounding a frantic rhythm against her ribs. She saw Jamal engaging Marcus's men, his movements desperate, fueled by a primal need to survive. He was outnumbered, outmaneuvered, and utterly betrayed. The carefully constructed facade of their operation had crumbled, revealing the rotten core beneath. This wasn't just about money or power; it was about survival, about the raw, brutal instinct to protect oneself, no matter the cost.

The buyer's crew, initially hesitant, now saw an opportunity. With Marcus's men occupied with Jamal, they moved in, not to aid or to escape, but to seize the bearer bonds, the very payment they were meant to deliver. It was a blatant display of self-preservation, a calculated move to salvage what they could from the unfolding disaster. They were opportunistic predators, and in the ensuing chaos, they saw their chance to profit from the internecine warfare.

Aisha watched in horror as the situation devolved into a free-for-all. Her own operatives, caught between the warring factions, were forced to make impossible choices. Some rallied to Jamal's side, their loyalty unwavering even in the face of certain death. Others, sensing the shift in power, the overwhelming odds against them, chose to flee, disappearing into the labyrinthine shadows of the warehouse, prioritizing their own skins above all else.

The realization dawned on Aisha with sickening clarity: this wasn't just Marcus's betrayal, orchestrated by Viktor. It was a deeper, more insidious betrayal. Silas, the architect of so much of their success, the one who had groomed Jamal, had clearly played both sides, setting up a scenario where the ultimate victor would be determined by whoever was left standing. And in this bloody tableau, the ultimate prize – the arms and the bonds – was being snatched by the opportunist buyer's crew, leaving everyone else to bleed for it.

Jamal fought with the ferocity of a cornered animal, but the odds were insurmountable. Aisha saw him go down, a guttural cry escaping his lips as a burst of automatic fire tore through him. Her vision swam. Jamal, her Jamal, the man who had promised her a future, was gone, a victim of a game he had been desperate to win.

She scrambled backward, the sounds of gunfire and shouting echoing in her ears. She had to get out. Silas's machims were far more complex than she had ever imagined. He hadn't just pitted them against their rivals; he had systematically dismantled their own ranks, turning allies into enemies, orchestrating their downfall from the shadows. The promise of power had been a lie, a carefully constructed illusion designed to lure them into a trap.

The weight of the betrayal was crushing, far heavier than any loss of money or weaponry. It was the shattering of trust, the annihilation of their shared dream. The camaraderie, the loyalty they had painstakingly cultivated, had proven to be fragile, easily shattered by the lure of self-preservation and personal gain. Silas had expertly exploited their ambitions, their vulnerabilities, their very desires, turning them against each other. He had ensured that no matter the outcome, he would emerge unscathed, perhaps even stronger, from the ashes of their destruction.

Aisha crawled through the debris, the acrid smell of gunpowder stinging her nostrils. She heard footsteps approaching, heavy and deliberate. It was Marcus. He found her huddled behind a fallen metal shelf, her body trembling. His face was a mask of exhaustion and grim satisfaction, a terrifying combination.

"You understand now, don't you, Aisha?" he said, his voice rough. "This is the real game. It's not about loyalty. It's about survival. And I survived."

He didn't offer a hand. He didn't offer comfort. He offered only the cold, hard truth of their reality. The bonds, the arms – they were secondary. The true prize was dominance, the elimination of threats, the consolidation of power. And he had achieved it, at the cost of their lives, their dreams, and their very souls.

As Aisha looked at him, at the hardened lines of his face, she saw not a survivor, but a ghost of the man he once was. The ambition that had driven them had consumed him, twisted him into something unrecognizable. And Silas, the unseen architect of this carnage, remained, a phantom in the shadows, ready to exploit the next wave of desperate souls who dared to dream of a better life. The desert of their ambition had proven to be a barren, treacherous landscape, littered with the corpses of broken promises and shattered trust. The weight of betrayal was a heavy burden, and for Aisha, it was just the beginning of a long, agonizing journey of reckoning. The desert was vast, and the path ahead was shrouded in an even deeper darkness than she could have ever imagined. She was alone, stripped bare, with the chilling realization that the true enemy had been among them all along, weaving a web of deceit with chilling precision. The echoes of gunfire faded, replaced by the deafening silence of absolute loss, a silence that screamed of treachery and the brutal cost of misplaced trust. The desert wind began to whisper through the shattered remains of their ambition, a mournful dirge for the fallen and the betrayed.

The chipped ceramic mug felt alien in Chloe's hands, its familiar weight now a jarring reminder of a life that felt increasingly distant. Each sip of the lukewarm herbal tea was a conscious effort, a small rebellion against the churning nausea in her gut. The sketchpad lay open on the cluttered kitchen table, its pristine white pages a stark contrast to the smudged charcoal and hastily drawn lines that littered its surface. These weren't the vibrant cityscapes or evocative portraits that usually flowed from her fingertips. These were meticulously crafted forgeries, tools of a trade she had never imagined herself a part of, a trade that was slowly, insidiously, chipping away at her soul.

The urgency in Marcus's voice had been palpable, a raw desperation that had bypassed her usual defenses. "They're closing in, Chloe. We need an exit strategy. A good one." He hadn't needed to explain what "they" were. The whispers had been growing louder, the surveillance more overt. Viktor's reach, it seemed, was longer and more suffocating than they had ever anticipated. The weight of their collective choices, the increasingly precarious tightrope they walked, had finally begun to snap. Marcus, always the pragmatist, the strategist, had turned to her, not with a weapon, but with a plea. "You're the only one who can do this. The only one with the skill."

And so, Chloe, the artist who found solace in capturing the essence of things, the observer who translated emotion into form, found herself tasked with distorting reality. Her fingers, accustomed to the gentle caress of a paintbrush, now moved with a jarring precision, replicating the subtle imperfections of age on forged identification cards, painstakingly recreating the distinctive watermark on a false passport. Each stroke of the pencil, each careful application of ink, felt like a betrayal of her craft, a perversion of the gift she had nurtured for so long. The lines she drew weren't about truth; they were about deception, about creating a new, fabricated reality that could shield them from the encroaching danger.

The process was agonizing. She'd locked herself away in the small, cramped studio space above their apartment, the scent of turpentine and oil paints now mingled with the acrid tang of freshly printed paper and specialized inks. The air was thick with the silent scream of her conscience. She would stare at the original documents, memorizing every flourish, every subtle curve of the lettering, before meticulously recreating them, imbuing them with a false history, a fabricated identity. It was a dance with the devil, a tango with the law, and with every finished piece, a part of her felt irrevocably lost.

The fear was a constant companion, a cold knot in her stomach that tightened with every shadow that flickered outside the window, with every unfamiliar car that idled on their street. She saw surveillance in every passerby, felt the weight of unseen eyes on her back even when she was alone. This wasn't the adrenaline-fueled danger of a heist or a confrontation; this was a creeping, insidious dread, the suffocating fear of being caught, of seeing her carefully constructed world crumble around her.

Marcus would check in periodically, his visits brief, his demeanor grim. He'd examine her work with a critical eye, his silence more damning than any criticism. "They look… real," he'd murmur, his voice tight, as if the very act of acknowledging their authenticity pained him. He never asked about her feelings, about the toll it was taking. He couldn't afford to. They were in survival mode, and survival, he'd made it clear, demanded a certain callousness, a willingness to shed the luxuries of morality.

Chloe found herself retreating further into herself. The vibrant conversations she once shared with Aisha, the easy camaraderie she had with Jamal, even the gruff affection she'd developed for Marcus – all of it felt like a distant memory. How could she explain the gnawing guilt, the shame that clung to her like a second skin? How could she articulate the feeling of being a fraud, of using her most cherished skill for something so fundamentally wrong? She started avoiding mirrors, afraid of what she might see reflected there – a stranger with haunted eyes and stained hands.

One afternoon, while meticulously aging a birth certificate, she paused, her hand trembling. She stared at the blank space where her own signature should have been, a stark reminder of the authenticity she was so adept at mimicking. Her own identity felt like it was fading, blurring into the fabricated lives she was creating. She remembered the pure joy she felt when she first discovered her talent, the innocent thrill of bringing a blank canvas to life. Now, that joy was a distant echo, replaced by a hollow ache, a profound sense of loss.

The pressure to produce more, to create even more convincing deceptions, was immense. Marcus had explained the plan: they would use the forged documents to slip through the cracks, to disappear into the anonymity of the digital age, to erase their footprints from Viktor's relentless pursuit. Each forged document was a key, a carefully crafted illusion designed to unlock a new, unburdened existence. But the price of these keys was her integrity, her very sense of self.

She found herself sketching not on the pad anymore, but in the quiet corners of her mind. The faces of the people they were impersonating, the phantom lives she was breathing into existence, haunted her waking hours. She saw them in the patterns of the wallpaper, in the flickering streetlights outside her window. They were a constant, silent testament to her complicity, to the widening chasm between the artist she was and the criminal she was becoming.

The guilt was a physical weight, pressing down on her chest, making each breath a conscious effort. It manifested in sleepless nights filled with fragmented nightmares, in the phantom touch of charcoal dust on her fingertips even after she'd scrubbed her hands raw. She'd started eating less, the vibrant colors of her paints now seeming garish and offensive. The world, once a source of inspiration, now felt tainted, a reflection of her own compromised soul.

One evening, Aisha found her hunched over the table, a half-finished driver's license splayed before her, her face buried in her hands. Aisha, usually so vibrant and full of life, approached cautiously, her brow furrowed with concern. "Chloe? What's wrong?"

Chloe flinched, unable to meet Aisha's questioning gaze. She couldn't confess the full extent of her actions, the depth of her deception. The words caught in her throat, a tangled mess of guilt and fear. "Nothing," she managed to choke out, her voice raspy. "Just... tired."

Aisha didn't push, but her gaze lingered, a flicker of something – suspicion? Sadness? – in her eyes before she turned away, leaving Chloe alone with the suffocating silence and the damning evidence of her artistic deception. The unspoken knowledge between them, the unspoken truth that Chloe was hiding, created a new, painful distance, a subtle yet profound fracturing of their bond. Chloe felt a pang of longing for the days when their secrets were shared, their burdens light. Now, her burden was a heavy, solitary one, a secret that isolated her in a way she could never have imagined. The artistic deception had not only changed her perception of herself but had also begun to poison the relationships she held dear, a stark reminder that every choice, no matter how well-intentioned, carried its own insidious cost. The weight of betrayal wasn't just about what Marcus and Viktor had done; it was also about what Chloe was now forced to do, the silent compromises she was making with her own conscience, the slow erosion of her artistic integrity and, with it, her very sense of self. The path ahead, paved with these fabricated documents, seemed to lead only deeper into the darkness.

The air in the back room of "The Labyrinth" was thick with the stale scent of cheap whiskey and desperation. David sat nursing a lukewarm beer, the condensation dripping down his fingers, a stark contrast to the calculated chill that had settled in his gut. He watched Marcus, his movements agitated, his words clipped and urgent as he spoke to Chloe. The conversation was a low hum in the background of David's thoughts, a soundtrack to his own internal monologue of departure. He saw the escalating risk, the tightening noose around their collective necks, and a cold, unyielding logic dictated his response. This wasn't about loyalty anymore; it was about survival, a primal instinct that superseded any prior commitments.

He'd always been the pragmatist, the one who saw the spreadsheets, the profit margins, the potential pitfalls long before anyone else. While Marcus chased the thrill of the gamble and Chloe got lost in the artistry of their illicit endeavors, David was meticulously charting the course towards the inevitable crash. He'd noticed the subtle shifts in Viktor's demeanor, the increased frequency of his 'discreet' meetings, the hushed phone calls that ended abruptly whenever anyone entered the room. Viktor's empire, once seemingly unshakable, was starting to show hairline fractures, and David knew that when an empire fell, the collateral damage was immense. He wasn't about to be buried in the rubble.

His escape wouldn't be a sudden, explosive departure. It would be a slow, deliberate unraveling, a series of calculated steps designed to detach himself from the sinking ship without raising immediate alarm. His financial acumen, honed over years of navigating the murky waters of illicit transactions, was his primary weapon. He'd begun by subtly rerouting small portions of their earnings, channeling them into offshore accounts under pseudonyms and shell corporations that were virtually untraceable. It was a painstaking process, requiring meticulous attention to detail and an almost obsessive level of discretion. Each transfer, each doctored ledger entry, was another thread he wove into the safety net he was constructing for himself, a net designed to catch him when the whole operation inevitably imploded.

He started spending more time alone, feigning preoccupation with 'inventory management' or 'client acquisition' to avoid the increasingly intense discussions about their next move. When Marcus or Chloe would seek him out, their faces etched with worry or a desperate plea for reassurance, David would offer them a carefully constructed facade of calm confidence. "We're fine," he'd say, his voice even, his gaze steady. "Viktor knows what he's doing. We just need to stay focused." The words felt like ash in his mouth, a bitter testament to the distance he was already putting between himself and the increasingly dangerous reality they were inhabiting.

The irony wasn't lost on him. He was the architect of their financial stability, the one who ensured their operations ran smoothly and profitably. Now, he was systematically dismantling his own involvement, siphoning off the very resources he had helped to build. But it wasn't greed that drove him; it was foresight. He saw the end of the road, and he was simply choosing a different path, one that led away from the precipice.

One evening, while ostensibly reviewing security protocols at a discreetly rented warehouse on the outskirts of the city, David met with a contact – a man whose face was as nondescript as his profession. The meeting was brief, held in the flickering shadows of a dimly lit alleyway, the city's ambient noise a convenient cover for their hushed exchange. David handed over a significant sum of cash, the bulk of his meticulously accumulated escape fund, and in return, received a package containing a new identity, complete with forged documents and a burner phone. The weight of the package in his hands was both a relief and a heavy burden, a tangible symbol of his impending betrayal.

He knew his actions would be viewed as a betrayal by Marcus and Chloe. They were bound by a shared history, by the risks they had taken together, by the implicit understanding that they were in this until the bitter end. David, however, had long ago abandoned the notion of 'until the bitter end.' He saw their shared plight not as an unbreakable bond, but as a ticking time bomb. His perceived disloyalty was, in his mind, a necessary act of self-preservation.

The first inkling of suspicion began to surface when Marcus noticed inconsistencies in their offshore accounts. It wasn't a large amount, a mere fraction of the overall funds, but for Marcus, who prided himself on his meticulous financial oversight, it was a glaring anomaly. He confronted David in the usual clandestine meeting spot, his voice tight with an unfamiliar edge of distrust.

"David," Marcus began, his eyes narrowed, scanning David's impassive face. "There's something… off. With the Argentinian account."

David feigned a moment of contemplation, tapping a pen against his chin. "The Argentinian account? I haven't touched that one in weeks. Everything should be in order." He manufactured a slight frown, a practiced expression of concern. "Maybe a system glitch? Those offshore platforms can be notoriously unreliable."

Marcus wasn't convinced. He was a man who trusted hard data, and the data, however small, was pointing in a direction he didn't want to consider. "I've cross-referenced everything, David. The transfers… they're subtle, but they're there. And they coincide with periods when you've been handling the 'disbursements.'"

The accusation hung heavy in the air between them. David maintained his composure, his heart rate steady, a testament to his practiced detachment. "Marcus, you know I'm dedicated to this. We all are. If there's a discrepancy, I'll personally look into it. But I assure you, my priorities haven't shifted."

But Marcus saw the flicker in David's eyes, the subtle tightening around his jaw. It was a tell, a minute crack in the meticulously constructed facade. He didn't press the issue further, not yet. He needed more concrete proof, but the seed of doubt had been sown, a poison that would spread through their already fragile unity.

Later that week, Chloe noticed David's unusual quietness, his increasingly withdrawn demeanor. He'd always been the steady hand, the calm presence amidst the chaos. Now, he seemed lost in his own world, his mind miles away. She tried to engage him, asking about his work, about the logistics of their upcoming phase of operations, but his answers were vague, evasive.

"David, are you okay?" she asked, her voice gentle, concerned. They were in the back room of "The Labyrinth," the usual cacophony of the bar a distant murmur.

David looked up, his gaze distant. "Just... thinking, Chloe. About the future. About what happens after all this."

"We'll figure it out," Chloe said, a hopeful note in her voice, clinging to the shared belief that had once bound them. "We always do."

David offered a thin, unconvincing smile. "Yeah. We do." He avoided her eyes, his hands busy rearranging empty glasses on the bar. He couldn't meet her gaze, couldn't bear to see the trust reflected there, a trust he was actively betraying. He knew Chloe was perceptive, an artist who could read the subtlest of human expressions. He worried that she, too, was beginning to sense his detachment, his growing disinterest in their shared fate.

His efforts to remain inconspicuous were becoming increasingly difficult. He started taking detours on his way to meetings, using different routes, varying his arrival times. He began carrying a discreetly worn shoulder bag, containing not only his usual business items but also a carefully packed go-bag with essentials, should he need to disappear at a moment's notice. He scanned every face in a crowd, every lingering glance, his paranoia amplifying with each passing day.

The fracturing of their unity was subtle at first, a slow erosion of trust and camaraderie. Marcus, now keenly aware of David's potential defection, began to sideline him from key financial decisions, attributing it to "streamlining operations." He'd present David with pre-calculated figures, carefully curated to obscure the full picture, and David, recognizing the shift, played along, his silence a tacit acknowledgment of his own impending exit. He no longer felt the need to defend his actions or explain his intentions. His objective was clear: extract himself cleanly.

Chloe, caught between Marcus's growing suspicion and David's increasing distance, felt a profound sense of unease. The vibrant energy that had once pulsed through their group had dissipated, replaced by an atmosphere of tension and unspoken accusations. She saw the sideways glances between Marcus and David, the way their conversations would abruptly cease whenever she entered the room. It was a familiar feeling, a echo of the isolation she already felt from her own clandestine activities, now amplified by the growing rift within the group.

One night, after a particularly tense meeting where Marcus openly questioned David's recent financial reports, David found himself alone in his apartment, the city lights blurring through the rain-streaked window. He opened a secure laptop, bypassing the usual passwords with practiced ease. He accessed the offshore accounts, initiating the final stages of his withdrawal. The numbers on the screen represented not just money, but his freedom, his future, a future divorced from the increasingly dangerous entanglements of their current life. He felt a pang of something akin to regret, a fleeting thought of the camaraderie they had once shared, but it was quickly overshadowed by the cold, hard logic of self-preservation.

He began meticulously erasing his digital footprint, deleting emails, scrubbing server logs, and disabling access to accounts that were no longer relevant to his new, solitary path. He was a ghost in his own life, systematically removing every trace of his involvement, preparing for the moment he would simply cease to exist within their world.

The final confrontation, when it came, was less an explosion and more a quiet implosion. Marcus, armed with irrefutable evidence of David's systematic embezzlement, cornered him in a secluded parking garage after a clandestine supply drop. The air was cold and damp, the only sound the rhythmic drip of water from a leaky pipe.

"You were always the money man, David," Marcus said, his voice low and laced with a bitter disappointment that cut deeper than any threat. "The one who kept us afloat. And you've been bleeding us dry."

David stood facing him, his expression unreadable. There was no anger, no defiance, only a weary acceptance. "It was inevitable, Marcus. You all saw it. Viktor's grasp is tightening. This whole thing was going to implode. I just made sure I wasn't standing too close to the detonation point."

"So you stole from us?" Marcus's voice rose slightly, the desperation evident. "From Chloe? She trusts you."

David's gaze flickered, a momentary flash of something akin to pain. "Chloe is using her talents to forge documents that could put her in prison for life. We're all making choices, Marcus. Mine just happens to be about ensuring I have a future beyond this mess." He paused, then added, his voice hardening slightly, "And I didn't steal. I merely... reallocated assets to ensure my own survival. Assets I helped generate."

The words hung in the air, a final, definitive severing of their ties. Marcus stared at him, his face a mask of conflicting emotions – anger, betrayal, a dawning realization of their shared peril and David's pragmatic, albeit ruthless, foresight. He knew, deep down, that David was right. The situation was dire, and their collective chances of survival were dwindling by the day.

"So that's it?" Marcus asked, his voice barely a whisper. "You're just... gone?"

David nodded, reaching into his coat pocket and pulling out the burner phone. He tossed it onto the damp concrete between them. "That's mine. Everything else is yours." He turned to leave, the weight of his decision pressing down on him, yet the lightness of freedom beginning to dawn. "Good luck, Marcus."

As David walked away, disappearing into the shadows of the parking garage, Marcus watched him go, the silence amplifying the hollowness that had settled within him. David's calculated exit wasn't just a personal betrayal; it was a stark, undeniable signal of their group's impending doom, a testament to the fact that when the stakes got high enough, even the strongest bonds could snap under the crushing weight of self-preservation. The loyalty they once believed in had become a luxury, a casualty of the dangerous game they were playing, and David, ever the pragmatist, had simply chosen to opt out before the final hand was dealt. He was alone with Chloe's artistic deceptions and the looming shadow of Viktor, the stark reality of their isolation hitting him with brutal force. The carefully constructed facade of their shared enterprise was crumbling, leaving only the raw, unforgiving truth of their precarious existence.

The oppressive silence in the apartment was a stark contrast to the usual thrum of activity that defined their lives. Aisha stood in the doorway of Jamal's study, the polished wood cool beneath her fingertips, her breath catching in her throat. The room was a sanctuary of ambition, shelves lined with books on strategy and economics, a gleaming mahogany desk dominating the space, a testament to the empire he was so relentlessly building. Jamal was hunched over a laptop, the blue light illuminating his face, a mask of intense concentration that seemed to have become his permanent expression. He looked up, his eyes, usually warm and full of shared dreams, were now hard, distant, reflecting the cold gleam of the screen.

"Aisha," he said, his tone flat, devoid of the easy affection that had once flowed between them. "What is it?"

She stepped further into the room, her heart a frantic drum against her ribs. "Jamal, we need to talk. Properly. Away from all of this." She gestured vaguely towards the window, towards the city that pulsed with the lifeblood of their dangerous enterprise. "This… this isn't us anymore. Not the us I fell in love with."

He sighed, a sound of impatience, and pushed back from the desk, though he made no move to truly engage with her. "What are you talking about? We're more successful than we've ever been. Everything we've worked for is finally coming to fruition."

"Success?" Aisha's voice trembled, a mixture of disbelief and a rising tide of despair. "Jamal, look at us. Look at what we're doing. This isn't success; it's a precipice. We're standing on the edge of something that's going to break us." She took a hesitant step closer, her eyes pleading. "I've seen the fear in your eyes, the late nights, the way you flinch at every unexpected sound. This is consuming you. It's consuming *us*."

Jamal leaned back in his chair, a flicker of annoyance crossing his features. "That's just stress, Aisha. It comes with the territory. You knew what this life entailed when you got involved."

"I knew there would be risks," she countered, her voice gaining a desperate edge. "I didn't know it would turn you into someone I barely recognize. Someone who is willing to sacrifice everything, everyone, for… for what? More power? More money? When does it end, Jamal? When are we enough?"

He finally turned to face her fully, his posture shifting from casual dismissal to a more assertive, almost condescending stance. "It ends when we're untouchable, Aisha. When we're so far ahead that no one can touch us. And that's what I'm building. This isn't just about us anymore; it's about legacy."

"Legacy?" Aisha laughed, a short, sharp burst of bitter amusement. "What legacy are we building, Jamal? A legacy of broken trust? Of ruined lives? Of fear? Is that what you want to leave behind?" Tears welled in her eyes, hot and stinging. "I'm begging you, Jamal. Let's walk away. We can still get out. We can disappear, start over somewhere clean, somewhere safe. We can have a normal life."

His expression hardened, his jaw clenching. "Walk away? Aisha, are you serious? We're on the cusp of something huge. To walk away now would be throwing away everything we've bled for. Everything I've sacrificed for."

"Sacrificed?" Aisha stepped back, the words hitting her like a physical blow. "And what about my sacrifices, Jamal? Did you even consider them? Or was I just another asset to be managed, another piece on your chessboard?" The chasm between them yawned wider, a dark, gaping void. "You're so focused on the power, on the control, that you've lost sight of what actually matters. You've lost sight of *me*."

Jamal stood up, his towering presence suddenly intimidating rather than reassuring. He walked towards her, not with an embrace, but with an air of finality. "Aisha, I appreciate your... concern. I really do. But you don't understand the stakes. You don't see the bigger picture." He ran a hand through his hair, his gaze drifting back towards his laptop, his focus already pulled away. "This is the only way. We're too deep in to turn back now."

"Too deep?" Her voice was barely a whisper now, the fight draining out of her, replaced by a chilling realization. He wasn't just stressed; he was completely consumed. His ambition had calcified into something ruthless, something that saw no room for sentiment, no room for compromise. "So that's it? You're just going to keep going, no matter what? No matter who gets hurt? No matter what happens to us?"

He met her gaze, and in those cold, hard eyes, she saw the definitive answer. There was no appeal, no softening, just the stark, unyielding truth of his chosen path. "I'm doing what needs to be done, Aisha. For all of us. For our future."

The words hung in the air, a death knell to the life they had once envisioned. The desperation that had fueled her plea began to transform into a different kind of resolve. It wasn't the fiery anger of betrayal, but the cold, quiet certainty of someone who had finally understood. He wouldn't change. He couldn't. And if he wouldn't pull them back from the brink, then she had to save herself.

"You're wrong, Jamal," she said, her voice steady now, the tremors gone. She met his gaze, her own eyes clear, though filled with a profound sadness. "This isn't for us. This is just for you. And I can't be a part of it anymore."

She turned, the movement deliberate, almost ceremonial. She didn't look back as she walked out of the study, out of the apartment, out of the life she had so desperately tried to preserve. The heavy oak door clicked shut behind her, the sound echoing the finality of her decision. The weight of betrayal wasn't just in Jamal's actions, but in the stark realization that the man she loved had become a stranger, blinded by a hunger for power that had consumed his very soul. She was alone, adrift, but for the first time in a long time, she felt a sliver of her own agency return. The path ahead was uncertain, fraught with its own dangers, but it would be a path she walked on her own terms, free from the suffocating embrace of his ambition and the crushing weight of his betrayal. She had to find a way to rebuild, to reclaim herself, even if it meant cutting ties with the people she had once considered family, severing the bonds that had become chains. The memory of their shared dreams, once a source of comfort, was now a painful reminder of what had been lost, a testament to the destructive nature of unchecked ambition. She walked through the rain-slicked streets, the city lights blurring around her, a solitary figure moving away from the wreckage of a life she could no longer inhabit. The plea had been made, the desperate attempt to salvage something from the ruins, and it had failed. Now, only survival remained, and survival meant distance. It meant creating a new life, one unburdened by the ghosts of their shared past, a past now irrevocably tainted by the shadow of Jamal's ambition. The weight of betrayal was heavy, but the lightness of her own emerging independence was a fragile, yet potent, new feeling. She wouldn't look back. She couldn't. The future, however bleak, was hers to build, brick by painstaking brick, without him.

Chapter 4: The Collateral Damage

The metallic tang of rain mingled with the exhaust fumes of passing cars, a familiar perfume of the city that Aisha now found herself navigating alone. The shelter of their once-shared apartment, a sanctuary that had become a gilded cage, was a distant memory. Each gust of wind seemed to carry whispers of Jamal's unwavering ambition, a chilling reminder of the chasm that had opened between them. Her plea, a desperate attempt to anchor him to the life they had built, had been met with the cold, hard certainty of his chosen path. He was too deep, he'd said, too far gone to turn back. And in his eyes, she had seen not just obsession, but a terrifying lack of recognition, a stranger occupying the space where the man she loved used to be. The weight of that realization had propelled her into the night, a fugitive from a life that had become synonymous with danger and moral compromise.

She walked with a determined stride, the sting of the rain a balm on her flushed cheeks. The initial shock of Jamal's transformation had given way to a cold, sharp clarity. He wasn't merely stressed; he was consumed. His ambition, once a shared dream, had become a ravenous entity, devouring everything in its path, including their connection, their trust, and ultimately, him. Her own sacrifices, the quiet compromises she'd made to support his ascent, now felt like concessions to a predator. The life she had envisioned, one built on mutual respect and shared aspirations, had been systematically dismantled, replaced by a landscape of escalating risks and moral ambiguity. The thought of their shared legacy, once a beacon of hope, now felt like a phantom limb, a painful reminder of what had been irrevocably lost. She needed to disappear, not just from Jamal's world, but from the suffocating grip of their intertwined past. The city, a sprawling, indifferent entity, offered a million hiding places, a thousand new beginnings, and the chilling possibility of anonymity.

Aisha pulled the collar of her jacket tighter, the worn fabric a meager defense against the encroaching chill. Her destination was a small, nondescript diner tucked away in a less-trafficked corner of the city, a place she'd scouted out weeks ago as a potential fallback, a contingency plan she'd hoped would never be enacted. It was here, in the anonymity of late-night coffee and lukewarm conversations, that she would begin the process of severing ties, of erasing herself from the narrative they had so carelessly woven. The thought of the others – of Karim, the loyal lieutenant whose unwavering devotion to Jamal had always felt a little too fervent, and of Layla, whose sharp wit and even sharper instincts had been a crucial asset – brought a pang of something akin to regret. They were all caught in the undertow of Jamal's ambition, their own destinies inextricably linked to his increasingly reckless trajectory. But her primary allegiance, she now understood with a stark finality, had to be to herself.

The diner was as she remembered it: a worn vinyl booth, a perpetually flickering neon sign casting a sickly glow, and the comforting aroma of stale coffee and frying onions. She slid into a booth by the window, the condensation blurring the world outside, a fitting reflection of her own uncertain future. She ordered a black coffee, the bitter taste a familiar comfort. The conversation with Jamal replayed in her mind, each word a shard of glass, cutting deeper with every recollection. His dismissal of her concerns, his framing of her pleas as naiveté – it was all a testament to how far he had fallen, how completely the darkness had enveloped him. He was no longer the man who had promised her a life of shared dreams and mutual respect; he was a phantom driven by an insatiable hunger, a phantom she could no longer follow.

The first casualty wasn't a stranger, not a nameless associate caught in the crossfire of their burgeoning empire. It was someone who had been a part of their inner circle, a familiar face whose absence would leave a gaping void, a stark and brutal reminder of the escalating stakes. News traveled fast in their world, a venomous whisper that could shatter illusions with brutal efficiency. Aisha heard it not from Jamal, nor from Karim, but from a hushed conversation overheard between two low-level runners huddled in a doorway as she made her way to the diner. The name spoken was Rashaad, a younger, ambitious member of their crew, someone who had always been eager to prove himself, too eager perhaps.

Rashaad. The name resonated with a chilling familiarity. He was the one who had handled the distribution for that last major shipment, the one who had dealt with the notoriously volatile Southside crew. He was young, cocky, but undeniably effective. He was also, Aisha realized with a sickening lurch, the one Jamal had sent to smooth things over after a recent, unsavory incident involving a stolen consignment and a very angry rival outfit. The details had been intentionally vague, a carefully curated narrative designed to shield Jamal from the uglier truths. But Rashaad had been the one on the ground, the one navigating the murky waters of street-level negotiations, the one who had to face the consequences when diplomacy failed.

The runners' hushed tones painted a grim picture. A meet gone wrong. A betrayal. A brutal, swift execution. The specifics were murky, lost in the sensationalism of rumour, but the outcome was undeniable: Rashaad was dead. Not wounded, not captured, but dead. The finality of it hung in the air, a dark cloud that seemed to eclipse the already grim cityscape.

Aisha's hand trembled as she reached for her coffee cup. This wasn't just collateral damage; this was a direct consequence, a brutal punctuation mark at the end of a sentence of escalating recklessness. Jamal's "legacy" was being built on a foundation of spilled blood, and Rashaad was the first to pay the ultimate price. The thought of his young, eager face, the ambition burning in his eyes, now extinguished in some grimy alleyway, sent a shiver down her spine. He had believed in Jamal's vision, had trusted in the protection that came with being part of their burgeoning operation. And that trust had cost him his life.

She felt a surge of anger, sharp and potent, directed not just at the faceless rivals who had committed the act, but at Jamal himself. He had orchestrated the situation, had sent Rashaad into the lion's den, and now his protégé was dead. Had he even paused to consider the human cost? Had he felt even a flicker of remorse, or was Rashaad's demise simply another data point in his cold, calculating ledger? The man she loved was gone, replaced by a ruthless strategist who saw people as disposable assets.

The news of Rashaad's death would undoubtedly cast a long shadow over their operation. Fear, once a distant threat, was now a palpable presence, a chilling reminder of their mortality. The illusion of invincibility, the carefully constructed façade of control that Jamal so desperately clung to, had been irrevocably shattered. This was more than just a setback; it was a turning point, a grim harbinger of the violence that was inevitably coming their way.

Aisha knew she couldn't afford to linger, to wallow in the grief or the anger. Rashaad's death was a stark warning, a brutal illustration of the dangers that now lay in wait. It meant that the people they were dealing with were not to be underestimated, that the lines they were crossing were not merely legal or ethical, but lines of life and death.

She paid for her coffee, the crumpled bills feeling strangely insignificant. Stepping back out into the rain, she felt a renewed urgency. Her mission was no longer just about escape; it was about survival. And survival meant putting as much distance as possible between herself and the escalating chaos that Jamal was so gleefully orchestrating. The city lights blurred through the rain-streaked windshield of a passing taxi as she hailed it, the flickering neon sign of the diner receding into the gloom.

The silence in the taxi was a welcome respite, a space where she could begin to process the enormity of what had happened. Rashaad's death was a clear message: the game had changed, and the rules were now written in blood. Jamal's pursuit of power had finally claimed its first victim from within their ranks, and the ripple effect of that loss would be felt by everyone. The confidence, the swagger, the almost casual disregard for consequences that had characterized their operations, would now have to be replaced by a grim, desperate vigilance.

She thought of Karim. Loyal, unwavering Karim. He would be devastated, no doubt. Rashaad had been like a younger brother to him, someone he had mentored and protected. How would Karim react to this loss? Would it temper Jamal's recklessness, or would it fuel his thirst for revenge, pushing him further down the path of destruction? Aisha couldn't predict Karim's response, but she knew that the loyalty he felt towards Jamal was a powerful force, one that might blind him to the true cost of their enterprise.

And Layla. Sharp-witted, pragmatic Layla. She had always been the voice of reason, the one who could see the flaws in Jamal's grand plans. But even Layla, with all her intelligence, had been drawn into the orbit of Jamal's ambition. Aisha wondered if this tragedy would be enough to shake Layla's conviction, to make her question the path they were on. Or would she, too, rationalize Rashaad's death as an unfortunate but necessary casualty?

Aisha's own path was now irrevocably altered. The idea of a clean break, a simple disappearance, seemed increasingly naive. The tendrils of their operation ran deep, and the consequences of Jamal's actions were now a tangible threat to anyone associated with him. Rashaad's death was not an isolated incident; it was a preview of what was to come. The rivals they had crossed, the territories they had encroached upon, the debts they had accrued – all of it was coming home to roost.

She felt a pang of guilt for leaving, for abandoning the crew when they were most vulnerable. But what choice did she have? To stay would be to invite the same fate that had befallen Rashaad. Jamal had made his bed, and he was dragging them all down into it with him. Her conscience, once a source of comfort and guidance, was now a tormenting voice, reminding her of the promises she had made, the allegiances she had formed. But self-preservation, she realized, had to take precedence.

The taxi pulled up to a less-trafficked street, a quiet residential area miles away from the heart of their operations. This was where she would go for now, a temporary refuge before she could truly disappear. The apartment she had secured was small, anonymous, and utterly devoid of the trappings of her former life. It was a blank slate, a place where she could begin to build something new, something untainted by the blood and betrayal that had come to define her recent existence.

As she stepped out of the taxi, the rain had begun to lighten, leaving the streets slick and gleaming under the streetlights. The city, which had once represented opportunity and ambition, now felt like a labyrinth of danger and deceit. Rashaad's death was a stark reminder that the stakes had been raised exponentially. The romanticized notions of power and control that had initially drawn them in were dissolving in the harsh reality of violence and loss.

Jamal's ambition was a wildfire, and Rashaad was the first branch consumed. Aisha knew, with a chilling certainty, that he wouldn't stop. He would push harder, take greater risks, all in the name of protecting what he had built, and in doing so, he would likely claim more victims. The question was no longer whether she could save Jamal, but whether she could save herself from the fallout of his destructive ambition. Rashaad's life, so carelessly extinguished, was a testament to the fact that in their world, loyalty was a fragile commodity, easily sacrificed on the altar of power. And Aisha, no longer willing to be a pawn in Jamal's game, was determined to break free before she became the next casualty. The path ahead was fraught with peril, but it was a path she would walk alone, guided by the bitter lesson learned from Rashaad's untimely end. The collateral damage was no longer a theoretical concept; it was a harsh, unforgiving reality that had claimed one of their own, a brutal awakening that would forever haunt the survivors of Jamal's escalating descent into darkness. The city, once a beacon of promise, now held only the echoes of violence and the chilling silence of loss.

The news of Rashaad's death hit Marcus like a physical blow, a brutal testament to the shifting tides of their operation. It wasn't just a loss of manpower; it was a gaping wound in the very fabric of their perceived invincibility. He saw the fear in the eyes of the remaining crew members, the hushed whispers that now carried the weight of genuine dread, not just apprehension. Aisha's departure had already fractured their unity, and Rashaad's demise threatened to shatter it completely. The carefully constructed edifice of power and control, built on a foundation of loyalty and a shared vision, was crumbling under the relentless pressure of escalating violence.

In the sterile quiet of his sparsely furnished office, the faint scent of stale cigar smoke clinging to the air, Marcus felt a cold, hard knot of rage tightening in his gut. He paced the length of the room, the worn Persian rug doing little to soften the impact of his heavy footsteps. Rashaad, so young, so eager to climb, had paid the ultimate price for Jamal's unchecked ambition. And while the immediate thought was of retaliation, of making the perpetrators pay dearly for their transgression, a deeper, more insidious current began to pull at him. It was the gnawing realization that he had, in some way, allowed this to happen. He had championed the aggressive expansion, had pushed the boundaries of their influence, and in doing so, had inadvertently paved the way for this bloodshed.

The guilt was a venomous serpent coiled in his stomach, its fangs dipped in the bitter bile of regret. He had pushed Jamal, had fueled his ambition, and now Rashaad was dead. The logic was undeniable, and it gnawed at him relentlessly. He saw his own reflection in the darkened windowpane – a man caught in a tightening noose, his carefully crafted image of leadership beginning to fray at the edges. The whispers of doubt from Aisha, the warnings he had so easily dismissed as feminine timidity, now echoed in his mind with a chilling prescience. He had been so focused on the prize, on the ultimate ascendancy, that he had blinded himself to the true cost of the journey.

He slammed his fist onto his desk, the force of the impact sending a stack of files skittering across the polished surface. This couldn't stand. He wouldn't allow Rashaad's death to be in vain, nor would he let his own burgeoning reputation be tarnished by what felt like his own failure. He needed to reclaim control, not just of the situation, but of the narrative. He needed to show them – show everyone, including himself – that he was still the one in charge, the one capable of navigating these treacherous waters. And the only way to do that, in his current state of mind, was through decisive, undeniable action.

Anya, his most trusted lieutenant, a woman whose loyalty was as fierce as her intellect was sharp, entered the office hesitantly. Her face, usually a mask of calm professionalism, was etched with a visible concern that mirrored the unease rippling through their ranks. "Marcus," she began, her voice low and steady, " Karim is requesting a meeting. He's... agitated. And a lot of the crew are talking. They need reassurance."

Marcus waved a dismissive hand, his gaze fixed on the city lights sprawling below, a constellation of potential targets and hidden dangers. "Reassurance comes from results, Anya, not from empty words. What's the latest on the Southside crew? Did they confirm the rendezvous point for that shipment?"

Anya's brow furrowed. "Yes, Marcus, they did. But it's... it's a trap, isn't it? The intel is too perfect, too easy. And after Rashaad..." She trailed off, the unspoken question hanging heavy in the air.

"After Rashaad," Marcus finished, turning to face her, his eyes burning with a desperate fire, "we hit them hard. We show them that crossing us, that taking one of ours, has consequences they can't afford. This shipment... it's our chance to hit them where it hurts, to disrupt their operations and send a clear message. We take this shipment, and we'll have leverage, Anya. Leverage we desperately need." His words were laced with a conviction that was as much about self-persuasion as it was about strategy. He needed to believe it, to project that unwavering confidence, even as a cold dread settled in his own heart.

"But the risk, Marcus," Anya countered, her voice gaining a sharper edge. "We're already stretched thin. Losing Rashaad has weakened us. And this particular shipment... it's rumoured to be heavily guarded. It's not just about retrieving product; it's about engaging directly with the people who killed Rashaad. This isn't just a business transaction; it's a war."

"War is exactly what it is, Anya," Marcus declared, his voice rising with a defiant intensity. "And we're not going to win it by hiding in the shadows. We need to strike, to strike hard and fast, before they can regroup, before they can consolidate their gains. This is our moment to seize the initiative, to turn the tide. We go in, we take the shipment, and we make them regret the day they ever laid a hand on Rashaad." He felt a surge of adrenaline, a reckless courage born of desperation and guilt. This wasn't just about business anymore; it was about personal vengeance, about restoring his own sense of control.

He saw the hesitation in Anya's eyes, the professional caution battling with her innate loyalty. He knew he was asking a lot, asking her to follow him into a situation that was fraught with peril, a situation where even his own conviction felt like a fragile shield. But he couldn't afford to show any doubt. He had to be the leader they needed, the one who could steer them through this storm.

"I understand the risks, Anya," he said, his voice softening slightly, trying to inject a measure of reassurance into his tone. "But we have Karim. He's still loyal, still our most capable enforcer. He'll lead the ground team. And we'll have backup positioned strategically. We won't be going in blind. We'll be precise. We'll be ruthless. This is the only way to ensure our survival, Anya. The only way to ensure that Rashaad's sacrifice wasn't for nothing." He was weaving a tapestry of justifications, each thread designed to strengthen his resolve and, more importantly, hers.

Anya studied him for a long moment, her gaze piercing. She saw the desperation, the raw, untamed emotion beneath the surface of his calculated words. She recognized the dangerous cocktail of guilt, ambition, and a burning desire for retribution that was driving him. She knew that Rashaad's death had profoundly shaken him, and in his vulnerability, he was making decisions that were more reactive than strategic. But she also knew that opposing him directly, at this moment, would be futile. His mind was made up.

"Very well, Marcus," she said finally, her voice heavy with an unspoken warning. "I'll assemble the team. But we need to be absolutely certain about our intelligence. One mistake, one miscalculation, and this will be more than just a collateral damage report; it will be our undoing."

Marcus nodded, a flicker of relief warring with the underlying anxiety. "Prepare the team, Anya. I want them ready to move within the hour. And get me Karim. I need to discuss the specifics with him personally." He turned back to the window, the city lights now seeming to mock him with their indifference. He was gambling, playing a high-stakes game with lives as his currency, all in a desperate attempt to reclaim the narrative, to bury the guilt of Rashaad's death under a fresh layer of decisive action. He was walking a tightrope, and the slightest tremor could send him plummeting into the abyss.

Karim arrived shortly after, his usual imposing presence amplified by a simmering rage. The loss of Rashaad, whom he had taken under his wing, had clearly taken a heavy toll. His jaw was clenched, his eyes hard and distant, the usual spark of camaraderie replaced by a grim, focused intensity. He moved with a coiled energy, like a predator pacing its cage, waiting for the signal to unleash its fury.

"Marcus," Karim greeted, his voice a low growl, devoid of any pleasantries. "You wanted to see me."

"Karim," Marcus acknowledged, gesturing to a chair. "Sit. We need to talk about Rashaad."

Karim's gaze sharpened, a flicker of pain momentarily crossing his features before being quickly masked by a steely resolve. "I know what happened. I want revenge, Marcus. I want to see the bastards who did this suffer. I want to make them pay for taking Rashaad."

"And we will, Karim," Marcus assured him, leaning forward, his voice taking on a carefully measured tone. "But not blindly. Not impulsively. We need to be smart about this. We need to hit them where it will hurt them the most, where it will cripple them." He paused, letting the weight of his words sink in. "The Southside crew. They're moving a major shipment tonight. A highly valuable consignment, according to our intel. This is our opportunity to strike back, to recover what's ours and to send a clear message."

Karim's eyes narrowed, a spark of interest igniting within them. "The Southside shipment? I heard whispers, but I didn't think... It's too risky, Marcus. They'll be expecting trouble. They'll be prepared."

"That's why we go in with overwhelming force," Marcus countered, his voice firm. "You'll lead the ground assault, Karim. You know the tactics, you know how to handle these situations. Anya will be coordinating from a distance, providing support and managing the extraction. We'll have eyes on every angle. This isn't a revenge mission, Karim, not entirely. It's a strategic maneuver. We cripple their operation, and we reclaim our lost ground. And yes," he added, his voice hardening, "we'll make them pay for Rashaad."

Karim remained silent for a moment, the internal conflict evident on his face. The primal urge for vengeance warred with the ingrained discipline of their operation. He had always been a loyal soldier, but Rashaad's death had ignited something deeper, something more personal. "Who's going with me?" he asked finally, his voice taut with anticipation.

"A select team," Marcus replied. "The best we have. Those who can handle themselves, those who understand what's at stake. We won't bring the entire crew into this; it's too risky. This needs to be surgical." He deliberately omitted the fact that he was also using this operation as a way to weed out those he perceived as weak, those who might falter under pressure.

"And the location?" Karim pressed, his gaze unwavering. "Where is this shipment being moved?"

"A disused industrial complex on the outskirts of the city," Marcus said, pulling out a map and spreading it across the desk. He pointed to a specific area. "The intel suggests they'll be using the old loading docks. Heavily fortified, but there's a blind spot on the north side, near the abandoned warehouse. That's where we'll make our entry."

Karim studied the map, his mind already processing the terrain, the potential entry and exit points, the likely defensive positions. He was a natural strategist, a warrior who thrived in the chaos of conflict. "It's a good location for an ambush," he conceded, a grim smile touching his lips. "But they'll have patrols, lookouts. We need to be in and out before they can react."

"Precisely," Marcus affirmed, a sense of urgency permeating his voice. "Anya has already mapped out the surveillance patterns. We'll have a window of opportunity, but it's a tight one. We hit them hard, we take the shipment, and we disappear. No unnecessary risks, no prolonged engagements. The objective is clear: disrupt their supply line and retrieve the product. Everything else is secondary." He hoped that by framing it as a calculated business move, he could mask the underlying recklessness of the entire operation.

The truth was, Marcus was operating on instinct, fueled by a desperate need to regain control and to alleviate the crushing weight of guilt. He knew, deep down, that this was a dangerous gambit, a move born of desperation rather than strategic brilliance. He was pushing his people into a situation that was far more volatile than he was letting on, all to appease his own inner demons. He saw Rashaad's death not as a consequence of their choices, but as a personal affront that demanded immediate, decisive action. He was blinded by his own need to prove himself, to demonstrate that he was still the man in charge, the one who could lead them to victory, even in the face of overwhelming odds.

As Karim left to prepare his team, Marcus felt a momentary sense of clarity, quickly followed by a fresh wave of anxiety. He had committed them to a course of action, a path that led directly into the heart of danger. He had disregarded Aisha's subtle warnings, Anya's professional concerns, and Karim's own deep-seated rage. He was gambling with their lives, all in a desperate attempt to erase the stain of Rashaad's death and to reassert his dominance. The city, a vast and unforgiving entity, held its breath, unaware of the reckless gambit that was about to unfold, a gambit that threatened to shatter what little remained of their fragile stability and plunge them into an even deeper abyss of violence and loss. The stage was set, the pieces were in play, and Marcus, driven by a potent mix of guilt and ambition, was about to roll the dice, hoping that fate would grant him the victory he so desperately craved, unaware that he was walking directly into a trap he himself had helped to set.

Jamal watched Marcus from a distance, a flicker of something akin to pity in his eyes, swiftly replaced by a chillingly pragmatic assessment. Marcus was unraveling, a potent blend of guilt, grief, and a desperate need for control morphing him into a liability. Rashaad's death had clearly exposed the cracks in Marcus's façade, revealing the fragile ego beneath the veneer of calculated leadership. This wasn't just about avenging Rashaad anymore; for Jamal, it was about seizing the moment, about stepping out of the shadow of Marcus's increasingly erratic decisions and claiming the future as his own. He saw the opportunity, stark and undeniable, a void opening up in the hierarchy that he was more than ready to fill.

His initial motivations had been simpler, born from ambition and a desire to prove his worth. But the streets, and the brutal calculus of survival, had a way of stripping away such niceties. Loyalty was a luxury, and sentimentality a fatal flaw. Marcus, consumed by his own internal turmoil, was no longer a formidable obstacle; he was a stepping stone. Jamal's mind, usually a whirlwind of strategy and anticipation, settled into a cold, sharp focus. He began to meticulously chart his course, not with the overt aggression that had characterized Rashaad's ambition, but with a calculated subtlety that would catch Marcus completely off guard.

The first move was almost imperceptible, a whisper in the right ear, a carefully placed seed of doubt. He knew the internal politics, the simmering resentments that Marcus had either ignored or inadvertently fostered. He began to cultivate these, not by direct confrontation, but by offering a different perspective, a seemingly more stable alternative. He reached out to Karim, not to conspire, but to engage in strategic "consultations." He framed his discussions around the perceived instability of Marcus's leadership, the dangers of his increasingly reactive approach. He spoke of Rashaad's death not as a catalyst for reckless retaliation, but as a stark warning.

"This Southside shipment, Karim," Jamal had mused, his voice low and measured, as they discussed the aftermath of the botched operation, "Marcus is playing with fire. He's letting emotion dictate strategy. You know as well as I do, Rashaad was good, but he was also reckless. And Marcus is taking that recklessness and amplifying it." He'd watched Karim's jaw tighten, the lingering grief for Rashaad a palpable force. "We need someone who can keep a level head, Karim. Someone who can see the bigger picture, not just the immediate enemy."

Karim, fiercely loyal to Rashaad and increasingly wary of Marcus's volatile state, had listened intently. He saw the truth in Jamal's words, the undeniable recklessness of Marcus's plan. While Jamal didn't explicitly ask for Karim's allegiance against Marcus, he planted the idea, the suggestion that a different kind of leadership was needed. He appealed to Karim's sense of order, to his innate respect for calculated strategy over desperate gambits.

Simultaneously, Jamal began to subtly leverage his connections with informants, not to betray Marcus directly, but to gather intelligence that he could present as vital foresight. He discovered that the "Southside shipment" intel Marcus had so readily embraced was indeed flawed, deliberately so. It was a lure, a trap designed to exploit Marcus's emotional state. He didn't reveal this directly to Marcus, knowing it would be met with defensiveness. Instead, he channeled this information through a trusted intermediary, an older, more seasoned member of their crew who had always been skeptical of Marcus's rapid ascent. This intermediary, concerned by the potential fallout, began to voice his own reservations, lending weight to Jamal's subtle campaign of doubt.

"Marcus is chasing ghosts," the intermediary, a man named Silas, confided in Karim, framing it as a shared concern. "Rashaad's death has him seeing enemies everywhere. This shipment... it feels too clean, too easy. I've got a bad feeling about it." Silas, under Jamal's quiet guidance, started to subtly question Marcus's operational decisions in front of other key figures, highlighting the increasing risks and the potential for devastating losses. Jamal ensured that these conversations happened organically, appearing to be merely an observer, a concerned member of the team.

The personal toll of their lifestyle was becoming increasingly evident, and Jamal was an expert at exploiting these weaknesses. He noticed how Aisha's departure had left a void, not just in their ranks, but in the sense of camaraderie that had once bound them. He subtly fostered a sense of exclusivity around his own operations, creating an aura of competence and stability that contrasted sharply with the growing chaos surrounding Marcus. He would host private meetings, ostensibly to discuss logistics for upcoming ventures, but in reality, to cultivate relationships with those who felt marginalized or undervalued under Marcus's leadership. He listened to their grievances, validating their concerns, and offering a quiet, understated promise of a more secure future.

His most daring move, however, involved indirectly feeding information to a rival crew. Not about Marcus's plans directly, but about vulnerabilities that Marcus himself had created. He let it be known, through a series of intermediaries and carefully managed leaks, that Marcus's operations were becoming increasingly predictable due to his emotional responses. He subtly highlighted the fact that Marcus was overly reliant on certain established routes, routes that Jamal himself was beginning to steer clear of, further cementing his image as a discerning strategist. He didn't betray Marcus's immediate plans, but he subtly undermined his general operational security, making Marcus a more attractive target for those looking to exploit weakness.

The industrial complex on the outskirts of the city, the designated rendezvous point for the "Southside shipment," was a perfect example of Marcus's flawed thinking. Jamal knew the area intimately, having scouted it himself during a period of independent exploration. He recognized the "blind spot" Marcus had identified, but he also knew it was a deception, a trap designed to draw opponents into a kill zone. He understood that Marcus, blinded by his desire for a decisive victory and driven by a reckless need to prove his mettle, would likely commit his best men to a frontal assault, focusing on the supposed vulnerability.

Jamal made sure he wasn't part of that assault. He claimed a severe case of the flu, a believable ailment that would keep him away from the front lines without raising suspicion. He used this time to further solidify his network, to ensure that his own loyalties were with him, not with Marcus. He would be physically absent, but his influence would be subtly at play, shaping the narrative and preparing for the inevitable fallout from Marcus's impending miscalculation. He was playing a longer game, a game of chess rather than checkers, and Marcus, consumed by the immediate threat, was merely a pawn to be sacrificed.

The night of the planned operation, Jamal was miles away, in a discreet, anonymous apartment on the other side of the city. He had no direct contact with the team Marcus had dispatched, no involvement in their preparations. His absence was a deliberate choice, a calculated maneuver to distance himself from the inevitable casualties. He knew, with a grim certainty, that Rashaad's death would not be the last. Marcus's obsession with retribution, his willingness to throw good people into a meat grinder, was a self-destructive force.

As the hours ticked by, Jamal didn't anxiously await news of the operation's success. He was already moving on. He was reaching out to Karim, not to offer support, but to gauge his reaction. He was consolidating his own resources, ensuring that any destabilization caused by Marcus's actions would benefit him. He had heard rumors of Marcus's plan to lead the operation himself, a foolish and reckless decision driven by ego. If Marcus fell, Jamal would be there to pick up the pieces. If he succeeded, Jamal would find another way to capitalize on his heightened recklessness.

His actions were a stark testament to the dehumanizing effect of their chosen path. The empathy that might have once guided him had been systematically eroded, replaced by a cold, predatory instinct. Marcus's instability was not an anomaly to be corrected; it was an opportunity to be exploited. The collateral damage, the lives that would inevitably be lost in Marcus's vengeful pursuit, were simply the unfortunate, yet predictable, consequences of a power vacuum. Jamal's ascent was not built on grand pronouncements or displays of brute force, but on the quiet, insidious work of a hunter, patiently waiting for the prey to weaken, ready to strike when the moment was right. He was the embodiment of survival of the fittest, a brutal Darwinian principle writ large on the unforgiving landscape of their illicit world. He was not driven by hatred, but by a chilling logic of self-preservation and an unyielding ambition for absolute control.

The vibrant canvases that once represented Chloe's escape, her silent rebellion against the grimy realities of their existence, now loomed over her like accusations. Each brushstroke, each carefully chosen hue, felt like a confession waiting to be unearthed, a tangible piece of her involvement that the authorities, or worse, Marcus's enemies, could seize and twist into damning evidence. She'd always been meticulous, almost obsessively so, about her artistic process. She used specific brands of imported pigments, sourced from obscure online suppliers, their invoices tucked away in the digital ether, a testament to her discerning taste and her deliberate attempt to create a separate, untainted identity. But now, those very details felt like a trail of breadcrumbs leading straight to her door.

Her studio, a sanctuary carved out of a forgotten loft space in the industrial district, had been her haven. The smell of turpentine and linseed oil was a comforting balm, a stark contrast to the metallic tang of blood and the stale scent of fear that permeated the rest of her life. She'd spent countless hours there, transforming scraps of salvaged canvas and discarded wood into explosions of color, abstract narratives that spoke of suppressed emotions and unspoken desires. She'd painted Rashaad's funeral, not the grim event itself, but the raw grief that had rippled through their crew, capturing the fractured expressions and the heavy silence in a palette of bruised purples and somber grays. She'd painted Marcus too, his face a mask of forced stoicism, his eyes betraying a turbulent inner storm, rendered in harsh, unforgiving blacks and stark whites.

These pieces, her most personal and raw, were hidden. Not buried, not destroyed, but secreted away in the hidden compartments of her studio, behind false walls and beneath loose floorboards. She'd always feared discovery, not of the art itself, but of the truths it held, the undeniable glimpses into the clandestine operations and the volatile relationships that defined their world. Now, that fear had intensified, morphing into a gnawing dread. The memory of Rashaad's brutal end, the subsequent crackdown by the police on anyone remotely connected to their activities, had cast a long shadow. They were being watched, scrutinized, and Chloe knew, with a chilling certainty, that her unique artistic signature, her distinctive materials, could easily become the linchpin of any investigation.

Her choice of materials was a deliberate act of defiance. She eschewed the common, readily available art supplies, opting instead for specialized mediums that hinted at a life beyond the confines of their street-level hustle. The imported cadmium reds, the rare cobalt blues, the fine Italian linen canvases – these weren't the supplies of a typical struggling artist. They whispered of disposable income, of access to resources that a street-level operator wouldn't typically possess. If discovered, these items could directly link her to the financial flows that the authorities were undoubtedly trying to trace. An invoice for a bulk order of specialized fixatives, for example, could easily be cross-referenced with known associates, their financial records, or even surveillance on their known hangouts. The very quality and exclusivity of her supplies, once a source of pride, now felt like a glaring beacon, a siren call to anyone seeking to unravel their network.

Chloe found herself replaying conversations, dissecting every interaction, searching for any slip-up, any accidental revelation that might have inadvertently exposed her artistic pursuits. Had she mentioned a particular supplier to anyone outside their immediate circle? Had an accidental smudge of her signature charcoal on a shared surface been noticed? The paranoia was a constant hum beneath the surface of her thoughts, a corrosive agent eroding her carefully constructed composure. She started to notice the casual glances of strangers, the way they lingered a beat too long, the subtle shift in their demeanor when she passed. Was it just her mind playing tricks, fueled by guilt and fear, or were they indeed observing her, cataloging her movements?

The city, once a canvas of endless possibility, now felt like a labyrinth of potential traps. Every shadowed alleyway, every dimly lit bar, every anonymous face in the crowd could be an informant, a rival, or worse, a law enforcement officer gathering intelligence. The sheer scale of the metropolis, its sprawling anonymity, offered no comfort. Instead, it amplified her isolation. There was no one to confide in, no one who truly understood the tightrope she walked. Her artistic endeavors, the very thing that had once provided her with a sense of self, now threatened to be her undoing.

She remembered a specific instance, a few weeks prior, when Marcus had been discussing a new strategy for acquiring resources. He'd been frustrated, his usual bravado tinged with desperation. Chloe, in an attempt to offer a different perspective, had gestured towards a discarded piece of abstract art leaning against the wall of their makeshift command center – a vibrant, chaotic swirl of colors she'd been working on. She'd spoken metaphorically, comparing the complex layering of paint to the intricate web of their operations, suggesting that a more nuanced, less direct approach might be more effective. Marcus, caught up in his own anxieties, had barely registered her words, his eyes glazing over. But she recalled a brief, almost imperceptible flicker of recognition in the eyes of one of Marcus's lieutenants, a man named Silas, who'd been present. Silas, a man of few words but sharp observation, had given her a long, assessing look. Had he seen the art? Had he made a connection between her passion and her involvement in their world? The possibility gnawed at her.

Silas was a wildcard. He'd been with Marcus's crew longer than most, a seasoned operative who valued loyalty and discretion above all else. While Jamal was subtly orchestrating his own rise, manipulating the existing power structures, Silas represented a more traditional, albeit dangerous, form of loyalty. He wasn't easily swayed by promises of power or ambition, but he was fiercely protective of the crew, and especially of Rashaad's legacy. If Silas were to discover Chloe's art, and connect it to the network, his reaction would be unpredictable. He might see it as a betrayal, a dangerous loose end that needed to be tied up, or worse, a valuable piece of evidence to be leveraged.

The thought of Silas, or anyone else, dissecting her artwork, searching for hidden meanings, for clues that could incriminate her, sent a shiver down her spine. She'd always kept her art separate, a private world where she could express herself without fear of judgment or reprisal. But now, the lines were blurring, the sanctuary invaded by the harsh reality of their lives. She considered the implications of her artistic materials being traced back to her. A specific type of canvas stretcher bar, for instance, might be a unique design or a specialty item that could be linked to a particular supplier, a supplier whose client list could be subpoenaed. Even the solvents she used for cleaning her brushes – rare, artisanal blends – could be tracked.

Her studio was more than just a place to paint; it was a carefully curated environment. She had bins of meticulously sorted pigments, each labeled with its chemical name and origin. She had journals filled with sketches, color studies, and detailed notes on her techniques. While she'd always maintained a high degree of secrecy, these were the very things that now represented her vulnerability. If law enforcement were to raid her studio, these materials would be the first things they'd seize. They would be analyzed, cross-referenced, and used to build a case against her, not just as an accessory, but as a central figure.

The weight of this potential exposure was crushing. Chloe found herself becoming increasingly withdrawn, her conversations with crew members becoming shorter, more guarded. She'd always been the quiet one, the observer, but now her silence felt deliberate, a shield against accidental disclosure. She started to avoid direct contact with anyone who might have seen her bringing art supplies into the city, or who might have glimpsed her carrying a canvas. Every trip to the art supply store, once a mundane necessity, now felt like a high-stakes operation. She'd begun using different disguises, varying her routes, employing a level of caution that felt unnatural, exhausting.

The increasing paranoia wasn't just about the law. Marcus himself was a growing threat. His descent into erratic behavior, his increasingly desperate attempts to regain control after Rashaad's death, made him unpredictable and dangerous. He was looking for scapegoats, for anyone to blame for the setbacks. If he discovered that Chloe's art, her perceived distraction or hobby, had somehow played a role in their operational security being compromised, even indirectly, he wouldn't hesitate to cut her loose, or worse, use her as a sacrifice to deflect suspicion. The thought of Marcus turning on her was almost as terrifying as the prospect of being arrested. He was a man who operated on impulse and ego, and his perception of betrayal, however misguided, would be absolute.

She remembered a conversation with Aisha, before she'd disappeared, about the dangers of leaving too much of a trail. Aisha, always more pragmatic and street-smart than Chloe, had warned her about the importance of anonymity, of blending in. Chloe, in her naivety, had dismissed the advice, believing her art was a harmless outlet, a separate world. Now, Aisha's words echoed in her mind, a stark premonition of the mess she found herself in. Aisha had understood the rules of their game, the ruthless calculus of survival. Chloe, blinded by her artistic aspirations, had seemingly forgotten them.

The idea of betraying former allies, a concept that had always seemed repugnant, began to creep into her thoughts. If the evidence against her became too overwhelming, if her own freedom and survival were truly on the line, what wouldn't she do? The thought was deeply unsettling, a betrayal of the very principles she'd tried to uphold through her art. Could she sacrifice someone else to save herself? Could she point a finger at another member of the crew, feed them to the wolves to divert attention from her own involvement? The moral compromise was a dark abyss, and the closer she got to the edge, the more appealing the idea of simply ceasing to exist within their world became.

She started to consider drastic measures. Destroying her art was a possibility, but the thought of erasing years of her work, her passion, felt like a form of self-mutilation. Moreover, she knew that simply destroying the paintings wouldn't erase the knowledge, the invoices, the suppliers. The trail could still be followed. She could move, disappear, but that too, would raise suspicion, make her a person of interest. Every option seemed to lead to a dead end, a new set of dangers.

The isolation was profound. She couldn't confide in anyone within the crew. They were either too compromised, too loyal to Marcus, or too caught up in their own survival to offer any real solace or help. Jamal, with his calculated moves and his chilling pragmatism, was a dangerous ally at best. He saw everything as a transaction, a means to an end. If Chloe's art became a liability, Jamal might very well offer her up as a sacrifice to secure his own position. The thought of him, cool and collected, explaining to the authorities how Chloe's art had led them to their operation, was a chillingly plausible scenario. He was an opportunist, and she was becoming an opportunity.

Her mind raced, desperately seeking a solution. She began to meticulously document every interaction, every piece of evidence that could potentially link her to the crew's activities. She started creating encrypted backups of her financial records, her communication logs, anything that could prove her level of involvement, or more importantly, her attempts to mitigate her risk. She knew the authorities would be looking for patterns, for connections, and she needed to control the narrative as much as possible, to present herself not as a willing participant, but as someone caught in the crossfire, a victim of circumstance.

The irony was not lost on her. She had sought solace and self-expression in her art, a way to process the violence and the moral compromises of their lives. Now, that very art, the tangible manifestation of her inner world, was poised to become the instrument of her destruction. The vibrant colors, the abstract forms, the very essence of her creative spirit, had become a liability, a damning testament to her entanglement. She was trapped, her artistic endeavors, once a source of freedom, now a gilded cage, her own creations the bars that threatened to imprison her forever. The city, vast and indifferent, offered no sanctuary, only an endless expanse of uncertainty, where every shadow held the potential for exposure and every familiar face could harbor a hidden threat. She was alone with her art, and her art was about to betray her. The weight of her secrets was no longer a burden she could carry in silence; it was a tangible threat, an imminent danger that demanded drastic action, even if that action meant sacrificing pieces of herself, or worse, the people she had once called allies.

Aisha's heart hammered against her ribs, a frantic drumbeat echoing the chaos that had become her life. The glitz and glamour of Vegas, once a dazzling allure, now felt like a gaudy, blood-soaked shroud. Each siren's wail, each unfamiliar car that lingered too long on her street, sent a fresh wave of panic through her. The faces of her friends, once etched with camaraderie and shared dreams, were now twisted in her memory by the shadow of violence and betrayal. Rashaad, gone in a brutal burst of gunfire. Chloe, her spirit seemingly fractured by the constant pressure, retreating into a world of her own creation. And Marcus... Marcus, the charismatic leader who had drawn them all into his orbit, now a man teetering on the precipice of self-destruction, his every decision a gamble with their lives.

The decision to leave had been a slow, agonizing burn, fueled by a growing certainty that staying meant certain doom. It wasn't just the threat of law enforcement, though their presence had become increasingly suffocating, their investigations a constant, chilling whisper. It was the internal rot, the way Marcus's thirst for control was poisoning everything, turning allies into potential liabilities. She'd seen it in Jamal's calculating eyes, a subtle shift from loyal lieutenant to ambitious rival. She'd heard it in the hushed conversations, the barely veiled threats, the palpable tension that now hung in the air like the desert dust. Aisha knew she couldn't fight it, couldn't change Marcus, couldn't salvage what was broken. Her only hope was to escape.

The logistics of her departure were a meticulous dance of deception. Every step was calculated to minimize her digital footprint, to erase any trace of her existence from the city's ever-watchful gaze. She'd spent weeks meticulously gathering cash, a small fortune accumulated through a lifetime of carefully managed side hustles and a few clandestine deals that now made her stomach churn. She avoided banks, paid for everything in crisp bills, and made sure her purchases were untraceable – burner phones, cash-only prepaid travel cards, discreetly purchased clothing that would help her blend into any crowd. She'd even acquired a new, nondescript vehicle, a reliable sedan bought with cash from a private seller in a neighboring town, its VIN meticulously scrubbed from any official records. The old car, the one that had witnessed too many clandestine meetings and late-night escapes, was left abandoned in a remote parking garage, a final, silent farewell.

Her packing was minimal, a testament to her desire to shed her past. A single duffel bag held the essentials: a few changes of clothes, a small first-aid kit, the precious cash, and a worn photograph of her and Chloe, their smiles bright and carefree, a stark contrast to the darkness that now enveloped them. She'd resisted the urge to contact Chloe, the thought of putting her friend at further risk a bitter pill to swallow. They had drifted apart in recent months, a silent acknowledgment of the growing chasm between Chloe's artistic world and Aisha's increasingly dangerous reality. Chloe's artistic endeavors, once a shared point of innocent fascination, had become a source of worry, a potential vulnerability that Aisha couldn't afford to acknowledge, let alone exploit.

The night of her departure was cloaked in a manufactured calm. She'd spent the evening meticulously cleaning her apartment, scrubbing away any evidence of her presence, emptying the trash cans, wiping down surfaces, ensuring that no stray hair, no forgotten receipt, could betray her. She moved with a practiced stillness, her movements economical and deliberate, the result of years spent navigating precarious situations. She avoided looking in the mirror, not wanting to see the fear in her own eyes, the haunted look that had become a permanent fixture.

Stepping out of her apartment building was like stepping into a different world. The familiar streetlights cast long, distorted shadows, making every alleyway seem like a potential ambush point. She walked with a measured pace, her senses on high alert, scanning faces, listening for any unusual sounds. The air was thick with the oppressive heat of a Vegas summer night, but Aisha felt a chill that had nothing to do with the temperature. She was leaving behind a life, a family of sorts, forged in the crucible of desperation and loyalty. The memories, however painful, were a part of her, and shedding them felt like amputating a limb.

Her destination was a small, anonymous bus station on the outskirts of the city, a place where people came and went with little fanfare. The bus itself was a relic, its seats worn and its engine coughing, but its anonymity was its greatest asset. She paid for a one-way ticket to a distant, nondescript city hundreds of miles away, a place chosen specifically for its lack of connection to her past. As she settled into her seat, the rumble of the engine a low thrum beneath her feet, Aisha felt a flicker of hope. It was a fragile thing, easily extinguished, but it was there, a small ember glowing in the encroaching darkness.

The journey was long and arduous. Hours blurred into a monotonous cycle of dim lights, snoozing passengers, and the constant hum of the engine. Aisha kept her gaze fixed on the window, watching the landscape transform from the stark, neon-lit sprawl of Vegas to the vast, indifferent darkness of the desert. Each mile that separated her from the city felt like a victory, a step further away from the abyss. But the weight of what she carried was immense. She had witnessed betrayals that would haunt her, losses that had hollowed her out. She had seen the best of people twisted into the worst, and the memory of Rashaad's final moments was a recurring nightmare, a brutal reminder of the price of loyalty in Marcus's world.

She replayed conversations in her mind, dissecting every word, every nuance. Had she missed something? Had there been a sign, a warning that she'd overlooked? The guilt gnawed at her. She'd been loyal, perhaps too loyal, to Marcus and his crew, blinded by the camaraderie and the intoxicating rush of their shared purpose. She had believed in their vision, in the idea of carving out their own destiny, free from the constraints of the system. But the system, it seemed, had a way of finding you, of ensnaring you in its web, and Marcus's ambition had proven to be a far more dangerous adversary than any external force.

The awareness of her own precarious position became a constant companion. She knew that Marcus, or anyone connected to him, would likely try to find her. She represented a loose end, a witness to events that could potentially implicate them. Her knowledge of their operations, however limited, was a liability. She'd seen enough to know that their business was built on a foundation of secrets and violence, and anyone who threatened to expose those secrets was a threat to their very existence. The thought of being hunted, of having to constantly look over her shoulder, was a daunting prospect, but it was a risk she was willing to take for the chance of a clean slate.

She thought of Chloe's art, her sanctuary, her refuge. Aisha had always admired Chloe's ability to create beauty amidst the ugliness, to find meaning and expression in a world that seemed determined to crush the spirit. But she had also worried about Chloe, about the way her art became a physical manifestation of their shared experiences, a tangible link to their illicit activities. If the authorities were to ever connect Chloe's distinctive materials, her unique artistic signature, to their network, it could unravel everything. Chloe, so fragile and sensitive, was not built for the kind of scrutiny and danger that would inevitably follow. This was another reason Aisha couldn't reach out.

The faces of Marcus's inner circle flashed through her mind. Jamal, with his smooth talk and his sharp mind, a man who played the long game, always positioning himself for maximum advantage. She'd always suspected Jamal was more than he appeared, that his loyalty was a carefully crafted facade. And then there was Silas, a man of few words but immense presence, a silent guardian who seemed to hold a deep, unspoken understanding of their world. Silas had always regarded Aisha with a quiet intensity, an unnerving gaze that seemed to penetrate her defenses. She couldn't fathom his motives, his allegiances, but she knew he was a formidable force, a variable that could tip the scales in unpredictable ways.

As the bus rumbled on, Aisha found herself wrestling with the moral implications of her departure. She was abandoning her friends, leaving them to face the consequences of their choices alone. Was this betrayal? Or was it self-preservation? She couldn't deny the fear that coursed through her veins, the primal instinct to survive. She had seen firsthand the brutal cost of involvement, the devastating impact of Marcus's ambition. Staying would mean becoming complicit, a silent partner in crimes that were escalating in severity and recklessness. Her conscience wouldn't allow it.

The bus stopped in a small, dusty town at dawn. Aisha disembarked, her legs stiff, her mind weary but resolute. She took a deep breath of the unfamiliar air, a scent that carried none of the oppressive weight of Vegas. This was a new beginning, a chance to build something different, something clean. She knew the road ahead would be challenging, that the shadows of her past would likely linger, but she was determined to face them, to forge a path towards a future where she wasn't defined by the choices of others. Her footsteps, now carrying her away from the familiar, were the first steps on a journey of reinvention, a testament to her resilience and her unwavering desire to escape the collateral damage of their world. The city of lost souls had lost one of its own, not to death, but to the desperate, hopeful quest for a life lived on her own terms.

Chapter 5: The Unraveling Web

The fractured state of Marcus's crew wasn't just a matter of frayed nerves and distrust; it was a gaping wound bleeding opportunity for those who knew where to look. Aisha's absence, though a significant blow, had also served to highlight the growing fissures within the group. The carefully constructed illusion of unity had shattered, revealing the rot beneath. Marcus, consumed by a potent cocktail of paranoia and wounded pride, was making mistakes, the kind that would have been unthinkable in the earlier, more cohesive days of their operation. His movements, once fluid and calculated, had become erratic, driven by a desperate need to prove his dominance, to reassert control over a situation that was rapidly spiraling beyond his grasp. He was no longer the maestro conducting a symphony of illicit endeavors; he was a desperate musician improvising wildly, hitting discordant notes that drew unwanted attention.

Marcus's misplaced confidence was a beacon for their adversaries. He'd always possessed an almost arrogant belief in his own invincibility, a trait that had served them well in navigating the treacherous currents of the criminal underworld. But now, that same hubris was a liability. He was taking risks, unnecessary ones, that put them all in the crosshairs. The discreet burner phones that had once facilitated their clandestine communications were now being used with a recklessness that bordered on suicidal. Calls were made from predictable locations, conversations were more open than they should have been, and the rhythm of their operations, once a ghost in the machine, was becoming a discernible pattern. The enemies they had amassed, the rivals they had outmaneuvered, were no longer merely specters in the periphery; they were closing in, their predatory instincts honed by the scent of Marcus's vulnerability.

The whispers that had once been confined to the shadowed corners of back alleys were now amplifying, reaching the ears of those who had the power to dismantle their empire brick by brick. Law enforcement, sensing the shift in the wind, the weakening of Marcus's grip, was tightening its noose. Surveillance intensified, informants, sensing opportunity, began to sing, and the carefully laid plans of Marcus's crew began to unravel like a cheap sweater. Each tactical misstep, each moment of unchecked ego, was another thread pulled from their tightly woven web, leaving them exposed and vulnerable. They had always operated on the fringes, masters of camouflage and deception, but now, they were being forced into the harsh glare of the spotlight, their secrets laid bare for all to see.

Jamal, ever the pragmatist, saw this unraveling not as a catastrophe, but as an opportunity for self-preservation and advancement. While Marcus was flailing, desperately trying to patch the holes in his sinking ship, Jamal was busy charting his own course. His ambition, a cold and calculating force, had always simmered beneath the surface, a quiet counterpoint to Marcus's volatile charisma. Now, it was coming into its own, fueled by the growing chaos. He was leveraging the situation, meticulously playing his cards, cultivating new alliances while subtly undermining Marcus's authority. His conversations, once filled with the outward appearance of loyalty, now carried a double edge, laced with veiled suggestions and carefully planted seeds of doubt. He was a master manipulator, a puppeteer pulling strings from the shadows, his own position solidifying with every misstep his former associates made.

Jamal understood the intricate dance of power and deception that governed their world. He knew that in times of crisis, loyalty was a currency that depreciated rapidly. He saw how Marcus's impulsive decisions were alienating even his most trusted lieutenants. Silas, a man of quiet observation and formidable loyalty, was beginning to show signs of weariness, his stoic facade cracking under the strain of Marcus's increasingly erratic leadership. Even the street soldiers, those who lived and breathed by Marcus's command, were beginning to question their allegiance, their faith eroded by the constant threat of exposure and the lack of clear direction. Jamal was adept at exploiting these cracks, offering a seemingly more stable alternative, a promise of survival in a world that was quickly becoming untenable.

He began to isolate Marcus, subtly at first, then more overtly. He would intercept communications, delay crucial information, and foster an environment where Marcus's orders were met with hesitation and whispered dissent. His own actions were meticulously crafted to appear as efforts to mitigate Marcus's mistakes, to salvage what could be salvaged, all while ensuring that the blame for any failures ultimately landed on Marcus's shoulders. He was planting the seeds of Marcus's downfall, nurturing them with every calculated move, creating a narrative of incompetence and recklessness that would justify his own eventual ascension.

The enemies they had made were not oblivious to this internal strife. They saw the cracks widening, the foundation weakening. They could sense the shift in power dynamics, the growing discord. The syndicate bosses they had crossed, the drug cartels they had muscled out of territory, the corrupt officials they had bribed – all were keenly aware of the weakening grip of Marcus's crew. They were circling, their agents and informants feeding them intelligence, piecing together the puzzle of

Marcus's unraveling operations. Each intercepted call, each witnessed clandestine meeting, was a confirmation of their suspicions, a stepping stone closer to their ultimate goal: the complete eradication of Marcus's influence.

The pressure was immense, a suffocating weight that bore down on every member of the crew. Fear, once a manageable undercurrent, was now a palpable presence, a cold dread that permeated their every interaction. The camaraderie that had once defined them had devolved into suspicion. Every glance was scrutinized, every word weighed for hidden meaning. They were no longer a united front; they were a collection of individuals, each desperately trying to navigate the encroaching storm, their own survival paramount. The hunter had become the hunted, not just by external forces, but by each other. The web they had so carefully spun was now a tangled trap, and the threads that once bound them together were now the very things that ensnared them.

Marcus, blinded by his own ego, remained largely unaware of the extent of Jamal's machinations. He saw the growing dissent, the whispers of doubt, but attributed it to the increased pressure. He believed he was still in control, that a few decisive actions, a show of force, would quell the unrest and reassert his authority. He failed to recognize that the true threat wasn't the external forces that sought to destroy them, but the insidious betrayal festering within his own ranks. Jamal was the serpent in their garden, patiently waiting for the opportune moment to strike, to claim the spoils of Marcus's impending downfall.

The narrative of their operations, once a tightly guarded secret, was now becoming a public spectacle, albeit one viewed through the distorted lens of rumor and speculation. The law enforcement agencies, though not yet in possession of irrefutable proof, were building a formidable case, their investigative teams working diligently to connect the dots, to bridge the gaps in the information they had. They were systematically dismantling the layers of secrecy that Marcus's crew had so expertly erected, peeling them back one by one, exposing the sordid reality beneath. The whispers of their activities, once dismissed as urban legend, were beginning to solidify into something tangible, something that demanded a response.

The streets, once their domain, were becoming increasingly hostile territory. The familiar faces of informants and rival crews were now tinged with a predatory glint. The subtle nods of acknowledgement had been replaced by averted gazes or outright hostility. The unspoken rules of engagement were being rewritten, and Marcus's crew was finding itself on the wrong side of the new order. The ease with which they had once operated was a distant memory, replaced by a constant state of vigilance, a gnawing awareness that at any moment, their carefully constructed world could come crashing down around them.

Jamal, meanwhile, was meticulously weaving his own narrative of survival and success. He presented himself as the rational voice, the one who understood the complexities of their operations and the inevitability of Marcus's mistakes. He was building a coalition of the disillusioned, those who had grown tired of Marcus's erratic leadership and the constant threat of imminent collapse. He offered them a vision of stability, a promise of a future where their efforts would be rewarded, where their risks would be managed, not dictated by the whims of a man losing his grip. His influence spread like a contagion, infecting the ranks with a growing sense of unease and a yearning for a new leader.

The unravelling wasn't a single event, but a slow, agonizing process, a gradual erosion of trust and control. Each betrayal, each tactical error, each piece of intelligence that fell into the wrong hands, chipped away at the foundations of Marcus's empire. The hunter, so confident in his prowess, had inadvertently led his own pack into a carefully laid trap. The web was tightening, its silken threads now a constricting noose, and as the walls closed in, the true nature of their predicament became terrifyingly clear: they were no longer the predators; they were the prey. The game had changed, and the rules had been rewritten by the very people they had once underestimated. Marcus's reign was nearing its inevitable, brutal end, and the chaos he had sowed was now poised to consume him. The once formidable crew was a ship adrift in a storm, its captain lost at sea, its crew adrift, each man for himself, as the waves of consequence crashed over them, threatening to drag them all down into the unforgiving depths. The hunters, in their relentless pursuit, had finally succeeded in turning the tables, transforming the once-feared predators into the hunted, their desperate struggle for survival now the only game in town.

The stale, recycled air of the underground poker room was thick with the scent of desperation, cheap cigar smoke, and the metallic tang of unease. Jamal, seated at a velvet-draped table in a private booth tucked away from the main room's cacophony, felt a prickle of something akin to triumph. Across from him sat a man whose name was whispered with a mixture of fear and grudging respect throughout the neon-drenched arteries of Las Vegas: Silas "The Serpent" Varga. Varga wasn't just a player; he was the house, the architect of fortunes and the architect of ruin, a man who moved through the city's underbelly with the chilling efficiency of a predator. His reputation preceded him – a reputation built on broken bones, double-crossed deals, and a network of influence that stretched from the glittering casinos to the desolate deserts surrounding the city.

Jamal, usually a master of projecting an aura of unwavering confidence, found himself subtly adjusting his tie, the silk feeling suddenly too tight around his neck. He had initiated this meeting, orchestrating it through a series of carefully veiled intermediaries and coded messages, a testament to his growing audacity. Marcus's increasingly erratic behavior had created a vacuum, a void that Jamal was determined to fill, and Varga represented the ultimate source of power, the kind of raw, untamed force that could either elevate him to unprecedented heights or crush him into dust. He had spent weeks gathering intelligence on Varga, piecing together fragments of information from hushed conversations and leaked reports, understanding that Varga's allegiance, if bought, would be a shield of impenetrable strength.

"You have a keen eye, young man," Varga rasped, his voice a gravelly purr that seemed to vibrate in the dimly lit space. His eyes, dark and piercing, scanned Jamal with an unnerving intensity, as if dissecting his very soul. Varga was a man of contradictions; his expensive tailored suit spoke of wealth and sophistication, yet his hands, resting on the table, were calloused and scarred, bearing witness to a life lived in the trenches of the criminal world. He took a slow drag from a slender, unlit cigar, his gaze never wavering from Jamal's face. "They say you're ambitious. They say you're smart. I prefer to judge for myself."

Jamal met Varga's gaze directly, refusing to flinch. This was his moment, the culmination of months of calculated maneuvering. "Ambition is what drives progress, Mr. Varga," Jamal replied, his voice steady and measured. "And intelligence is what ensures survival. Marcus has grown... sentimental. His leadership is becoming a liability to everyone involved. The operation is vulnerable. I believe I can stabilize it, but I need resources. Resources and protection that extend beyond the limited scope we currently possess." He paused, letting his words hang in the air. "Protection from... external pressures, and from those who would seek to capitalize on Marcus's shortcomings."

Varga finally took the cigar from his lips, a flicker of amusement playing around his mouth. "External pressures are a given. Internal shortcomings are opportunities. You want to use Marcus's weaknesses to your advantage. That much is clear. But what do you offer me, Jamal? Why should Silas Varga invest his time, his resources, his... reputation, in your ascent?" He leaned back, his eyes narrowing slightly. "You're playing a dangerous game. Marcus has friends. Powerful friends. And those who serve him out of loyalty, not fear, are still a force to be reckoned with."

Jamal had anticipated this. He had prepared his offering, the currency he believed would sway the seasoned crime lord. "Marcus's mistakes have not gone unnoticed by our… competitors. The same people who have been chipping away at our territory, looking for an opening. I've been observing their movements, their vulnerabilities. I have information, Mr. Varga. Information about supply routes, distribution networks, even the identities of key players within rival organizations. Information that could be… highly profitable for someone with your reach." He leaned forward, his voice dropping to a near whisper. "Furthermore, I can guarantee a level of discretion and loyalty that Marcus, in his current state, cannot. I understand the intricacies of this business. I understand that true power lies not just in brute force, but in calculated strategy and mutually beneficial alliances. An alliance with me is an investment in a stable, predictable future for our shared interests in this city."

Varga's gaze sharpened. Information was the lifeblood of his empire, the currency he truly valued. He had eyes and ears everywhere, of course, but the intimate details, the direct insights from within the heart of Marcus's operation, were gold. "Loyalty," Varga mused, the word rolling off his tongue with a cynical twist. "A rare commodity. And predictability… that's a luxury few can afford in this life. Tell me, what makes you so certain Marcus's reign is ending?"

"It's not a matter of certainty; it's a matter of inevitability," Jamal stated, the conviction in his voice unwavering. "Marcus is driven by ego, not by strategy. He's making rash decisions, alienating his most valuable assets, and leaving himself exposed. The recent… incident with the shipment was a clear indication of his declining judgment. He's becoming predictable in his unpredictability. Our enemies see it, our allies feel it, and soon, even his most loyal followers will question his leadership. I, on the other hand, am adaptable. I learn from mistakes. And I recognize that true strength lies in alliances, not in a solitary reign."

Varga's lips curved into a slow smile, a predatory baring of teeth that sent a shiver down Jamal's spine, despite his outward composure. "You have the courage of a lion, young Jamal. And perhaps, the cunning of a serpent, too. But you mistake vulnerability for weakness. Marcus may be faltering, but he's a cornered animal. And cornered animals are the most dangerous." He paused, his eyes boring into Jamal. "What assurance do I have that you won't simply be the next to falter, or worse, betray me, once you've achieved your objective?"

"Because my objective is not merely to replace Marcus," Jamal explained, choosing his words with extreme care. "My objective is to build something sustainable, something that benefits us both in the long term. You are an established power in this city, Mr. Varga. I am an emerging one. My success is intrinsically linked to yours. I need your network, your influence, your experience. And you, perhaps, need a trusted operative within a faction that, under my leadership, will become even more valuable to you. I am not looking for a temporary power grab; I am looking to build an empire. And an empire requires solid foundations, built on trust and mutual benefit, not on fragile loyalty to a sinking ship."

Varga was silent for a long moment, his gaze distant as if contemplating the intricate chess match unfolding before him. The air in the booth crackled with unspoken tension. Jamal felt the weight of Varga's appraisal, the silent calculation of risk versus reward. He had laid his cards on the table, hoping they were enough. He knew Varga was a man who respected audacity, who understood the language of power, and who was perpetually seeking an edge. If Jamal could provide that edge, perhaps he could secure the alliance he desperately needed.

Finally, Varga nodded, a subtle, almost imperceptible movement. "Very well, Jamal. You have my attention. Your information... if it proves as valuable as you claim, and your discretion as absolute, then perhaps we can forge a... mutually beneficial arrangement. But understand this," Varga's voice lowered, a chilling undertone of warning seeping into his words, "I do not tolerate incompetence. And I certainly do not tolerate betrayal. You are a pawn in my game now, Jamal. A valuable pawn, perhaps, but a pawn nonetheless. Your moves will be scrutinized. Your loyalty will be tested. And should you deviate from the path I lay out for you, the consequences will be... severe."

The word "pawn" landed with a dull thud in Jamal's gut. He had come seeking an ally, a partner, but Varga's pronouncement left no room for equality. He was a tool, a means to an end. Yet, he also recognized the brutal truth in Varga's words. He was outmatched, outgunned, and outmaneuvered. If he wanted to survive, to eventually seize the power he craved, he had to play this game, no matter the cost. "I understand, Mr. Varga," Jamal said, his voice a shade tighter than before. "And I assure you, my actions will speak louder than words. I will prove myself to be the most valuable asset you have acquired in a long time."

Their alliance was cemented that night, a pact forged in the smoky confines of a private booth, sealed with a handshake that felt more like a manacle being locked into place. Varga, true to his word, began to funnel resources and discreet support towards Jamal. Access to Varga's extensive network of informants provided Jamal with invaluable intel on Marcus's movements, his planned operations, and the weaknesses within his inner circle. Financial backing, channeled through shell corporations and untraceable accounts, allowed Jamal to subtly strengthen his own position, offering incentives to those within Marcus's crew who were already wavering, fostering a sense of burgeoning loyalty towards himself.

Jamal, armed with this newfound power, moved with increased confidence. He began to orchestrate minor disruptions within Marcus's operations, seemingly unrelated incidents that, in hindsight, would point towards Marcus's incompetence. A shipment delayed due to unforeseen "logistical issues." A high-stakes meeting compromised by an unexpected "informant leak." Each incident was carefully designed to sow seeds of doubt about Marcus's leadership, to erode the faith of his followers, and to paint Jamal as the steady hand amidst the growing chaos. He made sure Varga received timely updates on these "successes," reinforcing the narrative of his own strategic brilliance and Varga's sound judgment in backing him.

However, Jamal's ambition, coupled with Varga's influence, began to blind him. He started to believe he was more than just a pawn, that he was a player in his own right, capable of manipulating even the formidable Silas Varga. He relished the power he wielded, the clandestine meetings, the whispered conversations, the feeling of orchestrating events from the shadows. He saw Varga as a stepping stone, a temporary alliance that would serve its purpose and then be cast aside once he had solidified his own power base. This arrogance was a dangerous delusion, a fatal flaw that Varga, with his millennia of experience in the predatory arts, was keenly aware of.

Varga, for his part, watched Jamal's ascent with a detached amusement. He saw the young man's ambition, his hunger, his willingness to betray and manipulate. These were qualities Varga admired, recognizing them as essential traits for survival and success in their world. But he also saw the burgeoning hubris, the dangerous overconfidence that would inevitably lead to Jamal's downfall. Varga had no intention of letting Jamal become a threat, or an equal. Jamal was a tool, a disposable asset being used to destabilize Marcus's operation, to weaken any potential rivals to Varga's own established dominion, and to ultimately funnel Marcus's lucrative territory and client base directly into his own waiting hands.

The intricate web Varga was weaving was far more complex than Jamal could comprehend. While Jamal focused on undermining Marcus, Varga was simultaneously playing his own game, leveraging the chaos that Jamal was creating to position himself for a much larger takeover. He fed Marcus false intelligence, carefully curated to lead him further down a path of self-destruction, while subtly guiding Jamal towards actions that would further alienate Marcus's loyalists and expose him to increasing scrutiny from law enforcement. Jamal was merely a catalyst, an instrument of Varga's grand design, and he was playing his part with an eagerness that Varga found both useful and, ultimately, pathetic.

The first true crack in Jamal's carefully constructed facade appeared not from Marcus, nor from the law, but from within Varga's own operations. A clandestine arms deal, orchestrated by Jamal with Varga's tacit approval and under the guise of strengthening his own security, went disastrously wrong. The weapons cache, supposedly secure and hidden in a disused warehouse on the outskirts of the city, was raided by an unknown entity. The transaction was a setup, a betrayal orchestrated not by Marcus, but by Varga himself. The ensuing firefight resulted in the deaths of several of Jamal's newly acquired men, and the loss of a significant amount of capital that Varga had, ostensibly, provided.

Jamal was furious, blindsided by this unexpected turn of events. He immediately demanded answers from Varga, his newfound confidence replaced by a raw, desperate need to understand who had betrayed him. Varga, however, was uncharacteristically calm, his voice laced with an almost paternalistic disappointment. "You were too eager, Jamal," he said, his words delivered with the cold precision of a surgeon's scalpel. "You mistook my support for unconditional backing. You believed you were the one controlling the narrative. This was a lesson. A harsh one, perhaps, but a necessary one."

"A lesson?" Jamal's voice was a strained whisper. "My men are dead! My resources are gone! Who did this?"

"That, my young friend, is not your concern," Varga replied smoothly. "Your concern is to understand your place. You are not my partner. You are my tool. And like any tool, if it proves to be inefficient or to deviate from its intended purpose, it is either sharpened or discarded. You became too ambitious, Jamal. You started to believe your own press clippings. You allowed your ego to overshadow your purpose. The raid was a consequence of your own miscalculations, your own desire to operate independently, rather than under my direct guidance."

The realization struck Jamal with the force of a physical blow. He was not an ally; he was a disposable asset, a pawn being maneuvered and sacrificed for Varga's ultimate gain. The ruthlessness of it was staggering, a brutal testament to the true nature of the man he had allied himself with. Varga wasn't just a crime lord; he was a master manipulator, a puppeteer who saw every interaction as a means to an end, and every individual as a potential sacrifice on the altar of his insatiable ambition. The dangerous game Jamal had entered was far more perilous than he had ever imagined, and he was now trapped in its deadly embrace, realizing with chilling clarity that his quest for power had led him directly into the viper's den, with the serpent poised to strike. The web, once spun with his own calculated threads, was now tightening, its silken strands belonging to a far more powerful weaver, and Jamal was caught irrevocably within its deadly embrace. He had sought to become the predator, but he had inadvertently placed himself directly in the path of an apex predator, one who would undoubtedly devour him whole once his usefulness had been fully extracted. The true unraveling of Marcus's empire was merely a sideshow; the real drama was Jamal's own impending destruction.

The air in the abandoned printing press hung heavy and still, a sepulchral quiet broken only by the frantic thumping of Chloe's heart against her ribs. Dust motes danced in the slivers of moonlight that pierced the grimy skylights, illuminating a scene of desperate improvisation. Her fingers, stained with ink and sweat, moved with a practiced urgency, manipulating the levers of an old offset press. This wasn't about creating beauty anymore; it was about survival, a final, defiant act of artistry against the encroaching darkness. The familiar hum of the machinery, once a source of creative solace, now sounded like a death knell, a prelude to the inevitable reckoning.

She had been cornered, a corner she had painted herself into with every brushstroke, every whispered deal, every illicit transaction. The web, spun so intricately with her own hands, was now a cage, its silken threads tightening with each passing hour. Silas Varga's betrayal, a cold, calculated maneuver that had left her exposed and vulnerable, was a ghost that haunted every shadow, every creak of the dilapidated building. And then there were the authorities, their relentless pursuit a constant, suffocating presence, their sirens a recurring nightmare that echoed in the hollow spaces of her mind.

Chloe glanced at the pile of canvases stacked against the wall, each one a testament to a life lived on the edge, a life of vibrant creation born from the grimy underbelly of the city. Her art had been her sanctuary, her rebellion, her means of navigating the treacherous currents of Marcus's empire, and now, it was to be her last stand. The irony wasn't lost on her; the very skills that had brought her into this dangerous world might be the only thing that could pull her out.

The plan was audacious, bordering on suicidal. She needed to create a diversion, a grand spectacle that would buy her precious minutes, perhaps even hours, to slip through the tightening net. The printing press offered the perfect canvas for her desperate gambit. She had spent the last day meticulously preparing. Using the leftover ink and paper, she had been working on a series of large-scale prints, designed not for galleries or collectors, but for the streets. They were not her finest work, not in terms of aesthetic refinement, but in terms of impact, they were masterpieces of chaos.

The designs were deliberately provocative, a potent cocktail of sedition and spectacle. One depicted a grotesque caricature of Silas Varga, his serpentine smile replaced by a gaping maw of greed, his eyes hollowed out by insatiable ambition. Another showed a stylized representation of the city's corrupt underbelly, a tangled mess of power brokers and law enforcement officials entwined in a macabre dance, all illuminated by the cold, indifferent glow of neon signs. Her final piece, the most personal and perhaps the most dangerous, was a haunting portrait of Marcus, not as the charismatic leader he once presented himself to be, but as the broken, unpredictable man he had become, his eyes reflecting a terrifying void.

"This is it," she muttered to herself, her voice raspy, barely audible above the growing symphony of her own fear. She fed a large sheet of paper into the press, the rough texture scratching against the metal rollers. Her heart pounded with a mixture of adrenaline and a grim sense of resignation. Surrender was not an option. To cooperate, to become an informant, to trade her freedom for the dubious protection of the authorities, felt like a betrayal of the woman she had become, the artist who had dared to defy the suffocating norms of their world. She had to fight back, to carve out her own escape, no matter the cost.

She pulled the lever, the heavy machinery groaning to life. The printing plate, inked with a vibrant, almost violent shade of red, pressed down onto the paper. The image of Varga's sneering face emerged, stark and unforgiving. She repeated the process, her movements becoming more fluid, more economical, fueled by a primal instinct for self-preservation. Sheet after sheet of these provocative images began to stack up, a silent protest, a visual rebellion against the forces that sought to silence her.

As the prints accumulated, Chloe's mind raced, piecing together the final fragments of her escape plan. The noise from the printing press, she hoped, would serve as a beacon, drawing attention away from her intended exit. She had identified a weak point in the building's rear – a boarded-up service tunnel, forgotten and neglected, a relic of a bygone era. She had spent hours earlier that day prying at the boards, creating just enough looseness for a desperate shove.

But the plan hinged on more than just noise and a hidden escape route. She needed a contingency, a final, audacious move to ensure she wasn't immediately apprehended once she emerged from the tunnel. She had gathered a small arsenal of her own creations, not weapons in the traditional sense, but tools designed to sow confusion and create opportunities. Among them were several canisters of aerosol paint, specially formulated to create dense, disorienting clouds of color. She also had a few of her signature smoke bombs, designed not for combat, but for theatrical effect, capable of filling a space with thick, obscuring plumes.

The first patrol car's siren wailed in the distance, a mournful cry that sent a fresh wave of panic through her. They were closer than she anticipated. Time was running out. She intensified her printing, the rhythm becoming more frantic. She imagined the reactions of those who would find these prints, the confusion, the anger, the fear. She wasn't just leaving behind a message; she was igniting a fire, a small spark of defiance that she hoped would spread.

With a final, desperate push, she cranked out the last print – the portrait of a broken Marcus. She glanced at the clock on the wall; the hands seemed to be mocking her, spinning relentlessly towards her capture. She grabbed the canvases, her heart hammering against her ribs like a trapped bird. She needed to be efficient, to move with the precision of a seasoned operative, not the panicked desperation of a cornered artist.

She slung the rolled canvases over her shoulder, the rough material digging into her skin. The roar of the printing press was a deafening symphony now, filling the vast space with its mechanical fury. She grabbed the canisters of paint and the smoke bombs, stuffing them into her worn backpack. Then, she moved towards the back of the building, her eyes scanning the shadows, her senses on high alert for any sign of intrusion.

The air grew colder as she approached the rear exit. The moonlight, once a source of illumination, now felt like a spotlight, exposing her every move. She could hear the muffled shouts of approaching officers, the crunch of boots on gravel outside. They were closing in. This was it. Her last stand.

She reached the boarded-up tunnel. With a surge of adrenaline, she slammed her shoulder into the weakest section. The old wood groaned, splintered, but held. She braced herself and rammed it again, the impact sending a jolt of pain up her arm. A third shove, and a section of the boards gave way, revealing a dark, gaping maw of an opening.

She didn't hesitate. She scrambled through the narrow gap, the rough edges of the wood tearing at her clothes and skin. Once inside, she immediately reached for a smoke bomb, pulling the pin with trembling fingers. She tossed it into the printing room, the small device hissing as it ignited, filling the space with a thick, acrid cloud of black smoke. The noise of the printing press was now muffled by the expanding fog, and the shouts of the officers grew more frantic, more confused.

She could hear them entering the main printing area, their voices echoing through the smoke-filled space. "Where'd she go?" "What's all this?" "Damn smoke!" She knew she had bought herself a few crucial moments. She pulled out a canister of neon orange paint and sprayed a quick, jagged streak across the tunnel wall, a final, personal signature, a mark of defiance.

Crawling on her hands and knees, she navigated the narrow, debris-strewn tunnel. It smelled of damp earth and decay, a stark contrast to the sterile air of the city she was trying to escape. The darkness was absolute, pressing in on her, but she didn't falter. Her mind was a whirlwind of possibilities, of potential traps and unseen dangers. She knew Varga wouldn't let her go easily. He had invested too much in Marcus's downfall, and she was an unpredictable variable, a loose end that needed to be tied up.

Emerging from the tunnel felt like being born into a new world. The night air was cool and crisp against her skin, a welcome relief after the suffocating atmosphere of the printing press. She was in a dimly lit alleyway, a maze of overflowing dumpsters and discarded refuse. She could still hear the distant wail of sirens, but they seemed further away now, less immediate.

She unrolled the canvases, her hands still shaking. The images seemed to glow in the faint light, each one a testament to her struggle, her artistic rebellion. She needed to get them out, to ensure her message, her final act of defiance, would be seen. She had contacted a small, underground network of street artists and activists, individuals who valued authenticity and resistance above all else. She had given them a coded rendezvous point, a signal that would let them know when and where to collect her work.

As she waited, she heard footsteps approaching, not the heavy, purposeful tread of law enforcement, but a lighter, more cautious tread. A figure emerged from the shadows, cloaked and hooded, their face obscured. It was one of her contacts, a phantom known only as "Ghost."

"You made it," Ghost's voice was a low murmur, barely audible.

"Barely," Chloe replied, her voice tight with exhaustion and anticipation. "Are you ready?"

Ghost nodded, a subtle movement beneath the hood. "We are. The others are in position. We'll spread them across the district. They'll see them. They'll talk."

Chloe handed over the rolled canvases, the weight of them a physical and emotional burden lifting from her shoulders. She watched as Ghost melted back into the shadows, the canvases disappearing with them. Her art, her final stand, was now in motion, spreading through the city like a contagious idea.

But her own escape was far from secured. She was still exposed, still vulnerable. She knew she couldn't linger. The alleyway, while offering a temporary respite, was also a dead end. She needed to move, to disappear, to become a ghost herself.

She pulled the hood of her own jacket further down, her face hidden in the shadows. The printing press was a smoking ruin behind her, a testament to her desperate fight. She had left a mark, a final, indelible statement. Now, she had to rely on the very skills that had defined her life – evasion, misdirection, and the unwavering resilience of an artist who refused to be silenced. The unraveling web had nearly ensnared her, but in a final, defiant act, she had managed to snag a thread, to pull herself free, however precariously, into the uncertain dawn. Her stand was over, but her flight had just begun. She was no longer just Chloe, the artist. She was Chloe, the survivor, the phantom, a brushstroke of defiance painted onto the canvas of the city's underbelly, a testament to the desperate resilience that bloomed even in the darkest of soils. She knew the path ahead would be fraught with peril, that Varga's reach was long and his vengeance swift, but she had proven to herself, and to the world, that she wouldn't go down without a fight, leaving behind a trail of her artistry as a silent, powerful scream against the forces that sought to consume her. Her desperate stand had not been about victory, but about defiance, about leaving an imprint of her spirit before she vanished, like smoke, into the unforgiving night.

David, a phantom of the financial world, had meticulously scrubbed himself from the immediate vicinity of the unfolding chaos. His departure from the inner circle hadn't been a dramatic exit, but a slow, calculated fade, each step measured, each digital footprint erased with the precision of a surgeon. Unlike Chloe, who had chosen a path of fiery defiance, and the others who were being systematically dismantled by Varga's machinations, David's strategy was one of calculated detachment, a survival instinct honed through years of navigating the labyrinthine corridors of power and illicit finance. He was a man who understood that true control often lay not in confrontation, but in strategic absence.

He operated from a series of anonymous nodes, a ghost in the machine of the city's digital infrastructure. His knowledge of offshore accounts, shell corporations, and untraceable transactions was his armor, his escape route, and his arsenal. While Chloe was a painter of rebellion, splashing defiance onto the city's canvas, David was the unseen hand that moved the pieces on the board, a financial puppet master pulling strings from a distance. He was monitoring the unraveling of their shared enterprise, not with sentimental regret, but with a cold, analytical eye. He saw the collapse not as a tragedy, but as a predictable consequence of a system built on shaky foundations and fueled by unchecked ambition.

From his sterile, nondescript apartment, miles away from the smoke-filled printing press and the flashing blue lights that now surely assaulted its perimeter, David meticulously tracked the fallout. His screens displayed a constellation of data streams: financial transactions, encrypted communications, even public surveillance feeds, all feeding into his intricate web of information. He saw the panic ripple through the lower echelons of Varga's operation, the frantic attempts to cover tracks, the inevitable mistakes that would soon lead them to the same precipice Chloe had so dramatically escaped. He felt no kinship with these individuals; their fates were merely data points in his larger analysis.

His own journey had been a solitary one, a winding path that had begun with a fascination for the intoxicating power of capital, a fascination that had morphed into an obsession with its manipulation. He had seen the rot at the heart of the city's wealth, the gilded cages built on exploitation, the opulent facades masking desperate secrets. He had initially found a strange camaraderie with Marcus and his circle, drawn to their audacious disregard for convention, their willingness to push boundaries. But as the stakes escalated, as the lines between ambition and depravity blurred, David had recognized the inherent instability of their enterprise, the precariousness of their success.

He remembered the early days, the heady rush of illicit deals struck in dimly lit backrooms, the shared ambition that had bound them together. He recalled Marcus's charismatic pronouncements, his vision of a new order built on their collective will. He remembered Chloe's fierce artistic spirit, her ability to translate the raw energy of the streets into something potent and evocative. He had admired their boldness, their willingness to live outside the established norms. But he had also seen the seeds of their destruction sown in that very defiance, the hubris that would inevitably lead to their downfall.

Chloe's desperate gambit at the printing press, her audacious act of creating art from the ashes of their operation, had not surprised him. He had long recognized her resilience, her refusal to be merely a passive observer. He had even, in his own way, anticipated a move like hers, a final act of self-expression. He saw her prints, disseminated across the city by her underground network, as a testament to her indomitable spirit. He knew Varga would be furious, that this would only deepen his resolve to eradicate any lingering threat, Chloe included.

David, however, had made his exit weeks ago, long before the final implosion. He had seen the signs, the subtle shifts in Marcus's demeanor, the growing paranoia, the increasingly reckless decisions. He had started to subtly siphon funds, creating diversified escape routes, building a financial fortress that was impervious to the tremors that were beginning to shake their empire. He had felt a pang of something akin to regret, a flicker of loyalty to the men and women he had once considered allies, but it was a fleeting emotion, quickly overridden by the instinct for self-preservation. The psychological scars of their shared experience were not the adrenaline-fueled memories of daring raids or narrow escapes, but the quiet, gnawing realization of how easily trust could be broken, how quickly loyalty could evaporate under pressure. He had learned that the most valuable asset was one's own self, and the most effective strategy was to ensure that asset remained intact.

He continued to monitor Varga's movements through his own channels. He knew Varga was a predator, relentless and unforgiving. He anticipated that Varga's wrath would be directed not only at Chloe but at anyone remotely connected to her or Marcus. David's calculated detachment was his shield, but he was not entirely immune to the collateral damage. He had to ensure that his meticulously constructed invisibility remained absolute. He rerouted funds, created new digital identities, and maintained a constant state of vigilance. His survival depended on his ability to become a ghost, not just in the city, but in the very fabric of the networks he had once helped to build.

The psychological toll of this existence was subtle but profound. It wasn't the visceral fear of imminent capture, but the quiet, isolating burden of constant vigilance, the erosion of genuine human connection. He had witnessed firsthand the destructive nature of greed and ambition, the way it twisted relationships and corrupted souls. The shared experiences with Marcus, Chloe, and the others had left him with a deep-seated cynicism, a belief that everyone, eventually, would betray or be betrayed. He had chosen to shield himself from that pain by refusing to form meaningful attachments. His detachment was a form of self-protection, a way to avoid the inevitable heartbreak of loss.

He sometimes found himself reviewing old data logs, not out of nostalgia, but as a form of morbid curiosity, a detached observer studying the rise and fall of a powerful, albeit illicit, enterprise. He saw the moments of genuine camaraderie, the shared laughter, the belief that they were building something significant, something that would change the city. These were fleeting glimpses of a past he had consciously chosen to leave behind, a past that now seemed like a distant, almost alien landscape. The psychological scars were not in the memory of the thrill, but in the memory of the betrayal, the slow, creeping realization that the people he had trusted were capable of such ruthless ambition and self-preservation.

David's journey was a testament to a different kind of survival, one that prioritized intellect and foresight over brute force or passionate defiance. He was a man who understood that the greatest victories were often won not on the battlefield, but in the quiet, sterile rooms where data flowed and fortunes were manipulated. He had successfully navigated the treacherous currents of their shared downfall, emerging not unscathed, but certainly uncaptured. The financial ghost of their operation, he remained a silent witness to the wreckage, a solitary figure in the shadows, forever marked by the experiences but determined to forge a future defined by his own calculated solitude. His silence was his strength, his anonymity his sanctuary, and his financial acumen his enduring legacy, a testament to a survival strategy that prioritized foresight and detachment above all else. The city, in its own chaotic way, continued to churn, and David, the invisible architect of its hidden financial currents, continued to watch, to learn, and to remain one step ahead, forever a solitary player in a game he had mastered through sheer, unyielding detachment. He was a living ghost, a financial phantom haunting the periphery of a world he had once inhabited, a world that had consumed so many others, but which he had managed to escape through the sheer power of his intellect and his unwavering commitment to self-preservation. His survival was a quiet victory, a testament to the fact that in the treacherous landscape of power and corruption, sometimes the most effective weapon was simply the ability to disappear.

The chipped Formica countertop of the diner was cool beneath Aisha's forearms as she traced the faint condensation ring left by her iced tea. It was a small, insignificant gesture, a subconscious attempt to anchor herself in the mundane, the ordinary. Here, amidst the clatter of plates and the murmur of anonymous conversations, she could almost believe she was just another face in the crowd, another woman seeking refuge from the sweltering afternoon heat. But the illusion was fragile, as thin as the paper placemat beneath her elbow. The memory of Las Vegas, a city built on the shimmering mirages of chance and illusion, was a phantom limb, an ache that never truly subsided.

Her new existence was a tapestry woven with threads of caution and hyper-vigilance. She had traded the opulent, albeit corrupt, embrace of the city's underbelly for the quiet anonymity of a nondescript suburb, a place where the most exciting event of the week was the recycling truck's weekly pilgrimage. It was a stark contrast to the adrenaline-fueled nights, the hushed whispers of illicit deals, the intoxicating danger that had once defined her life. Now, her heart hammered a frantic rhythm against her ribs at the slightest deviation from the norm: a car lingering too long at the end of her street, a stranger's glance held a fraction too long, the unexpected ring of her doorbell. Each anomaly was a potential harbinger, a signal that the carefully constructed sanctuary she inhabited was about to crumble.

She had chosen a new name, a new history, a plausible backstory that held up under the casual scrutiny of neighbors and shopkeepers. She worked as a freelance graphic designer, a profession that allowed her to maintain a degree of isolation, her interactions largely confined to emails and fleeting courier exchanges. Her small, rented house was meticulously organized, every object in its designated place, a physical manifestation of her desperate need for control in a life that had, for so long, been dictated by forces beyond her command. She rarely ventured out after dark, and when she did, it was with a practiced nonchalance, a carefully cultivated air of someone simply enjoying the evening air, while her senses remained on high alert, cataloging every sound, every shadow.

The echoes of her past life were not just psychological; they were tangible, lurking in the periphery of her carefully curated present. She had escaped the immediate fallout of Marcus's implosion, the violent repercussions that had rippled through their operation like a shockwave. She had managed to slip through the cracks, a ghost in the machine, thanks to David's quiet, almost imperceptible, machinations. But David was a man who operated on a different plane, a detached strategist who had shed his allegiances like a snake sheds its skin. Aisha, on the other hand, was still tethered to the consequences of her choices, the indelible mark left by her entanglement with Marcus and his dangerous ambitions.

She had seen the news reports, the carefully worded articles that spoke of a major crackdown on organized crime, of arrests and indictments. They were sanitized versions of the brutal reality she had witnessed firsthand, but the underlying message was clear: Varga's reach was long, and his thirst for retribution was insatiable. The knowledge that Varga was still out there, a powerful, vengeful force, was a constant undercurrent of dread. She knew that if he discovered her new identity, her carefully constructed anonymity would shatter, and the forces that had once sought to control her would descend with unforgiving efficiency.

Aisha found herself replaying conversations, scrutinizing interactions for any hint of suspicion. Had that barista recognized her voice? Did the landlord's polite nod betray a deeper knowledge? These were the anxieties that gnawed at her, the constant, exhausting vigilance that defined her days. She slept with the blinds drawn tight, the doors locked, and a heavy crowbar by her bedside, a crude, unglamorous symbol of her fear. The vibrant, audacious woman who had once navigated the dazzling, treacherous landscape of Vegas had been replaced by a shadow, a woman perpetually braced for impact.

Her art, once a vibrant expression of her spirit, had become a source of both solace and renewed fear. She still sketched, still designed, but the subjects had changed. Gone were the bold, abstract compositions that had captured the city's electric pulse. Now, her work was characterized by a subdued palette, a focus on the subtle interplay of light and shadow, on the hidden anxieties that lurked beneath placid surfaces. She found herself drawn to imagery of isolation, of figures receding into the distance, their faces obscured by the encroaching gloom. It was a subconscious expression of her own predicament, a visual diary of her emotional landscape.

One afternoon, while browsing through an online art forum, she stumbled upon a series of prints that sent a jolt of ice through her veins. They were anonymous, posted by a user with a generic handle, but the style was unmistakably Chloe's. The raw energy, the defiant brushstrokes, the searing social commentary – it was her signature, unmistakable. The prints depicted Varga's operations, his opulent towers juxtaposed with stark images of exploitation and despair. They were a digital echo of the very rebellion Aisha had tried to flee.

A cold dread washed over her. Chloe, impulsive and defiant as ever, was still out there, still actively challenging Varga. This meant that Varga's grip had not entirely tightened, that there were still pockets of resistance, but it also meant that the net was tightening around them all. Chloe's actions were a beacon, drawing Varga's attention, and if Chloe was still on his radar, it was only a matter of time before he looked for any remaining loose ends. Aisha's breath hitched. She had hoped that by disappearing, she had effectively vanished from Varga's consciousness. Now, she feared that Chloe's continued defiance might inadvertently drag her back into the light.

She spent the next few days in a state of heightened alert. Every news cycle, every whispered rumor, every unfamiliar car parked on her street was scrutinized with an almost pathological intensity. She began to question the efficacy of her anonymity. Had David's careful planning accounted for the unpredictable nature of Chloe's artistic defiance? Had his meticulous erasure of their digital footprints been enough to shield them from Varga's relentless pursuit?

The isolation, once a chosen refuge, now felt like a cage. She yearned for connection, for a familiar voice, for a moment of genuine respite from the gnawing fear. But the very act of reaching out, of reconnecting with anyone from her past, carried an immense risk. The loyalty that had once bound them together had been fractured, replaced by the bitter lessons of betrayal and survival. Trust, a luxury she could no longer afford, was a forgotten language.

She tried to rationalize Chloe's actions. Perhaps Chloe believed that by exposing Varga, she was also protecting those who had been wronged, including herself. Perhaps it was a desperate attempt to reclaim some semblance of justice in a world that had offered them none. But Aisha couldn't afford such noble interpretations. For her, Chloe's art was a siren call, a dangerous beacon that threatened to illuminate her hidden existence.

One evening, as the sun bled orange and purple across the suburban sky, Aisha sat on her porch swing, the chains creaking softly with each gentle sway. She watched a neighborhood child chase a stray ball down the street, their laughter a bright, innocent sound that felt alien and distant. She clutched a worn photograph in her hand, a faded image of herself, Chloe, and Marcus, taken during a rare moment of genuine joy, before the darkness had fully descended. The smiles were genuine, the camaraderie palpable. Looking at it now, it felt like a relic from another lifetime, a testament to a naive optimism that had been brutally extinguished.

The memories were a double-edged sword. They offered a flicker of comfort, a reminder of the bonds that had once existed, but they also underscored the profound loss, the irreversible damage that had been inflicted. She had escaped the physical confines of Las Vegas, but the psychological chains remained. Her sanctuary was precarious, a fragile façade built on the shifting sands of fear and regret. She was free, technically, but the price of that freedom was a constant, gnawing anxiety, a life lived in the perpetual twilight of what-ifs and might-have-beens. The silence of her new life was a heavy shroud, muffling the vibrant spirit that had once thrived in the dazzling, dangerous lights of the city. She was safe, perhaps, but she was also profoundly alone, haunted by the ghosts of a past she could never truly outrun. The city of sin had left its indelible mark, and Aisha, in her quiet suburb, was a living testament to its enduring power. The fear was a constant companion, a whisper in the back of her mind, reminding her that freedom was a temporary state, a fragile illusion that could be shattered at any moment. Her every move was calculated, her every interaction scrutinized, a desperate attempt to remain invisible in a world that had a long memory and an insatiable appetite for revenge. The sanctuary she had built was not of brick and mortar, but of carefully constructed isolation, a fortress against the shadows that still threatened to engulf her.

Chapter 6: The Price of Ambition

The air in the abandoned warehouse hung thick and stagnant, a cloying miasma of dust, decay, and the metallic tang of old blood. Marcus, his once immaculate suit now torn and stained, slumped against a crumbling brick pillar. Each breath was a shallow, ragged testament to the toll the night had taken. His eyes, usually alight with a predatory gleam, were shadowed with a weary desperation, the swagger that had defined him for so long reduced to a faint tremor in his hands. He was cornered, the labyrinthine alleys of his ambition having finally led him to this dead end. The sirens, once a distant thrum, were now a rising crescendo, a relentless tide that promised to wash away the last vestiges of his empire.

His mind reeled, fragments of memory flickering like a dying flame. The glitz and glamour of Vegas, the roar of the crowd at a fight he'd orchestrated, the hushed reverence in the eyes of those who owed him their fortunes – it all seemed a lifetime ago, a cruel mockery of the man he had become. He saw Aisha's face, clear and sharp in his memory, her intelligence a quiet challenge he'd underestimated. He thought of Jamal, the loyal lieutenant whose quiet competence had always been a silent rebuke to Marcus's more flamboyant recklessness. Regret, a bitter, unfamiliar taste, coated his tongue. His ambition, a voracious beast that had driven him to scale impossible heights, had ultimately devoured him from within.

The metallic clang of heavy boots on concrete echoed through the cavernous space. Marcus pushed himself away from the pillar, his knees protesting. He scanned the shadowy interior, his senses, honed by years of survival, straining to pinpoint the approaching threat. Was it the Feds, their methodical approach as predictable as a sunrise? Or was it something more personal, more visceral? The thought of Jamal, his face a mask of grim determination, sent a fresh wave of unease through him. Had loyalty finally snapped under the strain of Marcus's relentless pursuit of power?

He fumbled in his inner jacket pocket, his fingers closing around the cool, familiar weight of his pistol. It felt like an extension of himself, a last resort in a world that had long since abandoned any pretense of fairness. He hadn't wanted it to come to this. He had envisioned a different kind of ending, a triumphant exit, not this ignominious surrender to the forces he'd so long defied. The thought of Varga, that shadowy puppeteer pulling strings from behind the scenes, sparked a flicker of defiance. He wouldn't go down without a fight, not for Varga, not for anyone.

The first shots rang out, sharp cracks that ripped through the heavy silence. Marcus instinctively dropped into a crouch, the bullets whining past his head, chipping fragments from the brickwork. He returned fire, his shots wild and unfocused, more an act of desperate assertion than a calculated attack. He was no longer the maestro of chaos; he was a trapped animal, lashing out in its final moments. He saw a figure silhouette against a broken window, the moonlight glinting off a weapon. He fired again, the echo of his own gunshot a deafening roar in his ears.

He scrambled for cover behind a stack of rusted crates, his heart pounding a frantic rhythm against his ribs. He could hear them now, the heavy breathing, the tactical commands, the sheer, overwhelming presence of armed men closing in. He was outnumbered, outgunned, and utterly alone. The carefully constructed edifice of his power had crumbled, leaving him exposed and vulnerable. He thought of Aisha again, her quiet strength a stark contrast to his own brash confidence. Had she escaped the fallout? Had she found the peace he had so desperately sought, only to betray?

The warehouse doors burst open with a violent crash, flooding the space with the flashing red and blue lights of police cruisers. Marcus knew, with a chilling certainty, that this was it. The end of the line. He raised his pistol, his finger tightening on the trigger, not in defiance, but in a desperate, final act of self-preservation. He would not be taken alive, not to face the humiliation, the imprisonment, the slow erosion of everything he had ever been.

But as he brought the weapon to bear, another figure emerged from the shadows, silhouetted against the chaotic brilliance of the flashing lights. It was Jamal. His face was impassive, his eyes betraying none of the turmoil that must have been churning within him. In his hand, he held not a weapon, but a small, unassuming data drive.

"Marcus," Jamal's voice was low, devoid of emotion, yet it resonated with a finality that chilled Marcus to the bone. "It's over."

Marcus stared at him, confusion warring with a dawning, horrific understanding. "Jamal? What are you doing?"

"What had to be done," Jamal replied, taking a step closer. "You pushed too hard. You took too many risks. You forgot who we were fighting."

"We were fighting for control, Jamal!" Marcus retorted, his voice hoarse. "For our own future!"

"Your future, Marcus," Jamal corrected, his gaze unwavering. "Not mine. Not Aisha's. Not anyone else's." He held up the data drive. "This is everything. All of it. The ledger, the contacts, the offshore accounts. It all goes to the Feds. It's the only way to guarantee your… retirement."

Marcus's world tilted. The betrayal, delivered with such quiet resignation, was more devastating than any bullet. "You… you're giving me up?"

"I'm saving myself," Jamal said, his voice softening almost imperceptibly. "And in doing so, I'm ensuring that Varga doesn't have a reason to hunt down anyone else. You were the head of the snake, Marcus. Cut it off, and the rest of us might just survive."

The sirens were deafening now, the shouts of law enforcement officers a chaotic symphony of his downfall. Marcus looked at Jamal, at the data drive clutched in his hand, and a profound, soul-crushing emptiness washed over him. His ambition, his drive, his entire life's work had culminated in this moment of utter, abject defeat, orchestrated by the very man he had trusted most.

He lowered his pistol, the weight of it suddenly unbearable. The flashing lights painted streaks across the dusty floor, illuminating the wreckage of his life. He saw Aisha's face again, a fleeting image of innocence lost. He had dragged her into his world, and he had failed to protect her. Now, he was failing himself.

As the heavily armed officers stormed into the warehouse, their weapons trained on him, Marcus stood his ground. He didn't resist. There was nothing left to fight for. The roar of the city, the intoxicating allure of power, the thrill of the chase – it had all led him here, to this dusty, forgotten tomb. His final stand wasn't a glorious battle, but a quiet surrender to the inevitable, a testament to the devastating price of unchecked ambition. He closed his eyes, the images of his past flashing behind his eyelids, a final, silent reel of a life lived too fast, too hard, and ultimately, too fatally. The story of Marcus, the king of his own destructive domain, had reached its tragic conclusion. The silence that followed the storm of sirens was, in its own way, the loudest judgment of all. He had built an empire on shifting sands, and the tide had finally come to reclaim its due. The city, ever hungry, had swallowed him whole, leaving only the echo of his rise and fall.

The air in the abandoned shipping yard was a symphony of decay, a metallic tang of rust mingling with the briny breath of the nearby docks. Jamal, no longer the quiet, unassuming shadow behind Marcus, surveyed his domain with a possessive gaze. The flickering sodium lamps cast long, distorted figures across the cracked asphalt, each one a testament to his ascendance. He had orchestrated Marcus's downfall, not with brute force, but with calculated precision, a chess master dismantling his opponent piece by piece. The data drive, a small, unassuming object, had been his ultimate weapon, delivering Marcus to the waiting arms of the law.

Jamal had always been a man of quiet observation, a student of human nature and, more importantly, a student of weakness. He had seen Marcus's ambition as a runaway train, a magnificent spectacle hurtling towards disaster. While Marcus reveled in the roar of the crowd, the flash of cameras, and the adoration of the desperate, Jamal was in the engine room, meticulously tending the fire, knowing precisely when and where to stoke it, and when to throttle it back. His loyalty, once a seemingly unshakeable bedrock, had been a carefully constructed facade, a means to an end. Marcus had seen him as a tool; Jamal had seen Marcus as a stepping stone.

The initial days after Marcus's arrest were a blur of controlled chaos for Jamal. He moved with an almost supernatural calm, smoothly assuming control of Marcus's remaining operations. The lieutenants, once fiercely loyal to Marcus, now looked to Jamal with a mixture of apprehension and respect. They had witnessed his quiet ruthlessness, his unwavering focus. He had a way of looking at you, a piercing gaze that seemed to strip away all pretense, leaving you exposed and vulnerable. He didn't need to threaten; his mere presence was often enough to elicit compliance. He met with them in hushed, clandestine meetings, the flickering candlelight casting stark shadows on their faces, making it impossible to read their true intentions. He offered them assurances, promises of continued prosperity, but beneath the surface, he was assessing them, identifying potential threats, and solidifying his own position. He knew that power, once seized, had to be constantly defended.

His patron, the shadowy figure known only as Varga, had been surprisingly pleased with the outcome. Varga valued efficiency and discretion above all else, and Jamal had delivered both in spades. The initial payout from Varga had been substantial, a reward for a job well done. It was enough to secure Jamal's future, to establish him as a player in the city's intricate web of power. But for Jamal, money was merely a tool. True power lay in control, in the ability to shape events, to bend others to his will. And he craved that control with a desperate hunger that burned hotter than any ambition Marcus had ever possessed.

He began to expand his reach, leveraging Marcus's network and his own newfound influence. He diversified, moving into new territories, brokering deals that Marcus would have considered too risky, too overtly aggressive. Jamal's approach was different. He was patient, methodical, a hunter who stalked his prey from the shadows, striking only when the moment was perfect. He cultivated an aura of inscrutability, a man who could be trusted implicitly because he revealed nothing, his motives shrouded in an impenetrable veil.

But the very traits that had fueled his rise also sowed the seeds of his destruction. Jamal had always been an observer, a man who understood the importance of caution. Yet, as his power grew, so did his arrogance. He began to believe his own carefully crafted image, mistaking his calculated moves for innate genius. He started to underestimate the very people he had so meticulously observed. He saw the fear in their eyes and mistook it for respect. He heard their hushed whispers and believed them to be declarations of loyalty.

His patron, Varga, had always been a pragmatic man, a businessman who understood the volatile nature of their shared underworld. Varga had invested heavily in Jamal, seeing him as a stable force, a reliable asset. But as Jamal's operations became more complex, more ambitious, Varga began to grow uneasy. Jamal was no longer content to operate within the established boundaries; he was pushing, probing, testing the limits of their alliance. He was making moves that Varga considered reckless, moves that threatened to draw unwanted attention.

The first sign of trouble came not as a direct confrontation, but as a subtle shift in Varga's demeanor. The phone calls became less frequent, the answers to Jamal's inquiries more guarded. Jamal, blinded by his own perceived invincibility, dismissed these changes as Varga growing complacent, a sure sign that Varga was no longer relevant in the new order. He began to operate with even less regard for Varga's counsel, convinced that he had surpassed his mentor.

He initiated a major deal, a clandestine operation involving the smuggling of highly illicit substances, a venture that Varga had explicitly warned him against. Jamal saw it as a bold move, a statement of his intent to dominate the market. He envisioned the immense profits, the solidification of his power, the ultimate proof of his superiority. He gathered his most trusted lieutenants, men he believed were as committed to him as he was to his own ambition. Among them was Rico, a seasoned enforcer whose loyalty had always been unquestioned, a man whose steely gaze had met Jamal's across countless clandestine meetings.

The meeting point was a derelict factory on the outskirts of the city, its skeletal frame silhouetted against the bruised twilight sky. The air was heavy with the scent of damp concrete and stale oil. Jamal arrived with his usual entourage, a quiet confidence emanating from him like a tangible force. He greeted Rico with a nod, a gesture that had always conveyed a shared understanding, a silent acknowledgment of their mutual commitment. But tonight, there was a subtle difference in Rico's posture, a tension in his shoulders that Jamal, in his hubris, failed to recognize.

The exchange was supposed to be swift and clean. The cargo was secured, the payment ready. But as the deal reached its climax, a chilling silence descended. The usual hurried exchange of goods and money was replaced by an unnerving stillness. Jamal's hand instinctively went to the inside of his jacket, the familiar weight of his firearm a small comfort.

Then, the betrayal. It wasn't a dramatic shootout, no hail of bullets tearing through the night. It was far more insidious, far more humiliating. Rico, with a chillingly calm expression, produced a small, compact device. He activated it, and a high-frequency pulse filled the air, disabling any electronic security measures, including the sophisticated tracking devices Jamal had embedded in his own contraband.

"Varga sends his regards, Jamal," Rico said, his voice flat, devoid of any emotion. "He said you've become... unpredictable. And that's bad for business."

Jamal stared, his mind struggling to process the sudden, brutal turn of events. The arrogance that had inflated his ego like a balloon had just been popped, leaving him exposed and vulnerable. He saw it then – the subtle shifts, the guarded responses, the gradual withdrawal. Varga hadn't been growing complacent; he had been preparing to cut his losses. And Jamal, in his blind pursuit of greater power, had provided Varga with the perfect excuse.

Before Jamal could even formulate a response, more figures emerged from the shadows, men loyal to Varga, their faces grim and resolute. They were armed, not with the crude weapons of street thugs, but with the cold, efficient tools of a professional outfit. Jamal's lieutenants, sensing the shift in power, had either scattered or, in a few chilling instances, joined Rico's side, their loyalty proving as fluid as the city's ever-changing tides.

Jamal was disarmed with brutal efficiency. There was no grand resistance, no desperate struggle for survival. The empire he had so meticulously built had crumbled around him in a matter of moments, not brought down by an external force, but by the very foundations of betrayal he had laid himself. His hubris had been his undoing, his overconfidence a gaping wound that had allowed his enemies to easily exploit him.

He was not killed on the spot. Varga, ever the businessman, saw a different kind of value in Jamal now. He was a loose end, a potential liability, but also a cautionary tale. Jamal was taken, not to a prison, but to a secluded location, a place where his actions could be scrutinized, his knowledge extracted, and his influence neutralized. His reign, though brief, had been a testament to the intoxicating allure of power and the devastating consequences of allowing that power to corrupt one's judgment. The city, with its insatiable appetite for both creation and destruction, had once again devoured one of its own, leaving behind only the bitter lesson of Jamal's fatal ambition. His downfall was not a dramatic explosion, but a quiet, chilling implosion, a stark reminder that in the unforgiving landscape of the underworld, even the most cunning players could be outmaneuvered and ultimately eliminated by the very forces they sought to control. The silence that followed his capture was not a victory, but an ominous prelude to Varga's next move, a chilling testament to the cyclical nature of power and betrayal that defined the city. Jamal's ambition had been a blazing comet, brilliant and all-consuming, but ultimately destined to burn out, leaving only the cold, empty void of his absence.

The stark white of the interrogation room seemed to amplify the silence, a suffocating blanket that pressed in on Chloe. Her hands, usually deft and sure with a brush or charcoal stick, were now clasped tightly in her lap, the knuckles white against the pale fabric of her pants. Outside this sterile box, the world was a maelstrom of flashing lights, urgent voices, and the sickening thud of boots on pavement. Inside, there was only the hum of fluorescent lights and the weight of unspoken accusations.

But even here, in this place designed to strip away identity and reduce a person to a series of answers, Chloe's artistic spirit refused to be entirely extinguished. It was a flicker, a defiant ember glowing in the ashes of their shattered lives. She had always processed the world through a visual lens, translating the cacophony of experiences into tangible forms. The lurid glow of the Vegas strip, the desperation etched onto the faces of those caught in its snare, the ephemeral beauty of a fleeting moment – it had all found its way onto her canvases, her sketchpads, her very soul.

Now, with Marcus gone, his ambition a supernova that had consumed them all, Chloe's art became something more. It was no longer merely an expression of her inner world, but a potential archive, a coded testament to the brutal ballet of their existence. The vibrant hues that had once celebrated life now seemed to hold a deeper, more somber resonance. Each stroke, each shade, could be a whisper of truth, a silent confession of what had transpired.

She thought of the pieces she had created during their ascent, the ones that Marcus had so eagerly displayed as proof of their burgeoning success. There was the sprawling cityscape, rendered in a palette of aggressive reds and electric blues, capturing the intoxicating pulse of the city that had promised them everything. But hidden within the intricate details, the shadowed alleyways, the distorted reflections in mirrored skyscrapers, were subtle visual cues. A particular shade of bruised purple bleeding into the neon, perhaps signifying the moral compromises they had made. A lone, broken bird trapped against a windowpane, a harbinger of the doom that was to come. She had painted these not just as art, but as a subconscious processing of the mounting darkness, a way to anchor herself amidst the escalating chaos.

And then there were the later works, created in the frantic, adrenaline-fueled days following their entanglement with Varga. These pieces were rawer, more visceral. One canvas, a chaotic explosion of black and crimson, depicted a distorted, fragmented face, its features obscured by streaks of paint that could easily be interpreted as tears, or blood. Was this Marcus, his ambition tearing him apart from the inside? Or was it a self-portrait, Chloe herself fractured by the weight of their shared secrets? The ambiguity was deliberate, a shield against direct interpretation, yet a clear cry for understanding.

The authorities, she suspected, would comb through her studio, dissecting every canvas, every sketchbook, searching for clues. Would they see the deliberate symbolism, the intentional obfuscation, or would they dismiss it as the fanciful ramblings of an artist caught in the crossfire? Her work was her truth, a parallel narrative running beneath the surface of their spoken words, a desperate attempt to make sense of the senseless.

She remembered a particular piece, a charcoal sketch of a solitary hand reaching out from a cage of intertwined bars. The bars were rendered with such stark realism, the shadows so deep, that they seemed to press against the very surface of the paper. The hand, though desperately clawing, appeared frail, its fingers splayed in a gesture of both longing and despair. This had been created after a particularly brutal meeting with Varga's enforcers, a chilling reminder of their precarious position. She hadn't shown it to Marcus; it felt too revealing, too much like admitting defeat. Now, it felt like a premonition, a visual prophecy of the trap they had fallen into.

Even now, as she sat in the sterile interrogation room, the images swirled behind her eyes. The glint of steel, the echo of whispered threats, the cold calculations in Varga's eyes. Her mind, a constant canvas, was already working, translating the present into potential art. The stark lines of the room, the vacant stare of the officer observing her, the subtle tremor in her own hand – these were the raw materials of her next creation, a testament born from the ashes of her current reality.

Could her art be a confession? Perhaps. The pieces undeniably chronicled their descent, the compromises made, the lives irrevocably altered. The portraits of the individuals they had crossed, subtly altered with features that hinted at their eventual fates, could be seen as confessions of guilt. The recurring motif of a shattered mirror, reflecting a distorted and fragmented reality, might be an admission of their own fractured selves. She had wrestled with the morality of their actions, the ethical compromises that had become as routine as breathing. Her art was the manifestation of that internal conflict, a visual diary of her soul's struggle.

Or perhaps, it was a coded message. A cry for help, hidden in plain sight. The specific arrangement of colors in one painting, the subtle distortion of perspective in another, could be a language only those who knew them intimately, or those with the patience to decipher it, would understand. She had always possessed a keen eye for detail, a knack for embedding subtle nuances into her work. If someone were to look closely enough, to analyze the composition, the symbolism, they might piece together the truth of what had happened, of how Marcus's ambition had spiraled out of control, dragging everyone in its wake.

She recalled a series of abstract pieces she had begun, inspired by the geometric patterns found in the city's architecture, the stark lines of the casinos, the intricate wiring of the underworld. In one piece, the stark black lines of a skyscraper were intersected by a jagged, crimson slash, a visceral representation of how their illicit dealings had violently disrupted the city's perceived order. Another featured a swirling vortex of blues and greens, representing the seductive allure of wealth, but with subtle undertones of grey and black, hinting at the decay beneath the surface.

Her most recent sketches, done in the hurried, clandestine moments before their final downfall, were filled with fragmented images: a hand reaching for a falling object, a distorted silhouette disappearing into the shadows, a single, watchful eye observing from the periphery. These were not mere artistic exercises; they were her subconscious desperately trying to record the unfolding tragedy, to capture the essence of their inevitable doom.

The possibility of her art serving as a testament to the lives lost was also a heavy burden. The vibrant portraits of the people they had encountered, the casual acquaintances, the fleeting allies, the unfortunate victims – they were etched into her memory, and onto her canvases. There was the hopeful gaze of a young woman she had sketched at a bar, a woman whose dreams had been as bright and fleeting as a shooting star, only to be extinguished by circumstances far beyond her control. Chloe had captured the spark in her eyes, the youthful optimism, but she had also subtly included a shadow in the background, a creeping darkness that foreshadowed her fate. Was this a betrayal, or a tribute?

The narrative had often been about Marcus's relentless pursuit of power, his insatiable ambition that had blinded him to the consequences. But Chloe had been a witness, a chronicler, and in her own way, a participant. Her art was the manifestation of her complicity, the tangible proof of her presence at the scene of the crime, even if she hadn't wielded the weapon. The vibrant colors she had used to depict their early successes now seemed to mock her, a reminder of the innocence they had so readily sacrificed.

She thought of a particular painting, a still life of wilting flowers in an ornate vase. The petals were a deep, velvety red, but they were tinged with brown at the edges, the life draining from them. The vase itself was intricately detailed, suggesting a facade of wealth and beauty, but a fine crack snaked its way across its surface, threatening to shatter it entirely. This painting, created shortly after their initial dealings with Varga turned sour, felt like a direct reflection of their situation. They had been beautiful, promising, but the rot had set in, and the cracks were beginning to show.

Even in this sterile environment, Chloe's mind was a whirlwind of imagery. She saw the potential for a series of interconnected works, each piece a chapter in their tragic story. The bold strokes of Marcus's ambition, the subtle shading of her own fear and complicity, the stark, unforgiving lines of Varga's influence. She imagined the critics, the art historians, poring over her creations years from now, trying to unravel the enigma of her life and the lives she had touched. Would they understand the context, the desperation, the sheer terror that had fueled some of her most powerful works?

She traced an invisible line on the tabletop, a phantom brushstroke. The chaos of the past few weeks had been overwhelming, a relentless tide that had threatened to drown her. Yet, amidst the wreckage, her creative spirit persisted. It was a stubborn, resilient thing, forged in the crucible of their experience. Even if her physical freedom was lost, even if her future was uncertain, the art remained. It was her legacy, a silent testament to the choices made, the paths taken, and the dreams that had been both realized and brutally shattered in the neon-drenched, unforgiving streets of Vegas. Her art would outlive them, a lingering echo of their story, a perpetual reminder of the price of ambition and the fragile nature of dreams. The art was her truth, her confession, and ultimately, her enduring legacy in a world that had tried its best to silence her. It was the whisper of her soul in the deafening roar of their downfall.

The metallic tang of fear had long since faded from David's mouth, replaced by the persistent, dry taste of apprehension. He moved through the pre-dawn city like a ghost, the chill of the air seeping into his bones, a physical manifestation of the hollowness that had taken root within him. He was out. He had escaped the vortex that had so spectacularly consumed Marcus and Chloe, emerging from its destructive gravitational pull with nothing but the ragged edges of his sanity and a memory bank overflowing with unspeakable truths. The escape hadn't been dramatic, no screeching tires or desperate sprints through darkened alleys. It had been a slow, agonizing disentanglement, a careful unpicking of the threads that bound him to the escalating madness.

He remembered the sheer, primal instinct that had driven him to sever those ties, the visceral revulsion that had curdled in his gut with every step deeper into the abyss. Marcus's feverish ambition had been a contagion, spreading its seductive, destructive tendrils, and David, once a willing participant in its initial allure, had found himself recoiling, his innate caution screaming at him to flee. Chloe, caught in the crossfire, a fragile bloom wilting under the harsh glare of their ambition, had been the catalyst. Her quiet despair, the unspoken fear that flickered in her eyes whenever Marcus spoke of their next audacious move, had been a mirror reflecting the terrifying trajectory they were on.

The moment of decision had been less a conscious choice and more a tidal wave of self-preservation. He had seen the path ahead, a precipitous drop into a chasm of moral compromise and ultimate destruction. He had seen Marcus barreling towards it with eyes fixed on a glittering, illusory prize, and he had seen Chloe, too trusting, too loyal, being dragged along in his wake. The memory of their last, strained conversation, the forced casualness of Marcus's tone as he outlined a plan that David knew, with chilling certainty, would be their undoing, was seared into his mind. He hadn't argued, hadn't pleaded. He had simply nodded, a silent farewell passing between them, a tacit acknowledgment that their paths, once so intertwined, had irrevocably diverged.

He hadn't looked back. The guilt, a heavy stone in his stomach, had been a constant companion, but the need to survive, to preserve some semblance of himself, had been a more potent force. He had shed the life he had known like a snake sheds its skin, leaving behind the glittering facade of aspiration, the intoxicating whispers of power, the dangerous camaraderie that had promised so much and delivered only ruin. His departure had been quiet, almost unremarkable, a whimper rather than a bang, which was perhaps the only mercy he had been afforded. He had simply... walked away. He had packed a single bag, his movements fueled by a desperate, gnawing urgency, and disappeared into the anonymous hum of the city.

Now, the city, once a symbol of boundless opportunity and intoxicating promise, felt like a gilded cage. Every flashing neon sign, every siren wailing in the distance, every shadowed doorway, served as a visceral reminder of what he had witnessed, what he had been a part of. He saw the ghosts of Marcus's fervent pronouncements in the harsh lines of the skyscrapers, the spectral echoes of Chloe's quiet anxieties in the flickering streetlights. He had survived, but survival had come at a steep price. He was an island, adrift in a sea of shared experience, the only one who truly knew the depth of the charade, the true cost of their ambition.

His new existence was a study in deliberate anonymity. He found work that was as devoid of connection as possible, menial tasks that required little thought and even less interaction. He scrubbed floors in a quiet diner until the early hours, the rhythmic swish of the mop a dull counterpoint to the ceaseless churn of his memories. He sorted mail in a soulless office building, the endless stream of envelopes a metaphor for the unread messages of their past. He craved the mundane, the predictable, the absence of any narrative that might draw him back into the orbit of their disastrous descent.

Sleep offered little respite. His dreams were a fragmented, recurring nightmare, a surreal tapestry woven with the faces of those they had wronged, the hushed tones of illicit deals, the chilling glint of avarice in Marcus's eyes. He would wake in a cold sweat, the phantom weight of unseen burdens pressing down on him, the silence of his sparsely furnished apartment amplifying the hollowness within. He would lie there for hours, staring at the ceiling, trying to piece together the fragmented narrative of his own escape, the moments of clarity that had allowed him to break free.

He carried the knowledge of what had happened like a shard of glass embedded in his soul. He knew the choices made, the lines crossed, the lives irrevocably altered. He knew the intoxicating lure that had drawn Marcus in, the way ambition could warp and twist even the brightest of spirits. He understood, with a clarity that was both a curse and a burden, how easily dreams could curdle into nightmares, how the pursuit of success could lead to a precipice from which there was no return. He had seen the unraveling, the slow, agonizing disintegration of everything they had once held dear.

He avoided any contact with their old circle, any familiar faces or places. The risk of recognition, of being drawn back into the narrative, was too great. He had burned his bridges, not with anger or recrimination, but with a cold, calculated necessity. He had seen the devastation that could be wrought by unchecked ambition, the way it could consume everything in its path, and he was determined to be the sole survivor of its destructive hunger.

His days were characterized by a profound solitude. He ate alone, walked alone, existed alone. He found a strange, somber comfort in this self-imposed isolation. It was a shield, a fortress against the chaos he had narrowly escaped. He had learned that true safety lay not in connection, but in detachment, not in shared dreams, but in solitary survival. The vibrant tapestry of his past had been torn asunder, leaving him with a stark, monochrome present.

He would sometimes catch himself staring out of a window, his gaze distant, his mind replaying scenes from their ascent, from their inevitable fall. He would see Marcus, brimming with an almost messianic self-belief, his words a torrent of promises and possibilities. He would see Chloe, her art a silent rebellion against the encroaching darkness, her spirit a fragile beacon in their storm-tossed world. And he would see himself, a quiet observer, a hesitant participant, always on the periphery, always a step removed from the heart of the storm, until the moment he finally chose to step entirely out of its path.

The psychological scars were deep, invisible wounds that festered in the quiet corners of his mind. He was marked by his brief but intense entanglement in the dangerous world his friends had so eagerly embraced. He had seen the underbelly of aspiration, the ruthlessness that lurked beneath the glossy surface, and it had fundamentally altered his perception of the world. The innocence he had once possessed was gone, replaced by a weary cynicism, a constant vigilance that had become second nature.

He understood that his survival was not a victory, but a testament to his own fundamental difference. While Marcus had craved the spotlight, the power, the intoxicating thrill of the chase, David had sought something far less ostentatious: peace. He had been present at the genesis of their downfall, a witness to the seeds of destruction being sown, and he had made the conscious decision not to nurture them.

The quietude of his new life was a stark contrast to the dramatic fates of the others. He imagined Marcus, perhaps facing judgment, his grand pronouncements silenced, his ambition finally meeting its insurmountable obstacle. He pictured Chloe, her artistic soul perhaps finding solace in a new form of expression, or perhaps broken by the weight of what had transpired. He didn't dwell on these thoughts for too long; they were a dangerous path, a descent back into the mire.

His solitary existence was not one of regret, but of a profound, unshakeable understanding. He had seen the ultimate price of ambition, and he had chosen a different currency. He had opted for the quiet dignity of survival, for the often-unseen strength of a life lived on its own terms, away from the seductive glare of what could be. He was the living embodiment of what happens when the pursuit of greatness leads to ruin, a silent testament to the fragility of dreams and the enduring, often solitary, journey of self-preservation. The memory of what had transpired was a heavy burden, yes, but it was also his anchor, the quiet reminder of the path he had chosen, the path that had led him, at long last, to the solitary, unyielding quiet of his own survival. He was free, but his freedom was a lonely one, a perpetual state of watchful solitude.

The silence in Aisha's small apartment was a stark contrast to the cacophony of memories that raged within her. Las Vegas, once a glittering beacon of possibility, had become a haunted landscape etched into her very being. The neon glare of the Strip was now a searing brand, a constant reminder of the choices made, the laughter that had turned to screams, the camaraderie that had fractured into irreparable pieces. She traced the rim of her mug, the lukewarm tea doing little to warm the perpetual chill that seemed to have settled deep within her bones. It had been months since she'd returned, since she'd meticulously erased any trace of her involvement, any whisper that might connect her to the unraveling spectacle. Yet, the escape felt less like a victory and more like a prolonged sentence of exile.

Her friends' faces, once vibrant and full of life, now flickered behind her eyelids like faulty projections. Marcus, his ambition a wildfire that consumed everything in its path, his charm a dangerous lure that had ensnared them all. Chloe, her gentle spirit crushed under the weight of Marcus's insatiable drive, her dreams reduced to ashes. And David, the quiet observer, the one who had managed to slip through the cracks, leaving Aisha to navigate the debris alone. She often found herself replaying their last interactions, dissecting every word, every subtle shift in their demeanor, searching for the precise moment where it had all gone irrevocably wrong. Had she said enough? Had she pushed hard enough against Marcus's escalating recklessness? Had she truly understood the depth of Chloe's quiet desperation? The questions were a relentless tide, eroding the fragile shores of her peace.

She worked at a small, independent bookstore now, the scent of aged paper and ink a welcome balm against the lingering stench of desperation that clung to her from her past. The quiet rustle of turning pages, the hushed conversations between patrons, the predictable rhythm of stocking shelves – it was an existence deliberately crafted for its lack of intensity, its profound ordinariness. But even here, amidst the comforting familiarity of stories bound in print, the echoes found her. A book title, a chance encounter with a phrase that mirrored a whispered threat, the distant sound of laughter that eerily resembled Marcus's boisterous pronouncements – each was a trigger, a small tremor that sent ripples of anxiety through her. She'd learned to school her features, to maintain a placid exterior, a mask of calm that hid the churning tempest beneath. The effort was exhausting, a constant battle to keep the past at bay.

Her social interactions were minimal, carefully curated to avoid any deep entanglements. Casual acquaintances at work, polite nods to neighbors – these were the extent of her connections. The thought of revealing the truth, of articulating the sheer, unadulterated horror of what she had witnessed, was too daunting. How could she explain the intoxicating pull of Marcus's vision, the blinding allure of the deals they had struck, the terrifying descent into a world where morality was a negotiable commodity? She imagined the disbelief, the judgment, the inevitable questions that would probe the very core of her complicity. It was easier, she told herself, to remain a ghost, a silent observer of her own survival.

Sleep offered little sanctuary. Her dreams were a recurring montage of fragmented images: the blinding flash of a casino floor, the predatory gleam in Marcus's eyes as he sealed a deal, Chloe's tear-streaked face bathed in the sickly glow of a hotel room lamp, the cold click of a lock as David made his escape. She'd wake abruptly, her heart hammering against her ribs, the phantom taste of stale air and fear in her mouth. The sheer helplessness she'd felt in those moments, the desperate yearning to intervene, to snatch them from the precipice, was a pain that never truly subsided. She was safe, yes, but safety felt like a hollow victory when it was built upon the ruins of others.

The counsel she had offered, the quiet warnings whispered in Marcus's ear, the pleas for caution directed at Chloe, now replayed in her mind with the crushing weight of hindsight. She saw the moments where she could have been more insistent, where a firmer stance might have altered the trajectory. But ambition, she had learned, was a powerful, blinding force. It distorted judgment, it deafened reason, and it fostered a dangerous complacency in those who were caught in its orbit. She had been a voice of reason, perhaps, but her voice had been drowned out by the siren song of success, by the seductive promise of a life beyond the ordinary.

She remembered Chloe's last phone call, the tremor in her voice as she'd spoken of unease, of a growing sense of being trapped. Aisha had promised to come, to help her find a way out. But the insidious grip of Marcus's influence, coupled with her own burgeoning fear, had made her hesitate. She had rationalized her inaction, telling herself that Chloe was strong, that she could handle it, that Marcus's charm would eventually smooth over any rough patches. That hesitation, that agonizing pause, was a regret that would forever gnaw at her. It was the moment she had chosen self-preservation over solidarity, a choice that left an indelible stain on her conscience.

David's departure had been a silent, almost imperceptible act. He had simply vanished, leaving behind a void where their shared anxieties had once resided. Aisha understood his need to escape, to preserve his own sanity. But his absence had amplified her isolation, leaving her to face the aftermath with no one to share the burden, no one who truly understood the intricate web of events that had led to their downfall. She often wondered if he ever thought of them, if the memories haunted his solitary existence as they did hers. She hoped, in a way, that he had found some measure of peace, some quiet corner of the world where the echoes of Las Vegas could not reach him.

The weight of what could have been was a constant companion. She saw Chloe, a talented artist, her potential stifled, her spirit broken. She saw Marcus, a man consumed by his own hubris, his vision warped into something monstrous. She saw the lives they had touched, the people they had inadvertently harmed, all caught in the crossfire of their unchecked ambition. It was a sobering realization, a stark reminder of the fragile line between aspiration and destruction.

Aisha's life had become a testament to the enduring impact of trauma. The events in Las Vegas had not simply been a series of unfortunate incidents; they had been a cataclysm that had reshaped her understanding of the world, of herself, and of the people she had once held dear. She had learned that ambition, untethered from ethics and empathy, was a dangerous force, capable of inflicting immeasurable damage. She had learned that loyalty, while noble, could also be a fatal flaw when misplaced. And she had learned that survival, while a fundamental instinct, often came at a profound emotional cost.

She tried to find meaning in her new existence, in the quiet rhythm of her days. She found solace in the written word, in the countless lives and experiences captured within the pages of the books she sold. She found a sense of purpose in the small acts of kindness she offered to strangers, a way of counteracting the darkness she had witnessed with glimmers of light. It was a slow, arduous process, this rebuilding of a life fractured by loss and betrayal. There were days when the weight of her memories threatened to crush her, when the silence felt too deafening, when the longing for what was lost became an unbearable ache.

But on those days, she would force herself to remember the strength she had discovered within herself, the resilience that had allowed her to walk away from the precipice. She would remind herself that while the past could not be undone, it did not have to define her future. She had survived, not unscathed, but undeniably alive. And in that survival, there was a quiet power, a testament to the enduring human spirit's capacity to endure, to heal, and, eventually, to find a measure of peace, even in the shadow of profound loss. The echoes of Las Vegas would always be a part of her story, a somber reminder of the price of ambition, but they would no longer be the only melody in the symphony of her life. She was learning to compose a new tune, one marked by resilience, by quiet strength, and by the hard-won wisdom of a survivor. Her journey was far from over, but she was moving forward, one page, one day, one carefully chosen moment at a time, carrying the weight of her experiences with a quiet dignity that spoke volumes.

Chapter 7: The Unheeded Counsel

The sting of hindsight was a venom that seeped into Aisha's every waking moment. It wasn't just the grand, earth-shattering decisions that haunted her, but the subtle nudges, the quiet whispers of caution that had been so easily dismissed. She remembered her uncle, Tariq, his weathered face etched with the wisdom of a man who had navigated the treacherous currents of business for decades. He had cautioned Marcus, not with overt disapproval, but with a gentle, almost paternal, concern. "Ambition is a fire, Marcus," he'd said, his voice a low rumble that carried the weight of experience. "It can forge steel, but uncontrolled, it will consume the very hand that feeds it. Always have an exit strategy, my boy. Always know when the heat becomes too much to bear." Aisha had watched Marcus nod, his eyes bright with the fire Tariq had spoken of, but his mind already miles ahead, charting courses that left no room for caution. Tariq had looked at Aisha then, a fleeting glance that held a universe of unspoken worry. He hadn't needed to say anything more. His gaze was a silent testament to his doubts, a premonition of the blaze to come.

Then there were the hushed conversations with Chloe, moments when vulnerability peeked through her friend's determined facade. Chloe had confided in Aisha about the growing pressure, the impossible deadlines Marcus was setting, the escalating risks he was taking. "I don't know, Aisha," Chloe had whispered one evening, her voice barely audible over the ambient hum of the Vegas strip. "Sometimes, it feels like we're flying too close to the sun. Marcus... he's so sure of himself, but it scares me. What if he's wrong? What if this all crumbles?" Aisha, caught in the intoxicating whirlwind of perceived success and her own desperate need for validation, had offered reassurances that now felt like paper-thin shields against an approaching storm. She'd encouraged Chloe to trust Marcus, to believe in his vision, to weather the temporary turbulence. "He's got this, Chlo," she'd said, her own voice laced with a manufactured confidence. "We're almost there. Just a little more, and it'll all be worth it." The words tasted like ash in her mouth now, each syllable a bitter accusation. She saw Chloe's hesitant smile, the flicker of doubt that never quite left her eyes, and ached for the chance to retract her own naive pronouncements.

Even David, the quiet, analytical one, had voiced his unease. He was the meticulous planner, the one who double-checked the figures, who spotted the discrepancies that others overlooked. He had approached Marcus with a detailed breakdown of potential legal ramifications, a cautious outline of liabilities that were being ignored in the relentless pursuit of profit. "Marcus, we need to be absolutely sure about the regulatory compliance here," David had said, his tone respectful but firm. "There are gray areas that could easily become black holes if we're not careful. I've outlined some alternatives, ways to structure this that mitigate the exposure." Marcus, however, had waved away David's concerns with a dismissive flick of his wrist. "Details, David, details," he'd said, his voice laced with impatience. "We're on the cusp of something massive. Don't let a few bureaucratic hurdles slow us down. You worry too much. Just trust the momentum." David had retreated, his shoulders slumped, his usual quiet confidence replaced by a weary resignation. Aisha remembered seeing the flicker of frustration in David's eyes that day, a silent acknowledgment that his counsel, like hers, had fallen on deaf ears. She wished she had stood by David, had amplified his warnings, had demanded that Marcus at least consider the meticulously crafted reports.

The tragedy wasn't that they had stumbled into darkness; it was that they had been shown the path away from it, and had stubbornly refused to turn. Each piece of advice, each intuitive prickle of doubt, was a breadcrumb leading away from the precipice. Tariq's steady hand, Chloe's worried whispers, David's reasoned analysis – these were the signposts that had been deliberately ignored, the warnings that had been drowned out by the siren song of a deal too good to be true, a dream too intoxicating to abandon. Aisha could almost feel the phantom weight of her own unexpressed anxieties, the moments when she'd bitten back words of caution, choosing the path of least resistance, of perceived loyalty, of a desperate hope that Marcus's charisma could somehow bend reality to his will. She had convinced herself that his audacity was genius, his recklessness was courage. She had been a willing participant in her own delusion.

She replayed the conversations, the subtle shifts in tone, the averted gazes. She saw how Marcus's charm, once a captivating force, had morphed into a tool of manipulation, adept at sidestepping any challenge to his authority or his vision. He had a way of making any doubt seem like a lack of faith, any caution seem like a weakness. And she, along with Chloe and David, had allowed him to cultivate that perception. They had been so eager to believe in the grand narrative Marcus spun, the tale of triumph over adversity, that they had blinded themselves to the escalating dangers. They had been so focused on the prize, the glittering promise of unimaginable success, that they had failed to see the widening chasm beneath their feet.

Her mind drifted to a specific afternoon, a tense meeting in a plush hotel suite. Marcus had been ecstatic, flushed with the success of a preliminary deal. Tariq had been present, ostensibly to offer his blessings, but Aisha had seen the deep furrows on his brow. Later, he'd pulled Aisha aside. "Aisha, my dear," he'd said, his voice low and serious. "This is a whirlwind. Marcus is a brilliant young man, but he needs anchors. If you see him losing sight of what truly matters, of the people who depend on him, you must be that anchor. Don't let the allure of the destination make you forget the importance of the journey, and the people you're taking with you." He had clasped her hand, his grip surprisingly strong. "Be his conscience, Aisha, when he forgets to have one." She had promised him she would. A promise that felt like a betrayal now, a vow broken by her own fear and her misguided sense of obligation. She had been so consumed by the need to prove herself, to keep up with Marcus's breakneck pace, that she had failed to be the anchor he so desperately needed.

Chloe had tried a different approach, a more emotional plea. She had shown Aisha a sketch, a raw, emotional portrayal of their group, but with a subtle undertone of distress subtly woven into the lines. "Look, Aisha," she'd said, her voice heavy. "I feel... trapped. Like we're all caught in a net, and the more we struggle, the tighter it gets. Marcus is building a beautiful facade, but I'm afraid of what's behind it. I'm afraid of what it's costing us." Aisha had seen the fear in Chloe's eyes, the genuine distress. But in her own desperation to maintain the illusion of control, she had dismissed Chloe's concerns as artistic temperament, as oversensitivity. "You're just stressed, Chlo," she'd said, attempting a reassuring smile. "We're all under pressure. But think of what we're building! It's going to be incredible." Chloe had simply nodded, her gaze distant, a silent acknowledgment that her fears were not being heard, or perhaps, not being understood.

And David, always the pragmatist, had presented a contingency plan, a detailed exit strategy should things go south. He'd spent days meticulously mapping out options, considering legal avenues, potential safe havens. He had brought it to Marcus, his presentation thorough and concise. "Marcus, if the worst-case scenario unfolds, these are our options. We need to have a plan B, and a plan C, to protect ourselves, and more importantly, to protect the innocent parties caught in the crossfire." Marcus had merely skimmed the document, a patronizing smile on his face. "David, you're a brilliant mind, but you think like a lawyer, not a revolutionary. We're not planning for failure. We're planning for victory. Your 'contingency' plans are just distractions from the inevitable." David had looked at Aisha, a silent question in his eyes. She had offered a small, apologetic shrug, a gesture that conveyed her own helplessness, her own inability to sway Marcus. She had felt a pang of guilt, a sense of shared disappointment, but had ultimately sided with the prevailing momentum, the intoxicating allure of Marcus's unwavering confidence.

These were the echoes, the unheeded counsel that now reverberated in the hollow chambers of her memory. Each missed opportunity to speak up, to push harder, to insist on caution, was a brick in the wall of regret that now imprisoned her. They had been given chances, glimpses of alternative paths, warnings that were clear and unambiguous. But the intoxicating allure of success, the blinding ambition, the sheer force of Marcus's will had rendered them deaf. They had been so eager to believe in the impossible that they had failed to heed the warnings of the possible. Their downfall wasn't a sudden, unforeseen catastrophe; it was a slow, deliberate descent, paved with the well-intentioned but ultimately ignored advice of those who saw the danger, those who tried to pull them back from the brink. Aisha understood now that true strength wasn't in audacious leaps, but in the quiet courage to listen, to consider, and to sometimes, just sometimes, choose the safer path. It was a lesson learned too late, a truth that would forever echo in the silence of her unlived futures.

David traced the condensation ring left by his water glass on the polished mahogany of the bar. It was a familiar habit, a small ritual performed in the sterile quiet of his self-imposed exile. The city lights blurred outside the tinted windows, a vibrant, chaotic tapestry that felt a million miles away from the meticulously ordered existence he now inhabited. He'd built this life brick by careful brick, a fortress of normalcy designed to shield him from the echoes of the past. Yet, the echoes persisted, quieter now, more insidious, like a phantom limb that still ached with phantom pain. His analytical mind, the very tool that had served him so well in navigating the treacherous currents of their ambition, now served as a relentless prosecutor, dissecting every decision, every calculated silence.

He remembered the hushed urgency in Marcus's voice, the almost desperate charisma that had swept them all up in its wake. Marcus had been a force of nature, a supernova of ambition, and David, the quiet observer, had been drawn into his orbit, much like the others. His role had been to anticipate, to plan, to identify the potential pitfalls before they became insurmountable obstacles. He'd presented Marcus with spreadsheets and risk assessments, legal disclaimers and contingency scenarios. He'd done his job, meticulously, dispassionately. He'd flagged the 'gray areas,' the 'bureaucratic hurdles,' the 'potential liabilities.' He'd offered solutions, alternative routes, pathways that skirted the precipice. But Marcus, high on the intoxicating scent of imminent success, had waved them away like so many gnats. "Details, David, details," he'd said, his voice a dismissive caress. "Don't get bogged down in the minutiae. We're building an empire, not a ledger book."

And David, ever the pragmatist, had understood the unspoken directive. To push further, to insist, would be to invite friction, to challenge the narrative Marcus had so expertly woven. It would mean becoming an obstacle, a wet blanket on the roaring fire of their collective dream. So, he'd acquiesced. He'd stored his concerns, filed away his meticulously crafted reports, and retreated into his shell of quiet competence. He'd told himself it was about loyalty, about trust in Marcus's vision, about the greater good that their success promised. He'd convinced himself that the calculated risks were precisely that – calculated. That Marcus, with his boundless energy and uncanny knack for persuasion, would somehow navigate the treacherous waters.

But the word that gnawed at him wasn't loyalty; it was complicity. Had his silence, his meticulous adherence to the plan even when he knew the foundations were shaky, made him an accessory? He'd always prided himself on his objectivity, his ability to detach himself from the emotional fray and approach problems with pure logic. It was a survival mechanism, a way to navigate the often-irrational world of business and ambition without getting consumed. But in this instance, that detachment had become a form of passive consent. He'd seen the storm clouds gathering, felt the shift in the wind, but instead of shouting a warning, he'd simply adjusted his umbrella, trusting that Marcus's ship would somehow weather the gale.

He recalled a specific meeting, a tense negotiation where the pressure had been palpable. Marcus had been all charm and bluster, deflecting probing questions with practiced ease. David had noticed a subtle inconsistency in the financial projections presented, a discrepancy that, while small, hinted at a deeper, more concerning pattern. He'd tried to catch Aisha's eye, to signal his unease, but she'd been caught in Marcus's magnetic field, her own face alight with a shared, albeit slightly anxious, excitement. Later, he'd approached Marcus privately, his voice low and measured. "Marcus, I've been looking at the Q3 projections again. There's a leakage in the capital flow we discussed. It's not significant enough to raise immediate red flags, but if it continues, it could create a significant deficit by year-end." Marcus had clapped him on the shoulder, a patronizing gesture that irked David to his core. "You're seeing ghosts, David. It's just accounting fluctuations. We're ahead of schedule, and the market is responding. Trust the momentum."

The momentum. It was a dangerous word, a seductive excuse for reckless abandon. David had always been the one to calculate the trajectory, to map the landing. He'd understood that momentum, unchecked, could lead to a catastrophic crash. Yet, he hadn't overridden Marcus. He hadn't staged an intervention. He hadn't called Aisha or Chloe, hadn't insisted on a full audit, hadn't demanded a pause. He'd simply...

watched. He'd watched as the small leaks became larger fissures, as the fluctuating currents turned into dangerous undertows. He'd watched as the carefully constructed edifice began to sway, its foundations eroded by a wilful disregard for the fundamental principles of sound finance and ethical conduct.

His guilt wasn't a sudden, overwhelming wave. It was a slow, persistent erosion, a quiet accumulation of small failures to act. It was the memory of Chloe's increasingly anxious texts, her veiled pleas for reassurance that he'd met with platitudes. It was Aisha's unwavering belief in Marcus's infallibility, a belief he had never challenged, never sought to temper with his own dose of reality. He'd always been the steady hand, the voice of reason in the background. But had he been too quiet? Had his very quietness, his preference for analysis over confrontation, allowed the situation to fester?

He'd often wondered about the true nature of his involvement. He hadn't been the architect of the grand, ultimately flawed, vision. He hadn't been the charismatic leader who had inspired the blind faith. He'd been the analyst, the one who saw the probabilities, the potential downsides, and then… stayed silent. He hadn't directly benefited from the illicit activities that had ultimately led to their downfall, not in the way Marcus or even Aisha might have. His gains had been more abstract: the satisfaction of a well-executed plan, the intellectual challenge of solving complex problems, the camaraderie of a shared endeavor. But that didn't absolve him.

His analytical skills, honed over years of academic pursuit and professional experience, had enabled him to see the truth with a stark clarity that others, blinded by ambition or loyalty, had missed. He'd identified the weak points, the ethical compromises, the sheer audacity of Marcus's schemes. He'd understood the risks inherent in their offshore dealings, the regulatory loopholes they were exploiting, the potential legal repercussions if their carefully constructed facade crumbled. He'd even drafted the contingency plans, the meticulously detailed exit strategies that Marcus had so casually dismissed. He'd laid out the paths to safety, the ways to mitigate the damage, the methods of extraction should the situation become untenable.

And then he'd done nothing with them. He'd presented them, dutifully, but had not championed them. He'd allowed them to be shelved, buried beneath the weight of Marcus's relentless optimism. He'd rationalized it as a matter of hierarchy, of Marcus's ultimate authority. But deep down, he knew it was more than that. It was a fear of ostracization, a desire to remain part of the group, to not be the one who doused the party's fire. It was the subtle comfort of consensus, even when that consensus was built on a foundation of increasingly shaky premises.

He remembered the day the first major domino fell, the day the authorities began their inquiries. Marcus had been furious, his composure cracking under the pressure. Aisha had been distraught, her usual poise shattered. Chloe had been a ghost, withdrawn and silent. David had felt a cold dread seep into his bones, a grim validation of his unheeded warnings. He'd still been the one to calmly gather the remaining documents, to discreetly liaise with the legal team, to try and salvage what little could be salvaged. His analytical mind, even in the face of utter devastation, had kicked into overdrive, seeking solutions, minimizing damage.

But the efficiency with which he'd operated then felt tainted now. It felt like a performance, a demonstration of his intellectual prowess in the aftermath of a disaster he'd passively witnessed, and perhaps, even, subtly facilitated. He hadn't actively participated in the deception, but he hadn't actively opposed it either. He'd existed in a liminal space, a quiet observer who possessed the knowledge to intervene but lacked the courage or the conviction to do so.

His anonymity now was a deliberate choice, a penance. He worked a mundane job, lived a quiet life, avoided any situation that might draw attention. He was a ghost, haunting the fringes of society, his past a shadow that clung to him like a second skin. He consumed news about financial markets, about legal proceedings, about the fallout from cases that mirrored their own, not out of morbid curiosity, but out of a desperate need to understand, to analyze, to find some logical framework for the illogical descent.

He often replayed the moments, not with Aisha's regret, but with his own brand of dispassionate self-examination. He saw his own calculated detachment as a form of self-preservation. He'd always known that diving too deep into the emotional currents of others could be dangerous. He'd learned to keep a professional distance, to analyze rather than empathize. And it had served him well, had protected him from the emotional toll that had clearly ravaged Aisha and Chloe. But in this instance, that detachment had curdled into a moral failing. He'd failed to see that sometimes, the most analytical approach required a leap of faith, not into the unknown, but into the realm of human connection and moral responsibility.

He picked up his glass, the condensation now a faint mist on his fingertips. He'd done his due diligence, he'd warned them in his own way. But had he done enough? Had he truly exhausted every avenue? Or had he, in his quiet pursuit of self-preservation and intellectual detachment, simply chosen the path of least resistance, allowing the momentum to carry him, and everyone else, towards the inevitable crash? The question hung in the air, unanswered, a silent reckoning that echoed in the sterile quiet of his solitary existence. The city lights continued to blur, indifferent to the quiet turmoil within him. He was safe, anonymous, and utterly alone with the ghost of what might have been, a testament to the insidious power of a silent complicity.

The weight of grief was a physical entity for Aisha, a heavy cloak that seemed to permanently drape over her shoulders. Each sunrise felt like a betrayal, a continuation of a world that no longer contained the vibrant laughter and unwavering support of her lost friends. David's meticulously crafted reports, once her compass in the whirlwind of their shared ambition, now felt like brittle fragments of a shattered mirror, reflecting distorted images of what was and what could never be again. The sterile silence of her apartment, once a sanctuary, now echoed with the phantom whispers of their past conversations, their shared dreams, their hopeful prognoses.

For weeks, she had existed in a state of suspended animation, going through the motions of life with a vacant stare. The legal proceedings had concluded, leaving behind a bitter taste of justice served, but offering no true solace. The public narrative had been etched, Marcus a villain, David a cautionary tale, and she, Aisha, a victim caught in the crossfire. But the labels felt insufficient, incapable of encapsulating the complex tapestry of her relationships, the nuances of their shared journey, the profound sense of loss that permeated every fiber of her being. She had attended the funerals, offered dry condolences, and accepted the sympathy with a numb politeness, all the while feeling like an impostor in her own life.

The turning point, if one could call it that, was not a sudden epiphany but a slow, insistent ache that morphed into a quiet resolve. It began subtly, a flicker of defiance against the suffocating darkness that threatened to consume her. She found herself staring at the framed photograph on her bedside table – the four of them, bathed in the golden light of a long-ago summer afternoon, their faces alight with an unburdened joy. Marcus, his arm slung carelessly around David's shoulders, a mischievous glint in his eyes. David, his characteristic reserve softened by a rare, genuine smile. And herself, leaning into Chloe, her hand gently resting on Chloe's arm, a silent testament to their deep bond. Chloe, with her infectious optimism and her unwavering belief in the inherent goodness of people. The ache intensified, but this time, it was accompanied by a nascent spark of something else: a desire to honor their memory not by succumbing to the shadows they had left behind, but by actively seeking the light.

She started small, reclaiming fragments of her routine that had been lost in the fog of her despair. A morning walk through the park, not to escape, but to observe, to feel the rhythm of the world continuing, to notice the tenacious bloom of a defiant wildflower pushing through the concrete. She reread journals she had kept during their early days, before the ambition had begun to warp their paths, searching for the innocent spark that had ignited their shared venture. She found passages filled with naive optimism, detailed sketches of innovative ideas, and earnest declarations of their collective purpose. It was a stark contrast to the ruthless pragmatism that had ultimately consumed them, and it served as a painful reminder of what they had lost, but also, a fragile beacon of what they had once strived for.

The impulse to speak out, to share her story and the lessons she had learned, grew stronger with each passing day. But the thought of reliving the trauma, of subjecting herself to the public scrutiny and the inevitable judgment, was daunting. She remembered the way the media had dissected their downfall, sensationalizing every detail, painting Marcus as a conniving mastermind and David as a passive accomplice. She knew that her narrative would be filtered through that same lens, and she feared that the truth, the complex interplay of ambition, loyalty, and ethical compromise, would be lost in translation.

Yet, the silence felt like a betrayal of a different kind, a silent acquiescence to the forces that had torn their lives apart. She thought of Chloe, whose gentle spirit had been so vulnerable to the manipulations of others. She thought of David, whose analytical mind, though ultimately used in a way that led to their undoing, was a testament to a desire for order and understanding. And she thought of Marcus, whose charisma had been both a gift and a curse, capable of inspiring greatness and masking profound flaws. They had all been individuals with their own strengths and weaknesses, caught in a vortex of ambition that had spiraled out of control.

One crisp autumn afternoon, while browsing in a quiet bookstore, she stumbled upon a collection of essays on ethical leadership. As she read, a new path began to form in her mind. It wasn't about seeking revenge or dwelling in the past, but about actively contributing to a future where such ethical failures were less likely to occur. The idea of advocacy began to take root. Could she, a woman who had been so deeply scarred by the consequences of unchecked ambition, now become a voice for integrity? Could she use her firsthand experience to educate others, to warn them of the subtle erosions of morality that could occur when profit and prestige overshadowed principle?

She began by seeking out organizations dedicated to promoting corporate social responsibility and ethical business practices. She attended seminars, read white papers, and engaged in quiet conversations with individuals who shared her commitment to a more principled approach to business. It was a slow, deliberate process, a painstaking act of rebuilding, not just of her own life, but of her faith in the possibility of positive change. She knew that her journey would be marked by the ghosts of her past, but she was determined to carry their memory forward not as a burden, but as a catalyst.

Her first tentative step into the public sphere was a small, local event focused on ethical decision-making in emerging businesses. She had prepared a short, personal reflection, weaving together the story of her own experiences without naming names or assigning blame, focusing instead on the universal themes of ambition, temptation, and the critical importance of ethical frameworks. Her voice trembled at first, her hands clasped tightly in front of her, but as she spoke, she felt a sense of liberation wash over her. The faces in the audience, initially a blur of polite attention, gradually sharpened into individuals, their expressions a mix of empathy and thoughtful consideration. She saw nods of understanding, felt the palpable connection that transcended the specifics of her story.

She spoke of the intoxicating allure of rapid growth, the pressure to cut corners when faced with daunting obstacles, and the insidious way in which small compromises could snowball into significant ethical breaches. She highlighted the importance of fostering a culture of transparency and accountability, where dissent was not only tolerated but actively encouraged, and where the pursuit of profit never overshadowed the fundamental responsibility to act with integrity. She emphasized that true success was not merely measured by financial gain, but by the lasting impact one had on stakeholders, the community, and the wider world.

When she finished, a profound silence fell over the room, not an awkward or uncomfortable silence, but one filled with a heavy, thoughtful resonance. Then, a young woman, her eyes bright with a mixture of admiration and trepidation, approached her. "Thank you," she said, her voice barely above a whisper. "I… I'm starting a company with a few friends, and we're facing some really tough decisions. Your words… they've given me a lot to think about." Aisha met her gaze, a genuine smile finally gracing her lips. "That's all I can hope for," she replied, her voice steady now, imbued with a newfound strength. "Remember that integrity is not just a guiding principle; it's the very foundation upon which lasting success is built."

This interaction, small as it was, solidified Aisha's resolve. She realized that her pain, though immense, could be transmuted into a force for good. She began to receive invitations to speak at universities, business schools, and industry conferences. Her narrative evolved, becoming more nuanced, more deeply explored. She spoke about the psychological traps of ambition, the importance of mentorship and guidance for young entrepreneurs, and the often-overlooked need for emotional intelligence and ethical foresight in leadership. She learned to channel her grief into empathy, her anger into a passionate advocacy for systemic change.

She even reached out to David. Their conversation was stilted at first, fraught with unspoken guilt and regret. But as they spoke, a fragile bridge of understanding began to form between them. Aisha didn't seek to assign blame; instead, she spoke of her desire to move forward, to find meaning in the ashes of their past. David, in turn, confessed the quiet torment of his own complicity, the analytical detachment that had ultimately failed him. They discovered a shared commitment to ensuring that such a tragedy would not be repeated, and while their paths diverged, a mutual respect began to grow from the ruins of their shared history. He admitted that her proactive approach was something he admired, a strength he had long since lost. He shared that he was now working with a non-profit that focused on financial literacy for underserved communities, a way of using his skills for a more constructive purpose.

Her journey was not linear. There were days when the memories felt overwhelming, when the weight of her loss threatened to pull her back into the abyss. But in those moments, she would recall the faces of the young people she had inspired, the words of gratitude she had received, the tangible sense of purpose that her advocacy provided. She was building a new life, brick by careful brick, not a fortress to hide in, but a beacon to guide others. She understood now that healing wasn't about forgetting, but about integrating the past into a meaningful present. It was about transforming the scars of betrayal and loss into a testament to resilience, a living tribute to the friends she could no longer hold, but whose memory she would forever carry forward, not as a burden, but as a guiding light. The lessons learned in the crucible of their shared ambition, however painful, had ultimately forged her into something stronger, something more profound. She was no longer just a survivor; she was a testament to the enduring power of hope and the quiet, unyielding strength of the human spirit.

Las Vegas, a sprawling monument to excess and aspiration, continued to hum with an energy that seemed oblivious to the quiet devastation that had recently rippled through its glittering facade. The iconic skyline, a jagged silhouette against the perpetual twilight, remained ablaze with a million points of light, each one a tiny testament to a dream being pursued, a gamble being taken, a life being lived, or perhaps, a life being lost. Aisha felt this indifference acutely as she navigated the city streets, a stark contrast to the profound personal reckoning she had undergone. The sheer, unyielding momentum of Vegas was a force unto itself, a relentless tide that swept over individual narratives, absorbing them into its vast, indifferent current.

The newspapers, once filled with the sensational details of Marcus and David's downfall, had long since moved on to newer dramas, fresher scandals, and brighter stars. The ephemeral nature of celebrity and infamy in this city meant that yesterday's headline was today's forgotten trivia, quickly buried beneath a fresh avalanche of manufactured excitement. Aisha saw it everywhere: the transient nature of success, the swiftness with which fortunes could be made and lost, the brutal efficiency with which the city consumed and discarded its players. It was a city built on the perpetual promise of a fresh start, a clean slate, a new hand dealt, and this promise extended to its collective memory as well. The tragedies that had so deeply impacted her were, for the vast majority of the city's inhabitants and its transient visitors, merely a brief, albeit dramatic, blip on the radar.

She walked past the grand casinos, their entrances like hungry mouths beckoning in the night, disgorging and absorbing crowds with equal abandon. The sounds of slot machines, a metallic symphony of chirps and jingles, mingled with the distant strains of live music and the muffled roar of a thousand conversations. Each establishment, a self-contained universe of hope and despair, operated with a singular focus: to entertain, to entice, to extract. It was a complex ecosystem, intricately designed to feed upon the universal human desire for more – more money, more excitement, more luck. And in this relentless pursuit, the individual stories, the personal costs, were easily obscured.

Aisha recalled the early days, the intoxicating belief that they, too, could conquer this city, that their ambition, tempered by integrity and intellect, would carve a unique path. Marcus, with his boundless charisma, David, with his sharp analytical mind, Chloe, with her unwavering optimism, and herself, with her own quiet determination, had arrived in Vegas with a vision. They saw not just the gaudy spectacle, but the underlying currents of opportunity, the potential for innovation within the established paradigms. They had believed, perhaps naively, that their personal values could not only withstand the city's relentless pressures but also offer a different, more sustainable model of success. The city, however, had a way of re-writing narratives, of imposing its own stark logic on even the most well-intentioned plans.

Now, as she observed the ceaseless flow of humanity, the eager faces of newcomers, the weary resignation of those who had been there for years, she understood the city's profound indifference not as malice, but as an inherent characteristic. Vegas was not designed to care about individual fates. It was a machine, fueled by the collective dreams and desires of millions. The tragedies that unfolded within its orbit were simply data points, statistical anomalies in the grand equation of its existence. The lights would continue to shine, the games would continue to be played, the hotels would continue to be filled, regardless of who won or lost, who soared or fell.

This realization was both a source of pain and a strange kind of liberation. It meant that her personal healing, her desire to create a new purpose, was not dependent on the city acknowledging or validating her experience. She didn't need Vegas to mourn with her, or to remember David and Marcus in the way she did. Her path forward was internal, a reconstruction of her own narrative that stood apart from the city's grand, impersonal spectacle. She could channel the lessons learned from her own shattering experiences into something meaningful, something that contributed to a more ethical framework for ambition, without needing the city itself to be the arbiter of that change.

She found herself drawn to the quieter corners, the establishments that existed on the periphery of the mega-resorts, places where the illusion of constant euphoria was less aggressively maintained. These were often places where the working people of Vegas congregated, the service industry staff, the builders, the artists, the individuals who kept the city running beneath its dazzling surface. Here, the indifference of the city felt less like a callous disregard and more like a pragmatic understanding of the daily grind, the constant effort required to simply exist, let alone thrive. There was a shared understanding of the precariousness of life in a city that was so heavily reliant on the whims of tourism and entertainment.

She observed families going about their routines, children playing in parks that offered brief respites from the relentless urban sprawl, couples sharing quiet meals in dimly lit restaurants. These were the lives that unfolded in the spaces between the neon glare, the ordinary moments that formed the bedrock of any community, even one as extraordinary as Las Vegas. And it was in these spaces, Aisha felt, that her new purpose could truly take root. Her advocacy for ethical leadership wasn't about changing the fundamental nature of Vegas – that would be an impossible task. It was about equipping individuals, the ones who were trying to build something meaningful, with the tools and the awareness to navigate the city's inherent challenges with greater integrity.

Her work with organizations focused on corporate responsibility took on a new urgency when she was invited to speak at a business ethics conference held in a convention center on the Strip. The irony was not lost on her – discussing integrity and ethical frameworks within the very heart of a city synonymous with high stakes and often questionable dealings. Yet, as she stood before the assembled professionals, she felt a quiet confidence, a resolve born from her own hard-won wisdom.

She spoke not of blame, but of the corrosive nature of unchecked ambition, the subtle compromises that could lead to profound failures. She shared anecdotes, anonymized and distilled, that spoke to the pressures faced by entrepreneurs and leaders in fast-paced, high-stakes environments. She emphasized the critical importance of establishing clear ethical guidelines from the outset, of fostering a culture where transparency and accountability were paramount, and where the pursuit of profit never overshadowed the fundamental responsibility to act with integrity.

"We are often drawn to cities like this," she began, her voice steady and clear, amplified by the acoustics of the grand hall, "because they represent the ultimate frontier of possibility. They are places where dreams can be forged from sheer will and ambition. But this very environment, this constant pressure to achieve, to win, can also be a breeding ground for ethical lapses. It is precisely in these crucible environments that our commitment to our values must be strongest. The allure of rapid success can be intoxicating, but it is the enduring strength of our ethical compass that will ultimately determine our legacy."

She spoke of the importance of building strong support systems, of seeking out mentors who embodied integrity, and of cultivating a resilience that was not solely dependent on external validation. She highlighted the psychological toll that the relentless pursuit of success could take, the way it could distort judgment and erode moral boundaries. She emphasized that true leadership was not merely about achieving ambitious goals, but about doing so in a way that uplifted others, that contributed positively to the broader community, and that left a lasting, honorable imprint.

The questions that followed her presentation were thoughtful, probing. Business leaders, many of whom had navigated their own ethical dilemmas within the city's vibrant but demanding landscape, sought her counsel on building ethical cultures, on managing whistleblowers, on the challenges of implementing robust compliance programs in rapidly growing companies. Aisha responded with clarity and conviction, drawing upon her own experiences not as a testament to failure, but as a powerful case study in the consequences of ethical compromise and the enduring rewards of principled action.

Leaving the conference, she felt a renewed sense of purpose. The city, in its vastness and its indifference, had become the very stage upon which she could enact her message. It was a place that embodied both the highest aspirations and the deepest pitfalls of human ambition, and by speaking within its confines, she was directly addressing the core of the issues she sought to address. Her journey had taken her from the depths of personal tragedy to a position of influence, not because the city had changed, but because she had. She had learned to harness the energy of this dynamic metropolis, to find her voice within its cacophony, and to use its very essence as a backdrop for her advocacy. The unheeded counsel she had once received, the warnings she had perhaps not fully heeded in her own past, were now being amplified, disseminated, and offered to a new generation of ambitious individuals navigating the seductive, and often perilous, landscape of urban opportunity. The city's indifference, rather than crushing her spirit, had inadvertently provided her with the perfect, unsympathetic audience for her message of integrity and resilience. It was a testament to her own enduring strength, a quiet defiance against the shadows of her past, played out against the dazzling, unblinking gaze of Las Vegas.

The ceaseless hum of Las Vegas, a symphony of ambition and desperation that had once been the soundtrack to her life, now served as a distant backdrop to Aisha's introspection. The city's enduring indifference, which had initially felt like a crushing weight, had transformed into a peculiar form of clarity. It was a vast, impersonal entity, a testament to the ephemeral nature of fame and fortune, and within its glittering confines, she had learned a profound, albeit painful, lesson: the deafening silence of ignored wisdom. The echoes of Marcus and David's unchecked drive, the intoxicating whispers of shortcuts and guaranteed successes, still resonated in the quiet spaces of her memory. They had been brilliant, driven, and possessed of a vision that, for a time, seemed capable of bending reality itself. But beneath the surface of their audacious plans lay a fundamental flaw, a disregard for the counsel that had been offered, both explicitly and implicitly.

She remembered the late nights, fueled by caffeine and an almost desperate optimism, poring over spreadsheets and projections. The air would be thick with the scent of possibility, but also with the unspoken tension of mounting pressure. There were moments, fleeting instances, when the sheer audacity of their ventures felt almost too good to be true. It was in these moments that the dissenting voices, the cautious recommendations, had been most easily dismissed. She recalled, with a pang of regret, a conversation with a seasoned financial advisor, a man whose own career had been built on a foundation of steady, ethical growth. He had looked at their aggressive expansion plans, their reliance on increasingly speculative investments, and had quietly, but firmly, advised caution. "Rapid ascent," he'd warned, his voice low and measured, "often comes with a hidden cost. Ensure your foundations are as solid as your aspirations are high." His words, delivered with the gravitas of experience, had been met with polite nods and a thinly veiled impatience. The prevailing sentiment had been that he simply didn't understand the unique opportunities Vegas offered, the sheer velocity of change that allowed for outsized returns if one was bold enough to seize them.

David, in particular, had possessed a remarkable ability to rationalize away any dissenting opinion. He had a way of framing pragmatic concerns as timidity, of reinterpreting caution as a lack of vision. Aisha, caught in the whirlwind of their shared ambition, had sometimes found herself swayed by his conviction, questioning her own instincts. Had she been too risk-averse? Was she hindering their progress by not embracing a more aggressive, albeit potentially volatile, strategy? The insidious nature of their downfall lay not in a single catastrophic decision, but in a series of incremental compromises, each one seemingly justified in the moment, each one a small step away from the path of sound judgment. The siren song of quick riches had drowned out the steady, persistent melody of earned success.

Marcus, ever the showman, had excelled at deflecting criticism with charm and an unwavering belief in his own charisma. He had a gift for making everyone around him feel like they were part of something extraordinary, something destined for greatness. Yet, when faced with the pragmatic realities of regulatory compliance, or the sober assessment of potential liabilities, his usual effervescence would be replaced by a practiced dismissiveness. He had often spoken of "outsmarting the system," of finding loopholes and workarounds. This was not the language of ethical leadership, but of a gambler willing to bend the rules to their limit. The counsel he had received, from legal experts and industry veterans alike, had been largely treated as an impediment to his grand vision, rather than a vital safeguard. He saw the system not as a framework for fair play, but as a puzzle to be solved, and he believed he held the master key.

Chloe, with her innate optimism, had often been the bridge between Marcus and David's more extreme viewpoints, and Aisha's more grounded perspective. She had a genuine desire for everyone to succeed, to share in the spoils of their endeavors. However, her optimism, while admirable, had at times prevented her from fully confronting the underlying risks that were being amplified. She had a tendency to believe that sheer willpower could overcome any obstacle, that positive thinking was a sufficient antidote to potential pitfalls. When Aisha had voiced her concerns about the escalating debt, or the increasingly opaque financial dealings, Chloe would often try to diffuse the tension with reassurances. "We're so close," she'd say, her voice soft, "Marcus and David have it all under control. We just need to keep the faith." This faith, however, was misplaced, built not on a solid foundation of due diligence, but on a desperate hope that their ambitious trajectory would somehow correct itself.

Aisha now understood that the most valuable counsel often comes not in the form of grand pronouncements, but in quiet, reasoned advice, delivered with the authority of experience. It was the kind of advice that, in moments of heightened emotion or overzealous ambition, could easily be mistaken for negativity or obstruction. The true cost of unheeded counsel wasn't merely a missed opportunity; it was the unraveling of everything built upon a flawed premise, the devastating ripple effect that extended far beyond the individuals at the center of the storm. The fragile edifice of their enterprise, so meticulously constructed, had been vulnerable not to external forces, but to the internal erosion of principles, a slow decay masked by the glittering facade of success.

The lessons were stark. The pursuit of wealth and influence, when untethered from a strong moral compass and a willingness to listen to wise counsel, was a treacherous path. It was a path that promised the moon but often delivered a harsh descent. The story of Marcus, David, and Chloe was a microcosm of a larger truth: that ambition, unchecked and unguided, could become a destructive force. It could blind individuals to the warning signs, deafen them to the voices of reason, and ultimately lead them down a path of ruin.

Reflecting on her own role, Aisha acknowledged her own complicity, however unintentional. She hadn't been the architect of their most reckless decisions, but she had been a witness, and at times, a hesitant participant. Her own youthful eagerness, her desire to believe in the seemingly invincible duo of Marcus and David, had muted her own voice of caution. She had wrestled with the internal conflict between loyalty and principle, a conflict that, in hindsight, should have been resolved with a far greater emphasis on the latter. The ethical framework she now championed was born from this very struggle, from the lived experience of watching integrity falter under the immense pressure of ambition.

The conferences and workshops she now led were not just about presenting theoretical concepts of business ethics; they were about sharing the visceral realities of what happened when those principles were abandoned. She spoke of the psychological impact of compromised integrity, the way it could erode self-respect, foster an environment of distrust, and ultimately lead to a pervasive sense of hollowness, even amidst outward success. The stories she shared, carefully anonymized but imbued with the emotional truth of her experiences, served as cautionary tales, vivid illustrations of the consequences of a misplaced focus. She would describe the quiet despair that settled in when the facade of success began to crack, the dawning realization that the foundations were not as solid as they had appeared.

"There's a seductive quality to ambition," she would often say, her voice resonating with a quiet authority that came from personal understanding. "It whispers promises of power, of recognition, of a life beyond the ordinary. But the most potent form of ambition is that which is tempered by wisdom, guided by integrity, and open to the counsel of those who have navigated similar paths. The loudest voices in the room are not always the wisest. The most compelling arguments are not always the most truthful. It is crucial to cultivate the ability to discern, to listen not just to what you want to hear, but to what you need to hear."

Her message often centered on the importance of building robust support systems, not just for business growth, but for personal and ethical development. She emphasized the need for trusted advisors, mentors, and even peers who were willing to offer honest feedback, even when it was difficult to hear. "The solitary pursuit of success," she'd explain, "is a dangerous endeavor. It allows for the unchecked growth of ego and the gradual erosion of accountability. True strength lies in the willingness to be vulnerable, to admit what you don't know, and to seek guidance from those who can help you navigate the complexities of the landscape."

She would often draw parallels to the structure of Las Vegas itself, a city built on calculated risks and elaborate systems designed to mitigate those risks. "Think of your own ventures," she'd encourage her audience, "as intricate ecosystems. For them to thrive, you need more than just a brilliant idea and relentless drive. You need sound financial management, ethical marketing, responsible labor practices, and a deep understanding of the regulatory environment. Ignoring any of these elements is like building a skyscraper on a foundation of sand. It might stand for a while, appearing magnificent to the casual observer, but it is inherently unstable, vulnerable to the slightest shift in the ground."

The stories of Marcus and David, in their tragic finality, served as a potent, if painful, reminder of this fundamental truth. Their ambition had been a wildfire, consuming everything in its path, leaving behind only ashes. They had been so focused on the immediate blaze of success that they had failed to see the tinderbox they were creating, the potential for widespread destruction. The counsel they had dismissed—the warnings about unsustainable debt, the advice to diversify their investments, the pleas for greater transparency in their dealings—had been the gentle breezes that might have prevented the inferno. Instead, they had been ignored, allowing the flames of recklessness to grow unchecked.

Aisha's work was now dedicated to ensuring that others did not suffer the same fate. She saw her own survival, her ability to emerge from the wreckage and forge a new path, as a testament to the enduring power of learned lessons, even if those lessons were paid for with immense personal cost. She understood that the true measure of success was not just about accumulating wealth or achieving recognition, but about building something sustainable, something that reflected a commitment to ethical principles and a respect for the wisdom of others. The city that had nearly consumed her had, in its own indifferent way, provided her with the ultimate classroom, a place where the abstract concepts of right and wrong were made brutally, undeniably real. Her voice, now a beacon of integrity in the glittering expanse of Las Vegas, was a testament to the profound, and often unheeded, power of listening. The legacy she sought to build was not one of grand pronouncements, but of quiet influence, of guiding others away from the precipices they might not yet see, armed with the hard-won knowledge that the greatest risks are often born from the most stubborn refusal to heed the wisdom offered.

Back Matter

Algorithmic Trading: The use of computer programs to execute trades at high speeds based on pre-programmed trading instructions.

Blockchain: A distributed, immutable ledger that records transactions across many computers.

Due Diligence: The process of investigation and analysis that a person or organization undertakes before entering into an agreement or contract.

Ecosystem: In a business context, the network of companies, individuals, and resources that interact and depend on each other.

Leverage: The use of borrowed capital to increase the potential return of an investment.

Regulatory Compliance: Adherence to laws and regulations governing business practices.

Speculative Investment: An investment that is made with the hope of large future profits, but with a significant risk of substantial loss.

Smith, J. (2020). *The Psychology of Risk-Taking in Business*. Business Press.

Lee, S. (2019). *Ethics in the Digital Economy*. Tech Publishing House.

Davis, R. (2021). *Vegas: A History of Ambition and Illusion*. City Lights Press.

National Financial Standards Board. (Annual). Report on Investment Trends and Market Volatility.

Made in the USA
Coppell, TX
19 February 2026